Eat, Drink, and Be Wary

Eat, Drink, and Be Wary

Satisfying Stories with a Delicious Twist

Edited by
Lisa Mangum

WFP
WORDFIRE PRESS

Ebook ISBN: 978-1-68057-293-3
Trade Paperback ISBN: 978-1-68057-292-6
Dust Jacket Hardcover ISBN: 978-1-68057-294-0
Case Bind Hardcover ISBN: 978-1-68057-295-7
Library of Congress Control Number: 2021951069

Cover design by Janet McDonald
Cover artwork images by Adobe Stock
Kevin J. Anderson, Art Director

Published by
WordFire Press, LLC
PO Box 1840
Monument CO 80132

Kevin J. Anderson & Rebecca Moesta, Publishers
WordFire Press eBook Edition 2022
WordFire Press Trade Paperback Edition 2022
WordFire Press Hardcover Edition 2022
Printed in the USA

Join our WordFire Press Readers Group for
sneak previews, updates, new projects, and giveaways.
Sign up at wordfirepress.com

Contents

WORDS OF WARNING   1
M. Elizabeth Ticknor

TICK TOCK   4
Aleksa Baxter

THE LAST RAMEKIN   12
Liz Pierce

THE GINGERBREAD CONTRACT   26
Jessica Guernsey

THE BOBA THIEF   44
Ken Bebelle and Julia Vee

THE LAST JARS OF PEACHES   60
Lauren Lang

LOVE POTION ON A LARGE #9   74
Kitty Sarkozy

THE WORLD'S GREATEST CHEF   88
CJ Erick

A RECIPE FOR HOME   94
Alicia Cay

THE HONEY PIE   107
Terry Madden

SPACE WITHOUT BREATH   123
Jen Bair

GALAXY EDGE CAFÉ   134
C. Michelle Jefferies

MISSION IMPOSSIBLE BURGER   150
Mike Jack Stoumbos

ROLL THE DICE   167
Mary Pletsch

WHY I WILL EAT EARTH: A MANIFESTO   183
M.R. Tevebaugh

AN OBSESSION OF PEACHES   188
Bonnie Elizabeth

MURDER IN THE ROUX MORGUE   201
Chris Mandeville

SOMEWHERE FAR   210
Ken Hoover

ROYAL WEDDING   225
Kevin J. Anderson

About the Editor   229
If You Liked ...   231
Other WordFire Press Titles Edited By Lisa   232
Mangum

Words of Warning
M. Elizabeth Ticknor

Don't trust the fairies, child. Beware the chitinous kiss of dragonfly wings against your peach-soft cheeks. Beware the delicate pitter-patter of flower-booted feet dancing on the surface of the goldfish pond. Beware echoes of laughter carried on gentle breezes, especially when you believe yourself to be alone. Beware their saccharine-sweet words, mixing truths and lies into every sentence until there's no way to tell the difference.

That's how magic works, you know—the fairies lie so well that reality reshapes itself to suit them.

Don't trust the fairies, child, but feed them daily. Leave saucers of milk or bread crusts on your kitchen stoop. Even if it's all the milk you have left, even if it's your last crust of rye, feed the fairies as best you're able. Far better to earn their favor than their wrath. If you must seek the fairies' aid, supplement your daily offerings with berries, cheese, and honey. Such generosity will endear you to them.

Fairy pranks can be both dangerous and deadly; protect yourself accordingly. Seek out an iron pendant—an arrowhead or a cross, a shape both sturdy and dependable. While you bear iron, no fairy can harm you directly. However, such protection is far from universal—spells and charms can still affect you. Keep bread crumbs on hand for emergency appeasement, and a pinch of salt to repel unwelcome advances.

Be on your guard should you ever venture into the dark and ancient wood. The pull of magic is strong there—it will confound your sense of direction and tempt you to stray from well-trod paths. Getting lost is the surest way to stumble into the Fae Realm, and nowhere is this easier to accomplish than in places where nature still holds sway.

Once you've crossed the threshold, you can't return the way you came—the paths are ever-changing. No matter which way you turn, sooner or later you're bound to wander headlong into the Fairy Court. Do not expect to find a castle. Fairies make their homes wherever they choose, and they far prefer a carpet of moss and the limitless expanse of a starry sky to the cramped, restrictive walls and ceilings that mortals use as protection from the elements.

Fairies, not being mortal, need no such protection.

Don't trust the fairies, child, and beware their hospitality most of all. Ignore the platters piled high with roast pheasant and boar. Shun the bowls piled high with fruits both familiar and foreign— bloodred apples as large as coconuts, bruise-purple mulberries that stretch as long as your fingers, dragon fruits that grow warm in your hands and pulse with something akin to a heartbeat. Drink not the aromatic wines made from elderberries, plums, cherries, and currants. Consume nothing while in the Fae Realm, for that will bind you in service to the Court forever.

Don't trust the fairies, child—but should you find yourself in the Fairy Court, steal a bottle of elderberry wine for me. I'll pay you well and teach you charms to turn away the Fairy Court's wrath. The wine will lose some of its potency when it's brought across the border, but it's still a fine draught, and it'll do these old bones good. There might even be enough magic left in the bottle to breathe life back into my tattered wings.

Words of Warning

M. Elizabeth Ticknor shares a comfortable hobbit hole in Southeast Michigan with her Wookiee husband and their twin baby dragons. An avid reader of science fiction and fantasy, Elizabeth also enjoys well-written horror. The authors who have inspired her include Douglas Adams, Ray Bradbury, Orson Scott Card, Neil Gaiman, C.S. Lewis, Chuck Wendig, and David Wong. Her other interests include drawing, painting, and tabletop roleplaying. Visit her at ticknortales.com or on Twitter @lizticknor.

Tick Tock

Aleksa Baxter

It's easy to kill someone. The hard part is not getting caught.

Or so Mildred Hense mused to herself as she stood in front of the full-length mirror her granddaughter had given her for Christmas the year before. It matched the rest of her room exactly, with the glue-gunned-on layers of beige lace and peach roses around the perimeter.

She was so proud of the girl. Twelve years old and skilled enough—mostly—to have done the work all by herself. Mildred, of course, wouldn't have left that hideous pool of dried glue in the bottom-left corner. Nor would she have allowed the lace to be the slightest bit crooked along the right edge.

But that was neither here nor there; it was a gift, and that's what counted. Although, were Mildred being honest with herself, the mirror was not going to be displayed in her new room in her new house that she was going to buy as soon as she disposed of her husband, Clive.

Whistling a happy little Christmas tune to herself, Mildred glanced once more at the article she'd found two weeks before, buried at the bottom of the tenth page of one of the papers her son had dropped by for her to use as lining in the birdcage.

It was a small article. One that might've slipped right by her,

4

but fortunately fate had intervened, and she'd caught a glimpse of the picture of a hideously ugly clock held by an equally hideously ugly man.

That clock. It was exactly like the monstrosity she'd been forced to feature on her living room mantel for the last fifty years. Fifty years of new couches and new wall colors and new carpet, all marred by that damnable clock that didn't match anything she'd ever owned or ever wanted to own.

But Clive was adamant that it stay. So year in and year out, she'd been forced to display that oversized, out-of-date piece of garbage that was too big to hide amongst a bunch of knickknacks.

Everyone commented on it. *Everyone.* She couldn't have a single person to her house for fifty years without them commenting on that awful clock. Did they notice her embroidery? No. Did they notice her crochet? No. Did they notice the lovely pale green carpet she'd had installed?

No. No. No.

It was always the clock. Where did you get that? Oh, how interesting. It's how old? Oh my.

Worthless piece of outdated ...

But it wasn't worthless, was it? Not according to the headline of that little article she'd found. Oh no. That clock she'd been forced to suffer through for the last fifty years of her marriage was, it seemed, worth more than a million dollars.

Had Mildred been a different sort of woman, she might have taken that article to her husband with a delighted smile and suggested that all of their money woes were solved. But Mildred was not that woman. Nor was Clive the sort of man to see the sense in selling off a family heirloom for the chance to retire to sunny Florida.

Which meant one thing: Clive must die.

Taking one last look at herself in the mirror, Mildred fluffed her snow-white curls and ran her hands down her ample hips, smoothing the fabric of her bright green dress with its reindeer trim along the neckline and sleeves.

She hadn't wanted to turn into the embodiment of Mrs. Claus, and for years she'd bitterly hated the thought that her outside appearance was so soft and cuddly. But she'd come around to it now that she was about to kill her husband. Suddenly being underestimated and overlooked had its advantages.

Giving herself one last dimpled smile in the mirror, she put on her wire-rimmed reading glasses and her snowman apron and turned toward the door.

It was time.

Mildred didn't bother with a recipe. Who needs one for cookies you've made every single year for the last sixty-five years? Plus, a little variation now and again was what made them homemade.

She removed the ingredients she needed from the fridge—butter, eggs, cream cheese, insulin—and stacked them neatly on the counter next to the flour, sugar, brown sugar, baking soda, vanilla extract, and powdered sugar.

As she mixed and stirred, she sang along to the Mariah Carey Christmas CD playing in the living room. It wasn't easy adding insulin to the frosting mix—those little bottles weren't built to dump right in like vanilla extract—but it wasn't exactly hard either. Not for someone with a plan.

Everyone knew Clive had a sweet tooth and was a bit spacy to boot. Just as everyone knew that once Mildred took her little pill at night she wasn't waking up until morning. And just in case they didn't know, she'd made sure to remind them more than once the last couple of weeks.

So who would question that he'd accidentally doubled-up his

dose and that she hadn't been awake to know until too late? These tragic things happened to the elderly, after all.

Mildred took a deep breath of baked sugary goodness as Clive clomped into the kitchen, leaving mud in his wake.

"Smells good," he grunted.

"Fresh out of the oven. Here, have one." She smiled at him, pointedly ignoring how he'd muddied up her floors and reached for the cookies with his grubby little hands before she could even offer them.

He, of course, took three. Fifty years of marriage and he never had listened to her about eating right or watching his weight.

She smiled. "Would you like another?"

"In a minute. I have something to show you in my workshop. Come on."

She grimaced. It was muddy outside and cold, and she didn't want to go to his messy workshop that stank of the cigars she wouldn't let him smoke in the house. She told herself it was one more night. She could put up with anything for just one more night. "Of course, dear. Let me just put on my snow boots."

As she did that, he grabbed three more cookies from the counter. She quietly smiled to herself, the thrum of accomplishment warming her against the bitter winter breeze that slapped her in the face as she opened the door.

There was a reason his workshop was away from the house. And it wasn't so she'd be forced to go there. "Like the cookies?" she asked.

"Yeah. Good stuff," he grunted as he shoved another one in his mouth.

Clive, as it happened, was not made of the same sort of stuff as his wife. He wasn't a planner. He was the kind of man who liked to live in the moment.

Which is why when he saw an article about the clock on a piece of newspaper wrapped around a gift from his youngest granddaughter and decided to kill his wife, he did it the good old-fashioned way. With a shovel to the back of the head.

Admittedly, it was a bit messier approach. Certainly not very elegant. Nor did it involve the karmic use of years of ignored advice.

But it worked.

Took a few tries, to be honest. Turns out that when you bash someone in the back of the head with a shovel it sometimes just knocks them down and makes them groan a lot. Especially if you're an older man with arthritis in his wrists who hasn't kept in the best of shape.

But the one positive trait Clive did have was his ability to stick to a decision once made. He'd stayed married to Mildred for fifty years, by gum, and when it came time to end that marriage, well, he stuck with that decision, too.

Of course, that did leave the issue of what to do with the body ...

Because it turns out that digging a hole in the ground in the middle of winter when there's been snow for the last week isn't exactly easy. And even though there might be a whole television show devoted to bodies buried in people's backyards, as Clive sadly learned, those people must've committed their murders in the summertime or lived in the south where the ground was not frozen as hard as a brick.

Or maybe they were just in better shape than an overweight diabetic whose hobbies involved drinking beer and watching sports on a little black-and-white television while pretending to work in his shop.

Either way, Clive quickly found that the killing was the easy part.

So, like all men of his ilk, he decided to give it some time and headed back into the house for a few more cookies. Which he ate in the living room with his feet kicked up and the television blaring in a way his wife would have never allowed, masking the sound of the wonderful, magical clock ticking away in the background.

Which is how his son, Ben, discovered him three days later when he finally dropped by to see why his mother hadn't called to make him feel guilty for spending Christmas at his wife's parents' house. Forget the notion of compromise and "happy wife equals happy life," Ben's mother had always insisted that she be the center of his world.

And until Ben had met said wife, he'd happily gone along. But Ben's wife was a formidable woman, and she'd put her foot down. It made for some cold family gatherings with the two women facing off across from one another, each smiling her most polite smile while exchanging sugar-coated daggers disguised as polite inquiries.

His wife's favorite such dagger, of course, involved complimenting Mildred on the clock featured so prominently on her mantel.

But such was life, and Ben skated through between the women, loving them both and happily oblivious to their tug-of-war for his heart. He was a simple man who liked football on Sundays, poker night on Wednesdays, and being the in-house accountant at a small engineering firm.

When he found his father's body, he didn't know what to do. This was not the sort of thing that happened in the life of a man like Ben.

His father looked peaceful with his feet kicked up, the TV on in the background, a plate of cookie crumbs at his elbow. But he also, after three days, did not look—or smell—very alive.

Ben immediately looked for his mother. She'd know what to do. But she was nowhere to be found, so he did the next best thing. He called his wife. She'd handle things. She always did.

And Ben's wife, Mary, did handle things. Even though what most people saw when they looked at Mary was a middle-aged stay-at-home mother of three whose crowning achievement the prior year had been taking over the PTA at her daughter's middle school, Mary was born to handle crises like this.

She settled Ben down in the guest room with a nice cup of tea, called the babysitter to pick up the kids, found the discarded bottles of insulin and tucked them away in her purse along with the two copies of the article about the clock she'd been so careful to plant in the path of her in-laws—thus also discovering her mother-in-law's body in the process.

She then took three deep breaths, channeled her experience playing Evita in her high school musical years ago, and called 911 to report the tragic death of her father-in-law from what was obviously natural causes and her mother-in-law from what was most obviously *not* natural causes.

When the detectives arrived and asked their questions, she managed that perfect balance of shaken tears and thoughtful observance as she reflected back on the tensions she'd seen over the years between Mildred and Clive. Because in fifty years there were always tensions, weren't there? Not generally the whack-them-in-the-head-with-a-shovel type, perhaps, but then one never truly knows the nature of someone else's marriage, do they?

She was perfect. Sad, composed, helpful, protective.

She deserved one of those shiny golden trophies for her performance, but she was happy to settle for the ugliest clock she'd ever seen in her life. Not like it was going to stay in her home for any length of time, after all.

No, she was going to sell that thing as soon as she could. She deserved it. It hadn't been easy to arrange for her husband's interfering parents to kill one another after all. She'd had to nudge them both in just the right way and at just the right time. She hadn't actually expected it to work out quite as well as it had, but life can be beautiful that way if you let it.

As she stared at the clock, feeling oh-so-proud of herself, her husband came to stand at her side.

"I've always loved that clock." He kissed her on the cheek. "It will look great on our mantel, don't you think?"

"Maybe we could see if it's worth something." She smiled at him, batting her cornflower-blue eyes.

"Oh, I'd never sell that clock. It's a family heirloom."

As he pulled her close in a one-armed hug, visions of that hideous monstrosity ticking away on her mantel for the next fifty years flashed through her mind, and she suppressed a shudder.

No. That was *not* going to happen to her.

As she leaned into her husband and stared at the clock, she thought about how easy it is to kill someone, but how much harder it is to get away with it.

But she'd figure it out. She always did.

Aleksa Baxter is the author of the Maggie May and Miss Fancypants cozy mystery series set in the Colorado mountains, starring Maggie May, her incorrigible Newfoundland Miss Fancypants, and a cast of quirky characters. The series is for those who like good friends, good food, cute dogs, and murder with a dash of romance on the side. You can find her online at aleksabaxter.com or at facebook.com/missfancypantsmysteries, where she occasionally posts photos of her very own Miss Fancypants.

The Last Ramekin

Liz Pierce

56:00

Molly's knife moved so fast it blurred, and, without looking up, she sensed the judges leaning forward in their seats, searching for any sign of magically-enhanced speed.

Let them look.

The speed of her knife was all in her hands, although if she were being honest with herself, some of the blur—at least from her point of view—was likely due to the fumes stinging her eyes as she turned the onion into a pile of small white bits, the knife chopping and scraping across the slightly textured surface of the nylon cutting board.

Damn!

She'd tossed a couple of onions in the freezer as soon as she entered the competition kitchen, before she'd even decided what she was going to cook, a move she was sure had gotten raised eyebrows from at least a few of the judges, scribbling on their scorecards and deciding whether or not to dock points for the action. In her favor would be those judges who were aware of the tear-prevention technique, and would be watching her closely.

The Last Ramekin

There hadn't been time for the first onion to chill enough for tear-free cutting, but Molly didn't dare blink to clear her eyes, or wipe the moisture away with the back of her hand, or she'd lose their support right out of the gate.

She ignored the fumes.

She'd started with onions. She almost always used onions. And garlic. And peppers. And a variety of herbs and spices. She could just imagine the television announcer's narrative as he reported her actions to the viewing audience in hushed tones: "In an unsurprising opening move, Molly McTavish, the *Kitchen Witch*"— there would be a definite sneer in his voice as he said those words—"has once again selected her standard set of ingredients. Can she truly hope to outperform the wizards and sorceresses in this competition with such humble fare?"

Whatever.

She *was* a kitchen witch, and proud of it. And she was the *first* kitchen witch in history to make it to the final round of the Culinary Conjurers competition. The narrator could sneer all he wanted, but Molly knew there were hundreds of kitchen witches out there in viewer-land cheering her on—including dear old Gran, who had taught her how to cook in the first place, and who would be watching on the tiny old television that just fit on the open cupboard shelf next to the cookbooks in her little Irish cottage.

Even her fellow finalists had come to acknowledge her skills and accept her over the course of the competition. They certainly treated her with less disdain than they had at the beginning of the week. It was possible—though she thought it unlikely—that they even respected her a little.

Molly took a deep breath, slid the minced onions into a small bowl, and went to work on the garlic. *No time for potions and politics now*, she chided herself, using one of her Gramps' favorite phrasings; she had a dinner to prepare.

She glanced at the stove as she slid the papery skins from the firm garlic bulbs. Bubbles were beginning to cling to the inside walls of the large silver pasta pot full of water on the back center burner. She didn't need it to boil too soon, so had filled it with cold water and tossed in pinches of salt and herbes de Provence, the thyme and lavender of the herb blend infusing the water and drifting over her kitchen like a simmering potpourri while she worked on other parts of the meal.

On the front left burner, nearest to her, the frozen butter she'd chopped and tossed into a pan over a low heat was finally beginning to melt.

She smashed the garlic to a fragrant, gooey pulp, scraped the blob off the cutting board and dropped it into the butter with one hand, her other hand reaching for the flat-edged wooden spatula in her apron pocket. She quickly stirred the garlic into the butter, which was just beginning to bubble, then dumped in the bowl of chopped onions, stirring them until they were coated with the garlicky mixture. With a deft shake of the skillet, the mixture spread out across the bottom of the pan, sizzling gently, the warm fragrance of onions and garlic coiling up out of the pan and swirling around her head.

It smells like Gran's cooking. It smells like home.

She spun around, retrieving the packet of chicken tenderloins from the refrigerator. She used a cooking fork to nick the plastic wrapping on the package, peel it back, then lift each of the six tenderloins and place them in the skillet, the thick, meaty ends nearly touching in the center of the skillet, the pieces fanning out toward the outer edges like a fleshy pink flower set in a bubbling bed of white-gold.

Molly heard the judges murmuring in approval, then covered the pan, steam instantly obscuring the glass lid as she noted the time.

52:00

She tracked the tasks in her head, like a mental checklist.
Proof the yeast for the breadsticks.

The Last Ramekin

Dredge the shrimp in flour and spices.
Turn the chicken in five minutes.

Competition cooking was all about timing and presentation, and, so far, Molly was on track with both. She flew to her next task, and the next, and the next, slicing and dicing, measuring and mixing, and clearing her workspace as she went so she'd have both clean tools and a space for the next task.

Around the competition hall, six other chefs in six identical kitchens also raced the clock, bright studio lights shining down on them, illuminating every action, every misstep for the cameras. This was the final round, and they were the last seven contestants —all that remained of the fifty wizards, witches, sorcerers, and conjurers; a veritable conclave of cooks, bakers, chefs, and sous-chefs who had begun the grueling competition a mere week ago.

They had one hour in which to prepare one last meal, and they were focused on their task. Steam *whooshed* from pans, meat sizzled in invisible tendrils of mouth-watering fragrance, knife blades hit cutting boards with rhythmic precision, and over it all, a large clock ticked the seconds like a metronome.

There was no time for anything else. There was almost no talking, very little of their usual banter.

And no magic.

This round—the final round—was a test of skill, of speed. Of their ability to mix and measure and cut and cook using only their own two hands, unaided by magic of any sort.

They'd had no advance warning of the rules for the round. They'd simply been led into their competition kitchens to discover them unusually stocked, with previously opened packages and containers of some items, while other items were brand new and still sealed. Dirty dishes and utensils were scattered on the counters or soaking in the sinks.

"Your kitchens have been prepared to simulate the average household kitchen on an ordinary weekday afternoon," the senior judge had told them. "In this scenario, your spouse is bringing home important guests for dinner. Your challenge is to prepare a simple, yet elegant, meal for six people, and be prepared to receive guests in your home in one hour."

Molly looked at the other chefs, all of whom were glancing as skeptically toward their kitchens as she had, but no one seemed particularly worried about completing the challenge in the time allotted.

"In the spirit of this scenario," the judge continued, "you will be allowed to borrow from your neighbors—no more than one item from each, please—but you are not required to do so. You gain no points for providing an item to one of your fellow chefs; however, each item you borrow will *cost* you one point."

This was a new twist, Molly thought. They'd not been allowed to share anything in previous rounds. On the other hand, the competition kitchens hadn't been presented in such a disorderly state in previous rounds, either. She wondered what key ingredients might be missing from her pantry.

"Finally," the judge said, "there is one last condition for this round: *You may not use magic*. Points will be deducted for any infraction—and to use sporting terminology, after three strikes, you're out."

Then the bell rang, and the large countdown clock on the wall behind the judges' table began ticking.

The chefs stood there, looking from the judges to the messy kitchens in stunned silence for a few critical seconds. Then, as one, they all rushed forward.

The race was on.

35:00

The first penalty was thrown twenty-five minutes into the competition. Molly didn't know what had happened at first, but, like the rest of the chefs, had stopped what she was doing and looked up in surprise when a loud buzzer sounded. They all watched in silence as a yellow silk ribbon fluttered down from the rafters toward Gustav's kitchen, at the opposite end of the half-circle of competition kitchens from her own.

The ribbon swam through the air like an eel, hungrily drawing golden sparks from the counter where the tall, lanky wizard had employed some minor magic in his preparations. As the ribbon sailed out of the kitchen, it settled on the floor in the shape of a large, glittering X.

Gustav said nothing, but even from across the room, Molly could see his mouth pressed in a firm line as he returned to his work.

Yikes!

Molly redoubled her efforts.

She wasn't nearly the baker that Gustav was, but her bread-sticks were rising nicely and would go into the oven soon, small fingers of dough dipped in butter and rolled in a mixture of herbs, garlic powder, and more shredded Parmesan. She'd found several packets of fast-rising yeast next to a partial tin of baking powder in her kitchen's pantry just as Maribel, the sorceress in kitchen number three, called out for baking powder.

None of the other kitchens had any to spare, so Molly had decided to risk the time to work up the yeast dough rather than make a much simpler recipe of drop biscuits, scooped out a couple tablespoonfuls of baking powder for the cake she'd decided to bake for dessert, and tossed the tin to Maribel. There wasn't much left, but Molly hoped there'd been enough for whatever the sorceress was making.

21:00

Molly's cake smelled almost ready, its warm, rich mocha permeating the air close to the oven. She glanced up at the clock. Four minutes before she could pull it out and swap in the breadsticks.

Just enough time to assemble the main dish.

She'd found a set of personal-sized ramekins in one of her

kitchen's cupboards, and scooped a tumble of pasta into each, topping it with portions of chicken and shrimp, over which she'd poured the bubbling hot spiced scampi sauce, garnishing the dish with a few curls of freshly shredded Parmesan and a sprinkling of parsley leaves. The ramekins only needed a few moments under the broiler to toast each dish to a lovely shade of gold.

Breathe.

If she got in a hurry, she'd forget about the rules and accidentally use her magic, like Gustav had. She was certain he hadn't been trying to cheat, automatically reaching for the power like he probably did every day. She'd nearly earned a penalty herself, almost leaving a spoon stirring the sauce while she dug through a cupboard for the paprika, and only remembered at the very last moment—fortunately, while the tips of two fingers and her thumb still grasped the utensil's handle.

That was really the hardest part of this challenge, Molly thought. Her competition kitchen had been ridiculously messy, but surprisingly well-stocked; once she'd decided on the meal she wanted to prepare, she'd had to make very few substitutions of ingredients, and she'd had enough other items on hand to loan something to almost every other chef in the round.

But not being able to magically whisk used dishes clean or clear the counter with a snap of her fingers—now that was hard.

17:00

She finished loading the ramekins, then took a few seconds to add still more items to the now nearly-full dishwasher, spinning the dial to the "fast wash" setting and switching it on before turning back to the oven.

Right hand, open oven door.

Left hand, grab pot holder and remove cake.

Right hand, grab tray of breadsticks and insert into oven.

Left hand, hold cake out of the way, while trying not to burn fingers on threadbare spot of pot holder.

Right hand, close oven door.

Turn, take two steps across room to refrigerator.

Left hand, do not drop cake in spite of the fact that heat is now zinging through fingers.

Right hand, open refrigerator.

Left hand, put cake on empty rack, cleared for this purpose.

Right hand, close refrigerator door.

Turn, take three steps to sink and dunk left hand in colander of slowly thawing frozen raspberries.

No magic, no magic, no magic.

07:00

Every time a yellow ribbon fell, it seemed to Molly that the clock ticked just a little louder, the hands moving across its face just a little faster. With seven minutes remaining, only Molly and a tiny, white-haired wizard named Nicholas in kitchen number four had managed to avoid collecting penalty ribbons.

Kamaria, a Kenyan sorceress who had confided to Molly a few days earlier that the secret to her wonderful doughnuts was a pinch of cardamom in the dough, only had one penalty ribbon. But Agatha, an accomplished conjurer who had borrowed a cup of sugar from Molly early in the round, had collected three, one right after another. Kitchen number six, right next to Molly's, now stood dark and empty.

Gustav had earned a second ribbon, which he'd batted away like a pesky insect. Maribel also had two, as did Joaquin, the Argentinian conjurer in kitchen number two who Molly had given a bag of baking potatoes. The tension radiated from their three kitchens as strongly as the varied cooking scents that filled the competition studio.

Think happy thoughts.

Molly tried to ignore the building tension and mentally reviewed her list. The ramekins of scampi were waiting in the still-warm oven, no longer cooking, but maintaining their tempera-ture until serving time.

06:00

She set a small dining table with plates and service for six.

05:00

She placed the breadsticks in a wooden bowl, covered with a towel, near the middle of the table. Next to it, in a matching wooden bowl, was a salad of spinach greens, thin slivers of red onion, mandarin oranges (canned, from one of the cupboards), and raspberries (from the freezer), tossed with a simple vinaigrette that she'd made while the cake was cooling. Pecans and feta cheese would have been nice additions, but her competition kitchen was lacking in those ingredients, and she was unwilling to risk losing the points borrowing them from another kitchen would cost her.

04:00

She placed the cake on the counter, covered in fluffy white frosting that she'd whipped by hand—the action helping relieve some of the tension of the rapidly evaporating time—and topped it with a pinch of tiny chocolate sprinkles she'd found in the pantry right next to the box of panko crumbs she'd tossed to Nicholas.

03:00

She pulled the lemonade from the refrigerator, the large glass pitcher instantly glistening with condensation, bright yellow lemon slices floating merrily amid the ice cubes as she carried the pitcher to the table. She wanted to drink it all down, let its tart sweetness quench her thirst. But there was no time.

02:00

Her hands still chilled from the lemonade pitcher, Molly quickly grabbed the potholders and swung open the oven door. Heat washed over her in a wave as she reached into the oven for the baking tray holding the six ramekins. She lifted it from the oven, using her foot to raise the oven door and her hip to push it closed as she turned, and was only two steps from the table when the threadbare section of the potholder slid away from the fingers of her right hand, exposing them directly to the heat of the baking tray.

Instinctively, she jerked her hand away from the heat.

Time seemed to stretch, the ticking of the clock booming in Molly's head, as the baking tray wobbled in her left hand then tipped, and the ramekins slowly began to slide, first one, then another falling off the tray.

No magic, no magic, no magic!

Molly righted the tray, diving toward the falling ramekins, her empty, burned hand outstretched in a futile attempt to catch the dishes. The first one crashed to the floor in an explosion of scalding shrimp and pasta. Heated shards of crockery shot across the floor in all directions, glistening trails of cream sauce marking their passing.

Tick, tick, tick, tick.

The next ramekin hit the floor less explosively, its fall cushioned by a piece of chicken from the first; but the third crashed into the second, sending a spray of pasta and sauce gushing upwards.

Molly saw a shrimp fly past her face as she fell, still struggling to balance the tray with the remaining ramekins. The unfortunate crustacean seemed to spin in the air in slow motion, momentarily mesmerizing her.

Mmm! It smells delicious!

And then she hit the floor, her left shoulder landing in the mound of pasta, her arm outstretched, the baking tray still in her hand. The remaining three ramekins shot forward, flying off the tray and spinning across the floor. One disappeared into the darkness at the back of the studio, its passage noted by a sharp "Hey!" from its hapless target.

The second crashed into the open doorframe with a loud crack, an explosion of pasta splattering the wall.

The last ramekin seemed to have caught a bit of a spin in its flight—whether from the angle of its fall, or a chance encounter with a splash of creamy debris, Molly never knew. It slid forward, out of her reach, its path curving slightly and slowing, bringing it to an undamaged stop on the floor directly in front of the judge's table.

Tick, tick, tick.

In less than a minute, the work of the past hour was undone.

As the large studio clock ticked its way toward the final minute of the competition, Molly pulled herself to her feet with as much dignity as she could muster, and retrieved the last ramekin. Gingerly, she carried it back to her dinner table, placing it gently between the bowls of salad and breadsticks.

01:00

Molly stepped back, standing next to her table, head held high, hands clasped behind her back, pasta and shrimp coating her shoulder and sliding to the floor with small *splooshing* sounds. Video of her ramekin debacle was going to go viral, no doubt about it—they were probably already replaying it for the viewing audience. She looked directly at the judges, a small, defiant smile touching her lips.

No magic. So there!

And then, from across the studio, a sharp sound broke the silence, as of someone snapping their fingers, followed immediately by the penalty buzzer. Molly started, looking over to see Nicholas, one hand raised and pointing at her table, even as a yellow ribbon drifted down, looping around his arm, and forming an X at his feet.

Molly's single ramekin had become three.

She stared at Nicholas, her mouth falling open in surprise. He simply smiled and nodded at her as the judges scribbled furiously on their scorecards.

00:45

There was a bright flash of light, accompanied so quickly by the penalty buzzer that they almost seemed to have occurred simultaneously, and once again the number of ramekins on Molly's table multiplied.

She whirled around, just in time to see a second yellow ribbon settling at Kamaria's feet. Like Nicholas, the sorceress was smiling at Molly, but she said nothing.

00:30

"What are you doing?" Molly hissed, not trusting her voice above a whisper.

"The rules placed no restriction on what could be shared," said Maribel. "You shared your extra ingredients with us, Kitchen Witch." She glanced at the ribbons at her feet, then looked back up at Molly. "They had extra magic to share with you. Don't waste it."

Molly looked around at the other chefs in amazement. She was a kitchen witch. She could cook up a storm, but her magical skills would never compete with any of theirs. Yet there they were, wizards, sorcerers, conjurers, all smiling broadly at her, yellow penalty ribbons at everyone's feet but her own.

They had done this for *her*.

00:15

Gran had often told Molly that the best meals often aren't those with the most elegant presentation or the most exotic ingredients—all of which are nice enough—but those that are shared with friends. And in those few critical moments, with wizards and sorcerers and conjurers and witches all around the world watching on live television, the other chefs had treated her as an equal, as a friend.

She had the advantage in points. She could win easily, assuming the judges hadn't docked her severely for the pasta and seafood now cooling in fragrant lumps around the studio.

But winning was no longer the only thing that mattered.

Molly turned to her table, quickly weaving a spell of her own. She spoke softly, but in the silence of the studio, the musical lilt of her Irish accent carried her words to the other chefs.

"May you live a long life, full of gladness and health," she said, as she placed ramekins at the two places on the far side of the table.

00:11

"With a pocket of gold as the least of your wealth." She placed a ramekin at the head of the table and another at the place at its left.

00:08

"May the dreams you hold dearest be those which come true." She moved the remaining two ramekins to the last two empty places.

00:05

"And the kindness you spread keep returning to you." With

that, Molly stepped away from the table and clapped her hands together.

The penalty buzzer sounded, and a yellow ribbon dropped, sparks dancing along the tabletop as it tried to find the spell Molly had woven. In its wake, loose threads unwound from the ribbon as it passed each place setting. As the ribbon slid off the table and folded itself into an X at Molly's feet, the threads it had left behind coiled into glittering patterns, forming a set of enchanted place cards spelling out the names Molly, Gustav, Joaquin, Maribel, Nicholas, and Kamaria.

"My friends," Molly whispered, "welcome to my table."

00:00

When not tinkering on an art project or conjuring in the kitchen, Liz Pierce writes what she calls "suburban fantasy"—stories that blur the boundaries between the real world and the fantastical, but are lighter and less edgy than their urban cousins. And hopefully, a little more fun. Whether it's the exploits of teenaged junior deities walking the halls of Olympus High, or the challenges faced by Faerie Folk trying to cope with jobs, neighbors, and mortgages, the results are often unexpected. You can find more of her work at lizpiercebooks.com.

The Gingerbread Contract
Jessica Guernsey

As the warm red liquid poured out, Andi tried hard to keep her hand steady. The flow was beautiful. Finally, she had managed a mirror glaze that streamed perfectly over the carefully tiered cake on the table below her. Andi tottered on a step stool because, at five foot three inches, she needed the height boost to reach the top of the five tiers. With her knee, she spun the base board, checking that the glaze covered evenly as the small rented kitchen space filled with the scent of warm gelatin.

She scooped the last of the red from her pot and grinned as the gorgeously shiny stuff made its way over the last of the surface.

Perfect. It was absolutely perfect.

Hard hands grabbed her thighs, and a roar echoed through the kitchen.

Andi screamed, a sound that was echoed by a much smaller voice across the table. Resisting the urge to hurl her red-coated pot at Darin, who stood laughing behind her, Andi stepped down from the stool and hurried around the table to the little boy seated there, his already large brown eyes even wider, his lip trembling.

"It's okay, Haden." Andi squatted down in front of the boy's chair and took his hands. "Mommy is okay."

"Geesh, kid." Darin leaned a hip against the table when Andi shot him a look. "I was just teasing. It's supposed to be *fun*."

Andi took in a deep breath through her nose and exhaled. Haden's big eyes peered up at her, but tears weren't flowing.

"See?" Andi smiled. "All fine. Darin is just silly."

Haden glanced at Darin, slipped his hands from his mother's, and went back to his plastic dinosaurs.

Andi breathed again as she stood. She said nothing, turning to a tray of gum-paste roses, colored with edible gold dust. She didn't want to look at Darin. His perfect lips and smoldering green eyes had a way of sucking all the annoyance right out of her.

"And I came here to share some good news for a change." He folded his arms.

Andi shifted slightly, giving him a little more of her attention. "Oh?"

"Yeah, but you don't even want to hear it. I swear, whenever I'm in a good mood, it's like you don't even care."

Andi set down the rose and, wiping her hands on her apron, went to stand in front of him. "Tell me your good news." She pumped her tone up with enthusiasm she didn't feel.

But Darin's arms stayed folded, his biceps stretching the fabric of his button-down shirt. Andi didn't understand why he insisted on dressing so nicely when he worked from home as a day trader. It wasn't like he met with clients. Today's shirt was a dark gray that complemented his tanned skin and still managed to accentuate his eyes.

Andi resisted the urge to wilt in her "mom jeans," T-shirt from a long-ago concert, and smudged apron. She wore a chef's jacket with her company name embroidered on it when delivering cakes so at least that looked more professional. And today she'd worn her blonde hair in a flipped ponytail, instead of the usual messy bun. Even used a little makeup that morning while Haden finished his cereal.

Andi wrapped her arms around Darin's waist and wedged herself in closer until his arms separated and wrapped around her.

"Tell me, tell me. Please?" she said, batting her eyelashes up at him.

Finally, a smile snuck through. "Okay. So we both know you're no good with numbers, right?"

This was a frequent refrain of Darin's, which was why he took over the finances for her business months ago, after he had moved in with them.

"And things have been ... pretty slim lately." He looked down at her, eyes full of sympathy. "So I was looking on some forums—"

"Which forums?" she asked.

"*Business* forums. Not important. Anyway, I found you a client."

"Okay." Andi hesitated.

He noticed and rolled his eyes. "Honestly, Andi, I'm just trying to help you achieve success here. Fulfill your dreams! It's not like Haden is of much use."

He had a point. Haden was three. He still hid when she turned on the big mixer.

"What kind of client?" she asked with narrowed eyes, head tilted to the side.

"A *big* one." Darin's grin grew to staggering wattage, and Andi couldn't help but start to smile, too.

Goodness, but the man was gorgeous. Sure, he had his flaws, but so did she. And he'd still asked her to marry him. They'd been engaged for more than a year with no set date, but that didn't matter, as long as they were together.

Darin pulled out his phone, one of the big, new ones that had all sorts of functions and stuff that he said she couldn't begin to understand. He tapped and flicked as he talked.

"It's perfect, really. Big payout, and it'll connect you to people on her level. This is exactly what your business needs. And once the money starts coming in, maybe you could afford to hire an assistant, not spend so many hours in here. Maybe get back to the gym." He winked at her, and before she could open her mouth to protest his last comment, he held the phone in front of her face.

The Gingerbread Contract

She didn't see much more than a very large number and one other word.

"Gingerbread?" Andi reached for his phone, but he held it away from her. "I make cakes, not gingerbread houses."

Darin scoffed. "Both get frosting dumped on them, right?"

Andi shook her head. "There's all kinds of structural considerations. I've never made one for a paying customer."

"So watch a few YouTube tutorials. It's not that hard."

"Why would anyone pay so much money for a gingerbread house?" Her gut went cold.

"Because this client is particular. It's the centerpiece for some big Christmas party. She's eccentric. I already sent her a message saying we accepted."

"You already ... what?"

"Did you see the *money*, Andi?" He looked at her, those green eyes pleading. "Your little business is struggling, babe. You can't make it on your own. Which is why I am trying to help you. Don't you want my help?"

"Well, yes, but—"

"But nothing." He raised a hand to cut her off, and she flinched a little. "I got you the client. You make it work."

He grabbed a rose from the tray and stuffed it in his mouth, the gold dust making his lips sparkle as he crunched. His perfectly straight nose crinkled, and he turned to spit into the nearest trash can.

"Ugh. That tastes like chalk rolled in sugar. People pay you for this? You should probably use things that taste *good*."

He stormed out of the kitchen.

Andi breathed out, dropping her shoulders. She didn't have time to smooth things over. She had a cake to deliver.

Andi watched hours of gingerbread tutorials, took pages of notes. Next came the sketches.

Checking the clock, Andi chewed her lower lip. The client was due in a few minutes. Hopefully the meeting wouldn't run longer than thirty minutes. Haden was tucked into her office with his favorite blanket, a juice box, and a dinosaur cartoon playing on her laptop. He'd stay put until the show ended.

She glanced toward the office, her hand almost going to her phone. Maybe her mother would be willing to come stay with him? But no. Darin was certain her mother was looking for a reason to fight for custody of Haden and asking her to help would give Darin more proof that Andi was unfit. Sure, her mother spoiled Haden every chance she got, but Andi didn't think her mother had ever said such a thing. Darin was adamant.

The bells over the front door jingled, and Andi put a welcoming smile on her face before turning to greet her new client.

Mrs. Kulcher looked like she'd stepped right out of a story featuring a fairy godmother. All softness and smiles, she pulled off white gloves and tucked them into an honest-to-goodness blue cape that was most likely velvet. White puffs of curls piled on her head, with only the tiniest hat to keep them contained.

"Hello," Andi said, reaching out a hand. "I'm Andi. You must be Mrs. Kulcher?"

Mrs. Kulcher strode forward and pumped Andi's hand, bringing the scent of cold from outside.

"So lovely, my sweet." As warm and soft as her grip, the woman's voice also held the faintest hint of an accent. "Shall we begin?"

"Of course." Andi motioned to the front counter where she'd spread her sketches.

Mrs. Kulcher trundled over, pink hands clasped underneath her wide chin. Instead of sitting on the stool, she bent over the sketches, cooing and squealing, taking several minutes to study each one.

Finally, Mrs. Kulcher stood up straight and tapped the third sketch. "This one."

Andi wanted to swallow hard but smiled instead. Mrs. Kulcher had picked the Tudor-style gingerbread house. It was definitely the most ambitious of Andi's designs. Of course that was the one selected.

"Great," Andi said, wearing her practiced smile. "Are there any adjustments you'd like to make to the design or colors?"

Mrs. Kulcher's tiny dark eyes darted over Andi's shoulder, and her smile grew even broader.

Andi didn't need to hear the small voice ask, "Mommy?" to know Haden stood behind her.

"Well, hello, sweet boy." The woman's voice was syrup.

Andi turned. Haden's already immense eyes were even wider, the rest of his face hidden behind his blanket.

"It's okay, baby. Mommy is working right now. Can you go back to the office, please?"

"Oh, no, such a precious gumdrop must stay right here with me," Mrs. Kulcher said, patting the neglected stool. "There is even a seat. Just for you."

Smiling broadly, Haden skipped over to stand beside Mrs. Kulcher, who bent over to pinch his cheek, then hefted him up to sit on the stool.

"Such a good boy," Mrs. Kulcher crooned, and patted his head. "Now, your mother has some lovely pictures. Do you like this one?" She held up the selected image for Haden.

"It's pretty." He nodded emphatically. "Mommy will make you a nice bread house."

"To be sure, my sweet." Mrs. Kulcher studied the sketch again. "This is just the sort of arrangement I was looking for."

Haden grinned at her and, accepting her as a friend, handed her one of his plastic dinosaurs. "This is a bronnasarus. He gotta long neck."

"Indeed, he does." Mrs. Kulcher looked suitably impressed before handing the dinosaur back. Looking at Andi, eyes twinkling, she said, "I would like to see a small version of this." She tapped the sketch. "Could you have it ready in two days?"

Andi didn't want to laugh at the woman's request—but two days? That was unrealistic. At the pause, Mrs. Kulcher's eyebrows bunched ever so slightly. Instead, Andi found herself nodding and agreeing to meet again in forty-eight hours.

With one last pat of Haden's cheek, the woman put on her gloves and swept out the door before Andi could do more than remind herself to breathe.

Bone-weary, Andi lifted a sleepy Haden out of his car seat. Good. He'd take a nice nap in the office while Andi got caught up on the orders she'd put off to finish the sample house for Mrs. Kulcher, delivered yesterday. It had been a busy forty-eight hours, and the next forty-eight promised to be just as packed.

Haden shifted in her arms. "Don't forget my candy," he mumbled.

"What candy?"

"Mrs. Kudder gived 'em to me."

Andi looked back in the car and found a baggie with a handful of gummy dinosaurs. When had her client slipped him candy? The kind old lady had gone over Andi's sample gingerbread with what felt like a fine-tooth comb.

Weren't the chocolate beam accents just lovely? And Andi would make it bigger, yes? She'd said repeatedly how impressed she was with the sample, only to have one more suggestion or adjustment. Noting with pouty disappointment that the windows were too small, and didn't Andi think the door looked better off-center?

Andi didn't feel quite so proud of her work, now with a full day ahead of her and so little sleep.

She tapped her ID badge against the door and pulled. But the light didn't turn green, and the door to her kitchen space remained locked. She groaned. It was far too early to call her landlord. She'd have to work through what she could at home and call when the office opened.

Heaving Haden up, she bundled him back in the car, relieved that the time out in the cold hadn't roused him.

Back at the house, Haden didn't look sleepy as he followed Andi around the kitchen. While she rolled out fondant, Haden lingered close by, dinosaurs making tiny prints in the soft stuff, powdered sugar dusting his cheek.

As soon as the leasing office opened, Andi called them, explaining the situation.

"Your account was terminated due to non-payment." The normally friendly agent went cold on her.

"What?" Andi switched the phone to her other ear. "That can't be right. I set up automatic payments more than a year ago. There's never been a problem before."

"Then I suggest you check your bank account, ma'am."

Ma'am? He'd never called her that before.

Andi muttered something about doing just that and disconnected.

She hurried to Darin's office, listening to make sure he wasn't on the phone, before tapping and opening the door.

Darin saw her and shut his laptop. "What?"

"I couldn't get into the kitchen space this morning." She told him what the leasing guy had said about not paying. "There's got to be a mistake, right?"

Darin's eyes had narrowed, but otherwise he hadn't reacted.

"Should I call the bank?"

He snorted. "No one *calls* the bank, babe. Let me finish up with this trade, and I'll check online."

"I could do it."

His jaw flexed. "You don't understand the accounts, Andi. This kind of thing goes over your head. I said I would handle it, and I will—"

A crash interrupted him.

Andi turned to see Haden sliding off Darin's leather sofa, dragging a stack of books off the coffee table with him.

"Get him out of here." Darin's face was a snarl.

"He's bored," Andi said, helping Haden stand, then restacking the books. "I'm busy in the kitchen, and his tablet is charging."

"Here." Darin shoved his tablet toward Andi. "He can use this. Just keep the kid quiet."

Andi murmured her thanks, but Darin dodged her kiss, so she quietly left his office with Haden in tow, closing the door behind them.

After opening a video app, she selected a kids' show and handed the tablet to Haden.

"Mommy, will you watch with me?" His eyes were large but sleepy.

If she cuddled him a little while, he would most likely fall asleep. Andi settled onto the couch next to him. Just a few moments.

The warm weight of her boy against her had Andi's eyes drooping.

With a chirp, a text notification popped up on the screen. Andi blinked awake. She carefully eased a sleeping Haden off her and tucked his blanket around him.

Tablet in hand, she headed back to Darin's office.

An email notification sounded next. Andi noticed the name "Kulcher," and before her right mind could stop her, she'd clicked on it.

The email contained a contract.

Good, Andi thought. *I had better see what all she expects.*

She scrolled through the legal jargon that made her eyes tired.

There. That section labeled "Item #1" referred to the ginger-bread house. Andi blinked and reread the specifications, briefly wondering if someone made a mistake and had used feet instead of inches.

She could hear Darin's voice in her head: "You can't understand these sorts of things. Just stick to frosting."

More stipulations for the client's supervision and some other things that were jumbled in legal terms. Andi skimmed, looking for words that made sense.

"Upon accepted completion of Item #1, Item #2 shall be exchanged. Receipt of the fresh chattel is to be determined by the Client."

Andi's eyebrows bunched. What did that mean? Darin never said there was anything else besides the gingerbread house. What was "fresh chattel" anyway? The phrase sounded familiar, but no definitions rose from the depths of her exhausted brain. She closed the email.

She had work to do.

"Your account is overdrawn."

Darin made the announcement as Andi piped a basket weave.

She nearly dropped the frosting bag. "How is that possible?"

Darin rolled his eyes. "I've been telling you for months. Your business is failing. There's no more money. You have to finish this contract for Kulcher, and then maybe, *maybe*, the leasing company will let you back in."

There was something about the way Darin nearly smiled. Something about the relaxed way he stood there, crushing her dream.

Something inside Andi woke up.

"Show me." She set down the bag and marched into Darin's office.

"There's nothing to see," he insisted.

She opened his laptop and turned it toward him. "Show me."

Darin scoffed. "Stop being so dramatic. It doesn't look good on you."

Andi lifted her chin.

"Fine." Darin slid into his fancy chair, tapped open a tab, and turned the screen to face Andi. "See? Those numbers in red mean you are overdrawn." He picked up his phone, giving it his attention.

Andi saw red alright. There was a lot of red on the page. She tapped the mouse and opened the transaction review. So many withdrawals. Nearly every time she'd made a deposit, there was a matching transfer to another account. She clicked, and a pop-up opened that showed the second account belonged only to Darin.

Maybe she made a sound. Or maybe he sensed something in her posture. Darin pulled the laptop back, shut the lid nearly on her fingers.

"Why are you transferring all my money?" Andi's stomach burned, and her hands balled into fists.

"That's not what that is, Andi," Darin said. His smile probably meant to be placating, but it just made her blood boil. "You don't get how these accounts work."

"I know how transfers work. It means money moves from one account to another. Why are you taking my money?"

His smile slipped, and he leaned in closer, the scent of his expensive cologne filling the space. "It's *our* money."

"That is my business account. The one that covers my expenses, like the lease. That's not a shared account."

"You're not the only one with a business, babe." Darin's eyes narrowed. "I've got expenses, too."

"So you drained *my* account to cover them?"

"It's temporary." He sat on the edge of the desk, arms folded. "Ever since crypto went down the crapper, I've had to improvise. It's how day trading works. You couldn't possibly understand the complexity. Besides, you'll have your big payoff from Kulcher soon enough. Let me handle this."

Andi wanted to scream that his "handling it" had gotten her kicked out of her kitchen. She wanted to grab his fancy laptop and smash it into his overpriced desk and maybe stomp on his stupid Italian shoes.

But she did none of that. She swallowed it down, letting it feed the fire that blazed in her gut.

"And where," she said, surprised at how calm she managed to sound with the bonfire raging inside, "do you suggest I bake the gingerbread? What supplies do I use for the decorations? With no money and no kitchen? You will have to cancel the contract."

Darin's face twisted. "That's not happening. I—uh—*we* need that money."

Andi turned toward the door. "Since you're so great at *handling* things, then it sounds like you'd better find a way to *handle* this."

———

Andi woke to her phone ringing. She lifted her head from Haden's pillow and slowly uncurled herself from around her sleeping boy. Still fully clothed, she dug the phone out of the pocket of her jeans.

"Hello?" Her throat felt raw from all the smoke in her belly.

"Andi, honeybun," Mrs. Kulcher's faintly accented voice greeted her cheerily. "Your business partner contacted me about your situation, and I have made arrangements. Do you have a pen?"

Trying not to sneer at the thought of Darin as her "business partner," Andi grabbed a loose red crayon and opened to the back of a coloring book, scrawling the address her client gave her.

A little stunned by the phone call, Andi changed clothes in the laundry room, not wanting to risk a run-in with Darin. There was no telling what the fallout would be after she'd stood up to him. Briefly, she considered calling her mom and asking her to take Haden, then squelched that idea, along with Darin's voice in her head saying it was a bad idea to give her mother too much control. She packed up Haden's bag and carried the boy to the car.

She didn't see Darin.

The drive to the new location took nearly twice as long as to her old kitchen. It was in an industrial park. She recognized the sleek blue car Mrs. Kulcher drove and parked beside it. As she unbuckled Haden, the fairy godmother herself opened a door. Andi found herself offering a weary version of the woman's smile.

"I have reserved this location for the duration of the contract." Mrs. Kulcher held the door open for them. "You will find that it is fully stocked, but should you require anything else, all you have to do is say the magic words." She winked.

Andi let Haden slide from her arms to standing.

"Hello, my pudding pie." Mrs. Kulcher gave her customary cheek pinch. "I do believe you have grown since I last saw you."

"Really?" Haden grinned.

"Most definitely." She offered her hand. "Come with me."

Haden took her hand and was led away without a backward glance at Andi. They went to a seating area with colorful chairs and an assortment of books. Andi managed to stop staring long enough to take in her new space.

It was an industrial kitchen, all white counters and stainless steel fixtures. Three immense refrigerators lined one wall and several ovens lined the other, with half a dozen long tables between them. The largest baking sheets Andi had ever seen were neatly stacked on one table. If Andi had read the contract right, she would need them.

"Mrs. Kulcher," Andi said, stepping into the sitting area. "Could I ask you a question? Just a clarification on the contract?"

Mrs. Kulcher blinked from her seat next to Haden. "You read the contract?"

Andi nodded. "Were the dimensions for the gingerbread correct? Were you expecting … feet instead of inches?"

Mrs. Kulcher let out a tinkling laugh. "Of course, sweet peach. How else am I to have a perfect creation if it fits on a simple table? No, I must have something grand!"

"So you want the base of the house to be … twelve *feet*?"

Mrs. Kulcher smiled. "It must be big enough to leave an impression. Isn't that right, Haden? Wouldn't you like to come visit me in my gingerbread house?"

Haden giggled and started chewing on a blue crayon.

"You want people to ... go inside?" Andi might have squeaked.

Mrs. Kulcher's smile was indulgent. "No, pumpkin. I am speaking figuratively."

"Oh."

The old woman turned back to Haden, removing the crayon and instead offering a wrapped chocolate.

Andi weirdly felt like she was intruding on their moment. She spun on her heel and headed back to the kitchen, her mind already working to expand the gingerbread recipe to fill those immense pans.

Andi should be asleep. She knew that. But sharing a bed with a toddler wasn't the most restful. And her brain wouldn't stop running the numbers on how much royal frosting she'd need to create the white stucco look of the Tudor-style house. At least the chocolate beams were finished. Those had been a bear to manage, but with the endless table space, she'd done it. She'd melted enough Isomalt sugar for the windows; she'd even made two extras to allow for breakage. Those should be cooled enough to handle by the morning.

But what Andi couldn't get out of her head was that odd phrase from the contract: "fresh chattel." It was so familiar. And it was obviously important; maybe even as important as the gingerbread. But what did it mean? Glancing at Haden and assured of his even breathing, she reached for her phone and opened a search window.

After an entirely sleepless night, Andi plastered on a smile as she made breakfast, listened to Darin drone on about bitcoin and penny stocks, wondering how much of what he said was real. She stoked the smoldering coals in her stomach to spark fire once more. She asked no questions, only endured his kiss as he slipped out the front door. Once his car was down the road and gone, she pulled an old backpack from the depths of the hall closet and headed to Haden's room.

A soft knock at the front door stopped Andi as she tied Haden's shoes.

She opened the door to an older version of herself. Curls grayer and clothes better fitting.

"Mom," Andi breathed out and felt a weight lift from her shoulders, only to move to her heart.

They embraced. Haden was all squeals and hugs at seeing his long-absent grandmother.

Andi quickly moved the spare car seat into her mother's sedan. She carefully buckled in Haden, smiling and tickling him as she struggled to not let tears fall. She breathed in the baby-boy scent of him one last time, then turned to her mother. Handing her the backpack with Haden's clothes and favorite dinosaurs, Andi let the tears come where her son couldn't see.

"Two weeks," she said. "No contact. No calls. No texts. I don't even want a postcard."

"Two weeks," her mother nodded, her own tears shining.

As they pulled away, Andi didn't watch. She had her own facade to build along with the gingerbread house.

It was done. In all its sugary glory, it was done. Andi feared her hands might never recover from the massive amount of royal icing she had squeezed, but there was time enough to heal. Setting down her frosting bag on the cold industrial table, she inspected the line of gummy dinosaurs along one cookie window ledge. She ignored the pang in her chest. She missed Haden with every cell, but it was for him that she had to complete this.

"You are finished?" Mrs. Kulcher's familiar voice held almost as much sugar as Andi's creation.

Andi didn't turn to the old woman, not trusting her face through her exhaustion. "It's finished. Just as you requested."

Mrs. Kulcher made pleased sounds as she walked around the house, holding a teacup and occasionally sipping as she murmured exclamations in another language, but Andi was certain she approved.

"And where is dearest Haden? I should very much like to see my sweet boy."

Andi hadn't even raised her head to answer when Darin came bursting through the door, his chiseled face a storm cloud. She flinched reflexively before she forced her shoulders straight and looked back at the client.

"The kid is gone," Darin said. Not to Andi. To Mrs. Kulcher. "I looked everywhere."

Mrs. Kulcher looked to Andi, who met the old woman with a gaze of steel.

"Then the contract is not complete," the woman said, the tone of her voice harder than set royal frosting.

"I never signed it." Andi flicked dried frosting from her apron, the blaze in her gut filling her with strength. "Darin did. You will have to speak to him about your 'fresh chattel.'"

Her web search for that odd phrase revealed that, along with the extravagant gingerbread house, Mrs. Kulcher would receive a person. A *young* person. Suddenly the extravagant price and Darin's insistence had made so much more sense.

Darin grabbed Andi's arm, jerking her hard enough to knock her off balance. "Where is the kid, Andi?"

She smiled, a real smile filled with the thrill of outsmarting this man who thought he was so much smarter than she was. "I don't know."

"Make the phone call." Darin shoved his phone in her face. "Now."

Andi shrugged as best she could in his grip. "You know I'm just no good with numbers." And she giggled.

She felt the burning sting before she realized he'd slapped her.

"Now, now." Mrs. Kulcher's tone sounded like she was addressing unruly schoolchildren. "There is no need for that."

Darin released Andi, and she stumbled away from him.

Mrs. Kulcher held a large key that sparkled with something other than sugar crystals and moved toward the gingerbread house. She smiled over her shoulder before pressing the key into the cookie door, just below the gumdrop doorknob. Where a keyhole might be. She turned the key and pushed open the door.

As the old woman stepped through, Andi's eyes widened. The gingerbread house now held a tidy room inside, complete with a rocking chair, table, and a large stone oven with a roaring fire.

"I have your payment here," she said, gesturing to the gold bar on the table, shimmering in the firelight.

Darin shot Andi a look that promised violence before stepping forward, crossing the threshold. His hand was already reaching for the big payoff.

But then there was no Darin. Only a small boy. One about Haden's size but dwarfed in Darin's tailored shirt and slacks.

Andi barely had time to suck in a breath before the gold bar landed with a dull *thunk* at her feet.

Mrs. Kulcher's smile held no warmth. "*Now* our contract is complete."

The old woman picked up her teacup and shut the door.

Jessica Guernsey writes urban and contemporary fantasy novels and short stories. A BYU alumna with a degree in journalism, her work is published in magazines and anthologies. By day, she crushes dreams as a slush pile reader for three publishers for a combined 12 years' experience. During November's NaNoWriMo, Jessica is a Municipal Liaison for the Utah: Elsewhere

Region. Frequently, she can be found at writing conferences. She isn't difficult to spot; just look for the extrovert.

While she spent her teenage angst in Texas, she now lives on a mountain in Utah with her family. Discover more stories at jessicaguernsey.com.

The Boba Thief
Ken Bebelle and Julia Vee

I stared hard at the modest storefront of Golden Dragon Pot Stickers. The most exclusive purveyor of dumplings on Lotus Lane enjoyed a near-legendary status amongst us Jiaren.

Having tasted these epic pot stickers but once, I hungered for them again. There was only one problem—Kelly, the chef and owner of Golden Dragon, hated my guts.

But today I had a plan. I reined in my aura, the solid gold corona of light around my head that announced to my kind that I was the Sentinel of San Francisco, the human extension of the magic sentience of the City. When my aura was just a bare sliver of light around me, I pulled on my ball cap to hide the distinctive silver stripe in my hair and donned a pair of oversized sunglasses.

The time to strike was now.

I strode across the street and kept my demeanor calm even as I trembled with anticipation on the inside. I pulled the door open with what I hoped was breezy indifference and stepped into the restaurant. The bell jangled cheerily, and the restaurant's bright green interior bustled with patrons.

A warm hug of umami scents washed over me, and I soaked in the clatter of a busy kitchen and the low buzz of diners packed into tiny stalls, slurping down tiny packages of pork wrapped in pan-fried dough. I paused as the thick aroma of meat slow-simmered in Shaoxing wine bathed me like a lover's caress.

A tidy row of to-go bags sat on the mobile order counter. I found one labeled "Emily." I'd even used a fake name. The lengths I was going to for these pot stickers. I picked up the bag, already savoring the pork and fried dough in my head.

A deep voice bellowed from the kitchen, prompting several patrons to look up from their succulent pot stickers. Oh, no. Queen Kelly, a woman built like a bank vault door and dressed in chef's whites, burst from the kitchen doors. The rich and savory taste of victory turned to bitter ashes in my mouth. Not just metaphorical ashes, either. A wisp of parchment with fading calligraphy hung from the ceiling. Bright embers devoured the edges of the thin paper, and in a second, it was gone but for a wisp of smoke.

Broken claw! I was both impressed and offended that Kelly had asked the local temple for a ward keyed to my power. Not enough to stop me, but effective for announcing my arrival. I wondered how many of them she had.

Kelly stopped inches from me and knocked the ball cap off my head. My short, distinctive dark hair spilled out.

I had enough power in my pinky to blast Kelly across the Pacific, but that wouldn't get me any pot stickers. So I reined in my annoyance and accepted my punishment.

Kelly grabbed the bag from my hand. "I'm far enough behind as it is without you making trouble for me. Out!"

My stomach rumbled as I stood outside the Golden Dragon. I sighed and mentally made plans for a mediocre lunch. A ping sounded on my phone showing a refund on my mobile order. Claws and fangs! I'd gotten so close!

I swiped away the notification on my phone and cursed the

dragon gods and their fickle ways. I hadn't expected the Sentinel gig to come with concierge service but buying some pot stickers didn't seem out of line.

I let my aura unfurl. No sense in hiding it now. I stalked back toward the newly erected Sentinel's Hall. A middle-aged balding man in a checkered shirt and a shopkeeper's apron paced in front of my door. He bowed at the waist when he saw me.

"Good afternoon, Sentinel. I'm Dan Takeichi, from Takeichi Mart and the president of the Lotus Lane Merchant's Association. We need your assistance."

I blinked in confusion. What could the merchant association possibly need from me? I was a retired assassin. It's not like I could operate a cash register or improve their supply chain. "I'm sorry. Yes. Mr. ...?"

"Takeichi."

"Mr. Takeichi. How can I help?"

"Please, call me Dan."

"I'm Emiko."

The man smiled and straightened up. "Yes, as you know, the Annual Lotus Lane Spring Feast is tomorrow night, and the merchants have been working hard to prepare."

I was aware because the security considerations for a festival on Lotus Lane were a logistical nightmare. Trying to keep thousands of talented, magical Jiaren hidden from outside eyes in a tiny city was hard enough. Trying to keep Wairen, outsiders, from noticing a flood of people heading into what should look like a deserted back alley was much harder.

I leaned in as I anticipated a new security concern. "I'm sure the merchants have been doing their best."

"Yes, well, several shops have noticed significant shortages in their inventory." He brought his hands together, twisting them back and forth.

I tilted my head. "What kind of shortages?"

Dan laughed nervously. "Sake, rice, and boba tea. Some other food."

I almost laughed. Lotus Lane had merchants with rare commodities that couldn't be found anywhere else. Even Jiaren from Vancouver came to Lotus Lane for their specific needs. Herbal concoctions, custom-crafted elemental powered tiles, fragrant hybrid fruits grown in special Realm fragments, gems and precious metals forged by gao-level talents. And this "thief" hitting Lotus Lane was passing all those things up for sake, rice, and boba tea?

"Who are the shops affected and how much was taken?"

"Our store, the Takeichi Mart, has had two bottles of sake taken each night for the past six nights. Moyoshi Sushi is missing rice shipments from the past week. Kelly from the Golden Dragon Pot Sticker has been missing two trays of frozen pot stickers each night, along with two pitchers of her brewed oolong tea that she uses for the boba. There are a few more."

No wonder Kelly's boba tea was so delicious. No powder mix for her; she brewed the tea. Argh. My recent defeat at her hands was too fresh. I couldn't go back in there now and investigate this gourmet thief.

Wait. No. I would be delighted to have respectable Mr. Takeichi, president of the merchant association, escort me into Golden Dragon Pot Stickers to conduct my investigation. Maybe I'd have to eat some pot stickers and drink some tea as part of my investigation!

I gave Dan a wide smile. "Let's walk through the places that have reported an issue. Tell me everything."

He dropped his hands to his sides, his relief obvious. "I'm so glad you can help us, Sentinel. Others scoffed, but I knew you were right for this task."

"Please, just Emiko."

It was true I wasn't uniformly loved by the occupants of Lotus Lane. But whether they loved me or hated me, they were all entitled to my protection. Usually I protected them from something far more unsavory, like demons from the underworld. Today, I had a hunch it was something altogether different. I'd lived in Japan near enough Shinto shrines to have some idea what might be going on.

We walked to the Takeichi Mart, a tidy shop stocked with mountains of fresh fruit and vegetables in wooden bins out front. Along the way, Dan explained that he and his brother, Walter, had recently taken over the store after their parents retired. Dan handled the morning shift, and Walter took care of closing. Despite Walter locking up at night, each morning, without fail, the liquor shelves were short two bottles of Junmai Daiginjo sake.

Patrons milled about the market with baskets filled to the brim with snacks and produce. It was a small space but stacked from floor to ceiling with delightful goods that I would have to peruse at length later. A round-cheeked teenager with a high ponytail manned the front cashier stand. She smiled at Dan as we came in, never stopping her rapid-fire scanning of produce for the waiting customer.

There were two cashier counters, each with a maneki neko, the familiar white lucky cat with the waving paw. Overall, the store was neat and orderly, with well-labeled aisles and clean displays. By contrast, a dusty waterfall display sat neglected in a front corner with some houseplants and an empty platform.

In the beverage section, Dan showed me the high shelf where the premium liquors were kept. "We stock the shelves at night until they reach this spot and then lock up."

"Any camera footage?"

"Nothing. No broken locks."

I walked over to the corner of the shop with the waterfall stand. "What goes here?"

"Hmm? Oh. My parents used to keep some art, and a plate with fruit. You know, offerings."

"Why is it empty?"

"The water fountain needs a new pump. I've been meaning to fix it. Seemed like a bad idea to leave food out too."

Interesting. "Why don't you take me to the other stores who have had missing items."

By early evening we were back where we started, and I smiled, thinking of Kelly having to allow me back into Golden Dragon Pot Sticker after unceremoniously booting me out earlier.

The crowd hadn't thinned out much at Kelly's. Dan pushed the door open, and we strode into the welcoming smell of fried dough and meat while the bell jangled behind us.

Crisp white bags with mobile orders lined up on the back counter, mocking me.

Dan poked his head into the kitchen. "Kelly? Do you have a minute?"

"Yes, yes. Let me finish this batch, Dan." I'd never heard her sound so friendly before.

Kelly didn't look up from the pan as she poured in the slurry. A delicate wafer of light rice batter crisped up and connected eight pot stickers together in fried harmony. It was culinary magic. After a moment, she slid the perfect square of pot stickery goodness onto a plate. She handed it to the server and stepped out of the kitchen.

Her face had a sheen of sweat from the hot kitchen and her eyes bugged out when she saw me. "What is she doing here?"

"She's the Sentinel. I've asked her to track down the missing festival food." Dan spoke slowly as if trying to soothe a wild beast.

I gave her a cheery little wave.

Kelly's eyes moved between me and Dan. Dan kept talking, and Kelly calmed down when she realized that the entire merchant association was backing me. Her eyes also warmed considerably as Dan spoke, and it occurred to me that maybe she was a little sweet on him.

Kelly had earned her title of Pot Sticker Queen the hard way. She started work at 4:00 AM, wrapping pot stickers and stocking her freezers. During the day, I'd seen her man the front desk, tired and irritable as customers flooded in. Dan told me he worked the morning shift, which meant that he was receiving the goods, sweeping and stocking the produce bins in front. Lotus Lane was usually hustling and bustling with commerce, but maybe that early in the day, it was just Kelly and Dan with their lights on.

"Kelly, would you show Emiko where the trays have gone missing?"

Kelly inhaled sharply, her chin jutting out. "This way."

The staff stared at us wide-eyed as we wound through the narrow kitchen to a floor-to-ceiling double freezer filled with trays. Each tray had rows of curved pot stickers neatly laid out. There had to be something like forty-eight pot stickers per tray.

If she'd been hit for two trays a day for a week, she was out something like six hundred pot stickers. I let out a low whistle.

"That's a lot of missing product, Kelly." Dan's voice was low and sympathetic.

She dropped her head, and I felt bad for her when she said, "Dan, I could barely make payroll this week."

He reached out and squeezed her forearm, commiserating. "That's hard. I'm sorry."

As happy as I'd been to barge back in here, I felt strange now witnessing this moment of vulnerability from my nemesis.

When she looked up, I gave her a short bow. "I will find the culprit."

I settled myself into a lawn chair in the middle of the sake aisle in Dan's store. I'd showed up just before closing, and Walter had gratefully let me in, even offering me a thermos of hot tea to fortify me through the night.

"Is it some sort of monster?" His eyes traveled over the sword at my hip, and he laughed nervously.

I hefted my backpack and showed him what I'd brought with me. "Probably not, given that your store is still standing. If it is what I think it is, we can still come out of this ahead."

With that, he had left me to it and locked me in the store. As night deepened and Lotus Lane grew quiet, the song of my city rose to fill the silence. I closed my eyes and listened, feeling the heartbeat of my city as it bedded down for the night. As I attuned my senses to San Francisco, my awareness spread out from me.

The magic of the city stretched away from me like a sheet of fabric. Each of the businesses on Lotus Lane shone in my senses like multicolored lights, different hues for the talents that had built the businesses, each business deforming the fabric of the city according to its relative strength.

I had a good hunch why the items had gone missing, but this next part was still a delicate dance. The Jiaren of Lotus Lane were depending on me, and I didn't want to let them down. I'd only had this Sentinel role for a month, and catching this thief would give me a small win that could go a long way to earning me some goodwill.

I waited in the shadows and assessed my city. Energy flowed around the businesses like rushing water, carrying luck and prosperity. The few people still out at this hour appeared as ghostly images, their brightness determined by the strength of their talents.

My heart rate had slowed into a deep resting state when two very strange beings crept along the outside of the building, skulking in the shadows and making their way to the back door. I turned my chair around to face the door.

With a flash of power, the back door glowed with brilliant white light and two short figures stepped into the T Mart. The glow faded, and the door reappeared. The shadowy outlines confirmed my suspicions.

They were kitsune, fox spirits, mischievous minor gods in service to Inari Okami, goddess of—what else?—rice, sake, and tea. They both had coats of pristine white and stood about two feet high at the shoulders. The larger fox had three lustrous tails with glossy fur, the smaller only two. Minor gods, messengers for Inari.

I had met a nine-tailed kitsune a few weeks ago and been completely humbled by her power. These kits were much closer to my level, and this time I had the home-turf advantage. I pulled the city's power to me and cloaked myself, bending the light to hide myself even as I sat in the middle of the aisle.

Either these kits were not as powerful as I thought, or they were simply too distracted. They padded across the store, whispering to each other, oblivious to me, and stopped in the middle of the aisle.

The larger fox stood on its hind legs to get a better look at the higher shelf. "Oh, look. Yuki No Bosha Junmai Daiginjo. That one was nice."

The smaller fox sat on the linoleum floor, right next to my foot, and began stroking one of its two tails, brushing the fine fur from end to end. "Whatever. They all taste the same to me. Just pick one, and let's get going already."

"Your palate is atrocious. You would drink sake from a plastic barrel if it weren't for me."

"Just hurry up already. I'm hungry."

The sake fox padded up and down the aisle. "You can't rush this. Since they've clearly forgotten to leave out an offering, it is our duty to select an appropriate bottle."

The younger fox lay down on the floor, covered its snout with its paws and closed its eyes. "I'm hungry. Let's go across the street. I want more of those pot stickers." A bright pink tongue poked out of its mouth and swiped across a row of very white, very sharp-looking teeth.

"I thought it was the tea you liked."

"That, too. Those boba pearls! So chewy! Rice never tasted so good."

These kitsune were hilarious. And clearly going to continue perpetrating mischief unless I brought them into line. I relaxed my grasp on the city's magic, and it trickled through my fingers, allowing the shadows to unfurl as I let my aura shine through.

The hungry fox hadn't stopped talking. "... so firm, yet soft on the outside. The delicate floral tea flavor. I may bring Inari a gallon of boba next time, see if she likes that better than the rice! Are you ready to go yet?"

The older fox had frozen in its tracks, hackles up, a massive bottle of sake clutched in its paws. It slowly turned until it met my gaze.

Perhaps sitting on an old lawn chair in the middle of a supermarket wasn't exactly the best power pose, but I felt my blinding aura made up for the poor staging.

The younger fox finally turned to me and jumped back, back arched and teeth bared. The older fox dropped to all fours and bared its teeth as well. The sake bottle clanked to the floor and rolled away.

"Welcome to San Francisco, honored servants of the great Inari Okami. To what does the Sentinel owe the pleasure of this unexpected visit?"

The foxes traded a wary glance. News of me assuming the mantle of Sentinel of San Francisco had blazed across the world just a few weeks ago. There was little chance they could claim ignorance of me, and to come to my city and not first pay respects would be an unforgivable slight. But I didn't want a fight with the kitsune, so I had given them an out in my greeting.

The older fox stepped forward, hesitant. "Good evening, honored Sentinel. Inari Okami sends greetings and blessings for a prosperous spring. I am Hisako, and this is Momoko."

I nodded to them both. "That is wonderful to hear. My people will be hosting an annual feast tomorrow night to celebrate the season. Perhaps you've heard of the event?"

The foxes looked at each other, brows furrowed with concern.

"You must stay! You will be my honored guests. There will be rice and tea and sake and pot stickers. I believe those are Inari's favorites?"

As I listed the items, Momoko's ears drooped lower and lower.

I made a face. "Sadly, this year's feast will not be the best it could be, for which I apologize. It seems many of our merchants are missing the very items we need for the event. Very strange."

I leaned forward, elbows on my knees, and really poured it on with my aura. I reached out for the city's power again and focused on the land beneath the store.

Both foxes' eyes widened as the magic under our feet solidified under my control. It was as if I had grabbed a rushing river and frozen it in place.

"This year's feast will be nothing compared to last year's spectacle." I sighed forlornly. "And that will make my people sad. Which will make me sad."

Hisako stepped forward. "Perhaps we might be able to help."

"Truly?"

"Yes, yes! My friend and I are ... resourceful, and we have supplies that will help make your feast as memorable as you hope."

I crossed my arms over my chest. "I will not have offerings that were meant for your master. I will not engender the ill will of Inari Okami for a mere party."

"No, no! The food was not given as an offering."

I squinted at her, and she squirmed under my gaze. "How do you come by this food? Did you steal it? I will not accept stolen property."

"Steal? No ... it was ... a gift. Yes, a gift, for which we no longer have a need for. We would be honored, great Sentinel, to be able to assist in your feast."

"Very well. In fact, I have a proposal for you. Kitsune are known to be clever and resourceful. It would be advantageous for my people if you would watch over their businesses."

The two kitsune traded a wary look. Now we were getting into the bargaining portion of the night. A timeless tradition and not my strongest suit, but I had planned ahead.

I reached under my lawn chair and pulled out my bag. Opening it, I revealed a lacquered wood bento box with a mother-of-pearl chrysanthemum inlaid into the top. Saito-san at Moyoshi Sushi had been more than willing to prepare my offering when I'd told him my plan. I'd brought the bento box from my house, a Hiroto family heirloom from my childhood.

Momoko edged closer as I lifted the lid off the bento and revealed eight freshly made inari zushi. Eight plump pillows of deep-fried tofu soaked in mirin and sake, stuffed with delicately tangy sushi rice and topped off with a variety of condiments— pickled cherry blossoms, toasted sesame seeds, umeboshi, and shichimi togarashi. Even Hisako moved toward the open bento box, compelled by the aromas of rice and sake.

I waved the box slightly. "I will ask the merchants of Lotus Lane to leave offerings for Inari Okami. They may not always be this fancy, but I believe they will please your mistress. In return, you will help me ensure the prosperity of the merchants of Lotus Lane."

Hisako's and Momoko's eyes remained glued to the bento box as I spoke. Hisako's tongue flicked out of the side of her mouth. "Yes. This is ... agreeable."

She seemed to be having trouble forming words in the presence of my offering. I placed the bento on the floor and picked up the rest of my things.

"Thank you for meeting with me, honored servants of Inari Okami." I picked up the bottle of sake that Hisako had dropped. "Oh. How did this get here?"

Hisako had the humility to look ashamed as I put the bottle back on the shelf. She seemed torn between trying to apologize and tearing into the inari sushi.

"The feast begins at eight tomorrow night. I will see you there."

I gave the two of them a small bow and turned and walked out the back door.

By the next morning, Lotus Lane was abuzz with the news that several stores that had been robbed had had nearly all the stolen goods returned in the middle of the night. Dan and Walter called me after sending me a photo of their back door, where several bottles of sake had been carefully lined up. I explained to them about the offerings, and they promised to spread the word through the merchants' guild.

When night fell, I made my way out to the feast. I checked and rechecked the wards that kept Lotus Lane invisible to Wairen. Tonight was a celebration, but I still needed to stay on top of security.

All of Lotus Lane had been blocked to regular traffic, and the vendors had erected stalls down the center of the road. Red and gold banners and paper lanterns were strung across the street from the rooftops. Throngs of people made their way slowly from one end of the street to the other, sampling delicious food and drink as they walked. This was more people than I'd ever seen on Lotus Lane at one time.

This was technically the third spring feast since I'd come to San Francisco, but this was the first one I'd attended. As I made my way through the crowd, I got more respectful nods than I was expecting. I still got my share of glowers and stares from people who hadn't forgotten my past, but I didn't let that keep me from relaxing and enjoying the night. I let my senses stretch out around me, and the warm feeling of home washed over me. My city was happy.

I found two petite young ladies standing in line at Moyoshi Sushi's stall. While most Jiaren wore nice clothing for the feast, the air was decidedly relaxed. These two women, however, had come dressed in fine summer yukata decorated with painted lotus blooms along the hems. Hisako's robe was tied with a deep red obi, and Momoko's obi was brilliant blue. I stepped in line behind them, blocking the view of anyone behind us who might notice the tips of their tails poking out from under their yukata.

"Good evening. Are you enjoying yourselves?"

Hisako smiled, flashing her sharp canines. "Oh, yes, we haven't had this much fun in years!"

"I think T Mart is holding a sake tasting," I said.

Momoko stifled a hiccup. "Yes, we were already there."

We stepped up to the stall where Saito-san was packing paper bento boxes with fresh nigiri sushi. The kitsune scanned the display, trying to decide.

I called out over them, "Saito-san. They'll have the feast special. On me."

"Hai!" He grinned and pulled two bentos from beneath the counter, both filled with inari zushi topped with pickled cherry blossoms.

The young ladies clapped with delight and took the boxes.

I leaned in close to Hisako. "The merchant association has made these inari zushi a tradition for the festival. To cement our continued friendship."

The fox spirit's eyes sparkled, and she inclined her head. "Inari will be most pleased."

The kitsune bowed again and wandered away, melting into the crowd. As they moved down the street, the lanterns brightened, and the voices of the crowd grew more boisterous. The kitsune would be good for my city, and it was good for my people to remember the old gods.

I waved to Saito-san and moved on.

The line in front of Kelly's stall was prodigious, and the smell of her frying pot stickers was enough to make my stomach gurgle. Her staff could barely keep up with the orders as their customers clamored for more. Kelly might never be friendly to me, but she was still a resident of my city, and I would protect her and her business. Even if I never got to eat her pot stickers again.

I turned to head up the street and nearly walked into a wall of a woman. Kelly's broad frame was clad in her usual chef's jacket, tonight sporting an additional bright green apron with her dragon logo on the front.

I gave her what I hoped was a not-too-cocky smile and nodded. "I'm glad to see business doing so well tonight. I hope the feast will be a resounding success for you."

Kelly's eyelid twitched, and she huffed a breath through her nose. She lifted an arm and held out a bag to me like it contained a bomb. "Here."

The porky goodness hit my senses like an avalanche, and I'm certain my eyes expanded to the size of steamed buns.

Kelly dropped the bag and I scrambled to catch it before it fell.

She huffed again. "One order per week. That's it. No more."

Behind Kelly, work had stopped at her stall as her entire staff watched our little drama. When I glanced in their direction, they all waved. As Kelly turned away from me, they all snapped back to their workstations like nothing had happened.

I called after Kelly's retreating back, "Thank you!"

She grunted and waved a hand in my general direction. It was likely the best I would ever get from her.

I reached into the bag and found a to-go box and a festive plastic cup filled with boba tea. Dark spheres of chewy goodness swirled at the bottom of the cup. I pulled out the white box, which had been carefully vented to prevent trapped steam from making the pot stickers soggy. I opened the box and broke off a pot sticker from the batch with a satisfying crack. I bit into the pillowy wrapper and the savory pork, decadent juices flooding my mouth. Contentment filled my body.

While I ate, the Jiaren of San Francisco celebrated the renewal of the spring season, their colorful auras blending together under the glow of endless lanterns. For today, my duties as the Sentinel had been simple enough, and as satisfying as these pot stickers.

I polished off the box and slurped my boba tea.

The Boba Thief

Julia likes stories about monsters, money, and good food. She was born in Macao and grew up in northern California, where she studied at UC Berkeley and majored in Asian Studies. She is a graduate of the Viable Paradise workshop.

Ken turned his childhood love for reading sci-fi and fantasy into a career in prosthetics. After twenty years he came back to books, writing about plucky underdogs and ancient magic artifacts with deadly secrets. He grew up in northern California and now lives in southern California with his wife, two kids, and too many tomato plants.

Ken and Julia have written together since middle school. Their modern Asian fantasy novel, *Ebony Gate*, will debut with Tor in 2023.

The Last Jars of Peaches
Lauren Lang

The air in the auction house is thick with anticipation and the stink of sweat. The converted warehouse is dim and hot; a bank of shattered windows high up on the walls allows only scant light and fresh air in. The poor ventilation combined with the collective heat from the gathered crowd of three hundred potential bidders in nothing but our underwear has warmed the large, open room to an uncomfortable temperature.

Sweat drips down my legs as the man next to me shifts from foot to foot, elbowing me in my bra cup as he does. The padding takes the brunt of the impact, but I'm still forced to step back. My calloused feet crunch against the cement floor. Whatever small bits remain of the rusting industrial machinery that once stood here are being ground into even finer particles under the weight of us.

We're standing shoulder to shoulder, pressed against the barricade that keeps the crowd back from the auctioneer's platform. The platform is a flat structure about six feet wide and three feet tall. It makes the auctioneer visible to the mass of unwashed bodies crammed together.

A smaller woman is standing in front of me, her ill-fitting panties sagging below her waistline. She's so thin, I can count the vertebrae in her spine. Her hair is brittle and matted in the back. It's a struggle to keep her greasy mane from touching my chest and face as the people behind us shove forward, impatient for things to get started.

We're all thirsty. The lucky few of us who brought water can't get to it until the event is over. Our belongings have been hidden away in secret stashes outside, scattered among the bricks of the decaying buildings that line Auction Row. Our canteens are inaccessible for the moment.

There's a rising murmur as the assembled bidders voice their disapproval. The auction was supposed to start a half hour ago. The auctioneers are ignoring the crowd's displeasure because they can afford to. They set the rules. We're so desperate for their wares that we'll do almost anything they say. Being half-naked does help us stay cooler in the sweltering heat, but there is another reason we're prohibited from wearing more clothing. Auctions are a magnet for petty criminals.

A few years ago, a pickpocket incited an all-out brawl and used the fight as cover to steal most of the bidders' payments before the auctioneers could collect them.

Now, the payment tokens are kept under guard, stored in small lockboxes behind a savage-looking doorman. Bidders aren't allowed to bring anything else of value inside the auction house. We also can't leave until the auctioneers have collected their fees. I always laugh at that last part. The auctioneers are the ones who bring the high-dollar items. After all, they're the ones with the food.

In the before-times, I would have laughed at the thought of doing this. What a difference a decade can make. As a twenty-something IT consultant wearing crisp, white-collared shirts and black pencil skirts to work every day, the thought of standing among the unwashed masses in holey granny panties would have been unfathomable.

Then, in 2032, the bees died en masse from a new, more lethal form of destructor mites. The mites had been causing

Colony Collapse for years, but previously, there had only been a thirty to fifty percent insect mortality rate among bees. The new breed of mites caused closer to ninety percent mortality. The mites quickly killed most of the honeybees in North America. The rest of the world isolated us, trying to keep the mites at bay and their bees safe.

With the North American bees dead, farmers had to grow more water-intensive, wind-pollinated crops like corn and wheat to feed people. But for years, the population of the Western United States had been growing as people who favored the West's dry climate and sunny weather moved in. There was already a burgeoning water crisis before the mites struck, and the additional strain of irrigating so many more acres of crops proved to be too much. The West's once-generous, natural aquifer ran dry, and seven states lost their ability to provide basic necessities.

Chaos ensued. People couldn't eat dollars and cents, so money didn't matter anymore. After that, the social order broke down.

With no official state to speak of, there isn't much left in the way of utilities. Luxuries like running water and power are long gone. Without maintenance, the roads have become impassable, trapping us here. We've been left to fend for ourselves.

The auction houses were our answer to the crisis. They became a lifeline for a starving populace, giving us a working barter-and-trade system and bringing back some semblance of order.

Currency consists of food, land, and water tokens, and each token has a redeemable value at the auction house. Water tokens are generally worth the most, but their value fluctuates depending on the season. During the July monsoons, when rainwater is readily available, food tokens are usually more desirable. Land tokens are never worth much, but the auctioneers created the option.

I work as a stand-in bidder for those who don't wish to visit the auction house themselves. The auctioneers announce what's available to bid on, and I participate in my client's stead. I don't get paid unless I place a winning bid.

Today, my client is the Calhoon family. They're richer than my typical client because they have a well that still produces. It's the source of their extravagant wealth. My clients sent forty-five water tokens with me today, a hefty sum that should be enough to win them what they want.

I glance around at my competition, trying to guess which clients they're representing today. It's hard to say. I recognize most of the faces, but clients change bidders frequently. In this game, you're only as good as your last win. Winning a can of green beans is what got me the Calhoon family as a client. If I can get the peaches, I'm almost guaranteed an even wealthier client at the next auction. If I don't, my value will decrease. I can't afford to have that happen again.

I picture my twelve-year-old daughter's face. I try to look past the dirt streaks on Cecile's cheeks. She's been crying from hunger a lot lately, her growing body demanding more nutrition than I've been able to give her. I see her sad hazel eyes, the same color as mine, and it breaks my heart. She's too small, barely four feet tall. Her growth has been stunted by a lack of food.

This morning, I had to chop off her long, brittle, blonde hair to keep it from tangling and matting. She sat stoically and allowed me to butcher her hair. I wept the entire time, my heart breaking. Cecile looks so much like I did when I was younger, but yet so different, her ribs always sticking out of her tiny frame. For her sake, I can't afford to lose the auction today.

I sweep the crowd again, mentally dividing up the people into three groups. The first group are pros, like me. We know how the system works, and we respect it—and each other.

The second group are tourists, people who come to see the spectacle but have no intention of bidding. They may be prospective sellers who come to see the process in action. People hoarded food before the catastrophe, and some still have enough that they can afford to sell the excess off via the auctioneers. Occasionally, the tourists are foreign journalists, here to document our downfall. Either way, they are mostly ignored.

The third group is the most dangerous: the amateurs. They're men and women who are just wealthy enough to bid but not rich enough to hire a pro like me. They are easy to pick out in a group. They may be cleaner than the rest of us, but they play dirty. All too often, they fall victim to a bidding frenzy, driving up prices. It's a shortsighted strategy. Even if they get their item, the rest of us are left to contend with a bidding history that makes the next can of peas or jar of tomatoes unattainable.

The auctions aren't just a numbers game. There's an art to winning that tourists and amateurs don't understand. They aren't hungry for it like we are. They haven't had to become as quick or as adept at judging people.

As pros, we've learned when we can push our clients to pay a higher price and how to dance around each other to place the lowest possible winning bid. It's possible to live on that margin, scraping by on the difference between the amount the client gives us and what we actually pay the auctioneers. It's understood that amount becomes ours, payment earned in exchange for our services.

Finally, the auctioneer and his patter, the man who calls out for bidders, appear off the side of the stage. Today's food hawker is Benjamin Bradford, a heavyset, balding, middle-aged man with a limp. He wears his navy-blue auctioneer's jacket with slightly too much pride for someone whose clothing is a size too small. The jacket stretches over the beginnings of a belly, a sign of the fantastic wealth he's accrued in his current position.

Behind Benjamin is a group of burly men in leather carrying an assortment of jars and cans. The brutes are better fed and look healthier than the rest of us. It's one of the benefits of working for the auctioneers, even as a grunt. There are no sunken cheeks or gaunt frames among their number, although their faces betray their boredom.

The men follow Benjamin up the small set of stairs to the platform. They arrange themselves across the stage in a line with the auctioneer and patter in the center. The angry murmurs from the crowd immediately die away. All eyes are on the food in front of us. There's a fantastic array of fruits and vegetables: a large can of hominy, a massive jar of whole pickles, and two cans each of black beans and pears. On the end is my desired prize—two large glass jars filled with preserved peaches.

"The auctioneers are thrilled to welcome you to today's event," Benjamin says, beginning his rehearsed spiel. "If this is your first time attending, please observe auction decorum. Use your paddles to place your bids. Shouting will not be acknowledged. Physical fighting will not be tolerated. Anyone who causes a disturbance will be banned from future events for life. And finally, payment must be made before you receive your goods. Anyone who fails to pay the agreed-upon price for any reason will be subject to the auctioneer's justice."

I cringe at that last part. There's always one person at every auction—usually an amateur—who thinks they're going to find some new and inventive way to cheat the auctioneers out of payment. The burly men aren't just for show. Professional bidders know better than to risk their hide for someone else.

With that, the auction starts. There's little fanfare since no one needs to be convinced to buy anything. Everyone knows what they came for. The burly man on the far-left side of the platform holds up the jar of pickles, and the paddles go up.

From the auctioneer's perspective, I imagine it looks like a sea of colored cardboard waving in the breeze. Each paddle is color-coded to represent the form of individual payment the bidder has brought with them: blue for water, yellow for food, and brown for land. Benjamin stares out at the various bids, calling out the minimum starting price and form of payment the auctioneer will accept for the item.

"Starting price is five water tokens," Benjamin announces.

There is a collective groan from the professionals sent here with other forms of payment. They won't be allowed to bid on the pickles today, though they may be able to make offers on the other items. Those who had hoped to bid with food or land tokens lower their paddles.

All interested bidders with at least five water tokens keep their paddles raised. About thirty people are competing at this stage. It's about average.

"Ten," the patter says, taking over from Benjamin. "Do I see ten?"

More paddles lower, but about fifteen stay up.

"Fifteen," the patter calls out. More paddles go down.

There are about five left now, and I can see the professionals shooting the other bidders dirty looks. This is the game we play with the auctioneers. If everyone were to lower their paddles, Benjamin would be forced to drop the price or refuse to sell the item, which would give us more negotiating power. Sometimes, we are able to silently collude with each other to successfully force the auctioneer's hand, though doing so isn't always voluntary. My fellow professionals have been known to "help" each other stop bidding. However, a few stupid amateurs are still waving their skinny arms in the air. They're allowing Benjamin to continue with the auction.

"Twenty water tokens," the patter says, eying the crowd. He knows when he's got a sucker hooked.

Two paddles stay up. The professionals are openly hissing at the remaining bidders now, their way of telling the idiots to stop running up the price without violating the rule about causing a disturbance. Both bidding amateurs ignore them.

"Thirty!" the patter exclaims triumphantly.

One of the paddles falls.

The other bidder wavers, his paddle hanging uncertainly in the air for a moment before he finds a nincompoop's confidence and triumphantly raises the paddle higher. The tension in the room is thick, and I can feel the hatred emanating from the professionals. The amateur appears oblivious to it all.

"Sold for thirty water tokens!" Benjamin yells.

The Last Jars of Peaches

The auctioneer moves right along. There are other items on the block today.

Thankfully, the auction proceeds in a much saner manner, with the cans of hominy, beans, and pears selling for much more affordable prices.

I watch with interest but don't bid. Only fools gamble with their own money at the auction house. While the house sells the goods, they don't guarantee that the products are safe. More than one bidder has walked away with spoiled food, and there are no refunds here. The auctioneers are not responsible for what happens to an item once it leaves their hands. Best to leave risks like that to the people who can afford to take them.

When the peaches come up on the block, I feel my anxiety start to rise.

"Paddles up for peaches!" Benjamin yells.

I'm glad to see that the majority of the bidders left are offering water, though there are a few land paddles as well. If all anyone has to bid is water, it is more likely that Benjamin will select it as the accepted payment method.

"Starting price is ten water tokens," Benjamin yells out.

There must not be enough land paddles left to make bidding competitive.

I keep my paddle up, as do many of the other attendees.

"Twenty," the patter says.

I cringe at the increase but keep my paddle up. We are bidding on two jars, so it's not an entirely unexpected jump.

"Thirty!"

My paddle begins to waver. I can see many other professionals glancing at one another, silently gauging their competition's willingness to continue. Enough paddles stay up that the patter continues.

"Forty water tokens!"

Most of the paddles fall, but across the room, I can see an idiot amateur with a frenzied look on his face. My stomach falls. If he were smart, we could both drop our paddles and duke it out at a lower price. But he's fallen prey to bidding frenzy. There's no reasoning with him now.

"Fifty water tokens!"

The rest of the paddles drop. No! We're the only two bidders left, and the price has gone over my allotted amount. If I keep my paddle up, I won't be able to pay, but if I take it down, I lose the chance at a better life for my child. My paddle hangs in the air while I desperately try to decide if I can squeeze another five tokens out of my client.

Before I have a chance to think, the choice is made for me. The man next to me intentionally elbows me in the boob. I hiss in pain, and I drop my paddle with a clatter as my hands fly to my throbbing breast. I cradle my bosom, tears stinging my eyes.

I haven't been paying attention, but the other pros must have decided the price is too high to allow *anyone* to pay.

Benjamin sees the assault, and while he doesn't acknowledge it, he glances at the patter, who pauses at fifty, giving me a chance to reenter the bidding process.

"Fifty water tokens going once ... Going twice ..."

I listen anxiously, but I know that worse awaits me if I don't take my neighbor's "gentle" hint. I can't take care of my daughter if I've been beaten half to death.

"Sold for fifty water tokens!" Benjamin yells across the cavernous room. His voice reverberates in my ears, ringing through my mind over and over again.

A smile breaks out on the amateur's stupid face. If the professionals did something to try to discourage him from placing his winning bid, I can't tell. I'm focused on the pain in my chest, but it's the sinking feeling in my stomach that brings tears to my eyes. The gathering begins to break up, with a few people heading toward the exit. I hang back, staring at my lost treasure. We won't be released until payment has changed hands anyway. There's no reason to rush.

The smiling fool who won the peaches approaches the platform with the other winning bidders. They're waiting for their payment to be brought out. Within a few minutes, a burly man appears with a series of small lockboxes containing the bidders' tokens. The tokens exchange hands without incident until Benjamin gets to the peaches.

"Fifty water tokens," he says to the man. As a former patter, Benjamin's voice naturally carries, so it's not difficult to listen in on their conversation.

The man opens his lockbox and triumphantly presents Benjamin with the tokens, but Benjamin's expression sours as he stares at the man's outstretched hand.

"I'm sorry, sir, but that's only thirty. You won the bid at fifty."

"And you'll accept thirty," the man says, his voice projecting confidence that is either false or too foolhardy to comprehend.

"I'm sorry, sir, but you must be new to our establishment. The rules were laid out before the auction. I require fifty tokens. Now."

I can see the burly men gathering around Benjamin. Their early boredom is gone. The promise of violence shimmers in the air, rising off the men like heat waves in the sweltering building.

"You'll take what I give you!" the man yells, throwing the tokens at Benjamin.

It's such an entitled motion that I'm taken aback. It reminds me of the before-times when people regularly screamed at service workers. I'm not sure how this mentality could have persisted despite the events of the past decade. Maybe there's something wrong with him; the heat has caused his brain to short circuit, perhaps. I have no logical explanation for his behavior.

Benjamin stares at the man for a moment. He doesn't bother responding verbally. Instead, he turns to one of the brutes next to him, the look in his eyes silently giving his permission. The group of leather-clad enforcers grab the amateur by the arms and drag him away from the platform. I watch as the brutes shove their way through the crowd gathering near the exit, pulling the man along with them.

"Stop! Stop, you're hurting me!" the man screams.

I shake my head. If he thinks he's in pain now, the poor fool has no idea what's coming to him.

Suddenly, a voice rings out behind me.

"You!"

I turn to look, and Benjamin is pointing at me.

"You were the next highest bidder. The peaches are yours if you can pay."

My eyes light up. I jump the barricade, and Benjamin slowly descends the stairs and meets me in front of the raised platform.

"Thank you, thank you! I can pay!" I exclaim.

"Fifty water tokens," Benjamin says.

I take a step back from the auctioneer in shock.

"No. I'm sorry, but that's not correct. My highest bid was forty."

"You had your paddle raised at fifty," Benjamin says, a dangerous edge to his voice.

"I dropped it," I insist, careful to keep my tone neutral.

"Only because the man next to you forced you to," the auctioneer says with a sneer. "You would have bid fifty."

"But I didn't bid at that price. I bid forty, and I'll be happy to take the peaches for that amount."

Benjamin eyes me up and down, his eyes wandering over my half-naked form. His gaze makes my skin crawl.

"I've seen you here before, haven't I?" he says with a smile.

"I won the can of green beans at the last event."

"And you'll be back, I take it?"

I don't like where this conversation is heading, but I might be able to use the direction to my advantage.

"I come when I'm hired to be here. If I take those peaches to my client, I'm sure they'll be happy with me. They'll probably even recommend me to some of their friends. That would mean more work."

"Forty it is then," Benjamin says. "As a *personal favor* to one of our most loyal bidders."

The look in Benjamin's eyes makes me shiver in revulsion, but I have my daughter to think of.

"Thank you, auctioneer. I'll go get my payment from the front."

"No need," Benjamin says. "You're a professional. I'm sure you're good for it."

"But I insist," I say, panic sneaking into my voice.

If Benjamin empties my lockbox, he'll get the extra five water tokens that I should take home as my fee. So that's his game: extortion. No wonder he's got a gut. He's getting rich stealing from the bidders.

"Here," Benjamin says, handing over both jars at once. "They're all yours."

He knows precisely what he's doing. Once the jars are in my possession, the transaction is complete, and I'll have no choice but to pay. I push the glass jars away from me even as Benjamin shoves them into my grasp. He lets go, and in horror, I watch as both jars of peaches crash onto the floor and shatter.

The sound echoes across the warehouse. The crowd gathered near the exit goes silent, slowly turning to look at us.

I stare down at the peaches, the bright orange fruit staring up at me cheerfully from the filthy cement. A pleasant aroma I haven't smelled in years wafts up to my nostrils. I can almost taste the sugar in the syrup splattered all over the ground. My mouth starts to water.

It only takes a moment for the crowd to realize what's happened.

The next thing I know, the warehouse is filled with the sound of pounding feet. The bidders run at us, screaming and pushing as they shove each other out of the way in their desperation. The sight of the peaches on the ground has sent the starving men and women into a frenzy. There's no precedent for what's just happened, and without the brutes to maintain control, people are fighting to reach the peaches first. I can barely hear the doorman screaming to his companions for help, but they'll be too late to stop the riot that's about to happen.

The filthy, beleaguered woman from earlier is the fastest, diving over the barrier, falling into the mess, and snatching at the fruit. She whisks it off the ground, ignoring the shattered glass, and shoves a peach slice into her mouth before grabbing at another piece. She's beaten to it by another desperate bidder who crunches down hard on a shard of glass and spits the bloody fruit back onto the ground.

The rest of the crowd hits the barrier. I'm shoved back into the platform and away from my would-be extortionist. Desperate people fall to the floor, sucking the syrup off the cement. My stomach heaves.

When I'm finally able to tear my eyes away, I can't find Benjamin. He seems to have fled, and I would be wise to do the same. I know I will be blamed for this. At best, I'll be banned for life. At worst, I'll be hauled out onto the street and beaten before being banned.

I kick, elbow, and punch my way through the crowd until I'm finally on the edge of the melee. I take a few licks in the face for my efforts, but it's worth it. From my position, I can see the brutes coming back through the front door. The doorman joins them, and together, they run full tilt toward the crowd.

Desperate not to be caught, I use the crowd as a shield. I wait until the brutes reach the center of the crowd and start hurling people away from the platform. Then, I make a break for the unguarded door. My head is spinning, but a plan begins to develop as I flee.

When I reach the entrance, I see all of the boxes containing the bidders' tokens. I only hesitate for a second before I grab every single box I can carry. I'll need a way to make a new life for my daughter and me, and this is how I'm going to do it.

Despite what's happened, I would say today's auction turned out just peachy.

The Last Jars of Peaches

Lauren Lang is a former broadcast journalist and current freelance photographer and videographer living in Denver, Colorado. In her spare time, she writes fiction, cooks, bakes, crochets hats for stuffed animals, gardens with the intent of taking pictures of the flowers that survive, and terrorizes local residents by pretending to be a wildlife photographer and running through area parks with her camera screaming, "Birds!" Occasionally, she does actually take a picture of a bird. She can also occasionally be found in a tree with the birds.

Love Potion on a Large #9
Kitty Sarkozy

Have you ever known you shouldn't do something, but you do it anyway? I don't mean spur of the moment— we all do stupid shit without thinking—I mean premeditated. Bad idea from the second you think about it, but you plan it out, put everything together, wait days or weeks, and the whole time the smart part of you is screaming "WTF?!"

Asking my ex-husband, Neal, out to dinner was a bad idea from the start. We broke up more than a year ago, and I was moving an hour away. I guess I got sentimental, thinking about how I was going to miss being able to see him. But I didn't see him, even though he lived a mile away; I hadn't seen him in months. That was a good thing. But for some reason I texted him, inviting him to meet me for dinner the following week.

I think I was hoping he would say "No," then I could get that righteous vindication high you get when someone you know is a jerk acts like a jerk. It would have created some solid angry energy for packing and squelched the pesky nostalgia I was feeling, but he said "Yes."

I could have cancelled, but I didn't.

I could have gone, had an awkward dinner, and felt slightly sad.

That isn't what happened either.

Instead I made a love potion.

I know, right?! First, off, you have to believe me when I tell you I didn't think that stuff worked. So, if I didn't think magic worked, why did I make a love potion? I don't know. Maybe after everything he had done to me, I needed to feel a bit of power? Maybe my life changing so fast had made reality a little fuzzy?

Two days before our "date"—which I thought he might not tell Mandy, his new girlfriend, about because he is a lying, cheating piece of shit—I remembered seeing a love spell in one of the books I had packed up recently. It had belonged to my grandparents. They'd been in some kooky cult back in England before my mother was born.

The books were beautiful, hand-transcribed and illustrated. There were pressed herbs and flowers between the pages, very witchy and romantic. I was thinking that maybe instead of leaving them in musty old boxes I could display them at my next place. They would be awesome conversation pieces.

I found "To Ensure True Love Requited" in the third book.

It had a list of ingredients, some of which I already had, and there was an occult shop fifteen minutes away where I could get the rest. The instructions weren't hard either. I told myself it would be fun and silly, an embarrassing story to tell in a few years. How I made a love spell to win back my ex-husband, ha ha. How I gathered the ingredients and put it together, but didn't use it. I wouldn't ever add something to someone else's drink or food, right?

I made the potion.

Two days later, I took it with me to the restaurant, a place in the square I knew he liked, with its fancy, overpriced "authentic" woodfire pizza. Ordering would be easy, and the food would come quickly. The host recognized us, and things got tense for a minute as he clearly thought we were still a couple.

Neal was dressed the way Mandy liked, khaki pants and a hideous Hawaiian shirt. His hair was a bit too long, and there was more gray in his beard. He looked tired. I wondered what he was thinking about how I looked. I'd lost a few pounds and was certainly in better shape, because exercise was one of the ways I deal with stress. My outfit was meant to look just thrown on, but it was one of at least ten I'd tried.

The spell said to mix the powder with red wine, because the color red has a sympathetic bond to love and passion and the acid would hide the flavor.

When the waiter asked what we wanted to drink, I asked, "What Sangiovese do you have?" I figured it sounded classy. Neal was older than I was, and better educated. I was always trying to sound more grown up around him.

The waiter said they only had one type.

I casually said to my ex, "I don't mind buying a whole bottle, if you want to share it."

I was sure it would work. Neal loved to drink and was the cheapest person I knew. There was no chance he would say "No."

He said, "No."

He ordered beer. I only ordered a single glass of wine. My little adventure in witchcraft should have ended there.

We looked at the pizzas, finding one we could agree on. We ordered a large thin crust #9, with artichoke hearts, breaded eggplant, and feta.

My predictions for the awkwardness of the evening were accurate.

We made small talk while waiting for the pizza. He talked about the university, about how the head of the history department was an idiot, and how the administration was plotting against him, and how his students were all simpletons.

I talked about my newest cozy mystery that would be out in a few months. I used to be interested in his work, but after a year I found it boring. Neal was never interested in my "paperback chick-lit," telling me I should be a "serious, literary" writer.

I talked a little about the new house, but that could so easily lead to talking about the house I was leaving, the house we lived in while we were married. The topic was quickly abandoned.

We talked about the cats. He said he wanted to stop by and see them before I left. Anger boiled inside of me when he said he "loved them." I wanted to yell, "If you loved them so much, why haven't you bothered to see them in the last six months?" Instead I smiled and said, "I'm sure they would like that."

We talked about the weather, how we had been getting good rain and temperatures, good for gardening. That trailed off when he realized I wasn't doing much gardening in a house I was about to leave. After that was a long uncomfortable pause. I was wishing the pizza would come so we could leave and both forget this happened when he stood and excused himself to the restroom.

Right after he left, the pizza came. Small talk with this older, less fun, less interesting version of a guy I once loved was going to be over as soon as we ate. I reached out to take a slice when I noticed the red, acidic, flavorful tomato sauce coating the crust.

I pulled the small plastic cosmetics jar out of my purse, lifted up the cheese on a few slices, softly said the magical chant, sprinkled on the powder, then turned the pan so the enchanted pieces were directly in front of his plate.

I'd just returned the jar to my purse when he came back. He looked upset as he sat down across from me.

"You okay?" I asked.

"Yeah, I have to go soon. I can't really hang out, sorry," he said.

"No worries!" I chirped. I guessed that Mandy had texted him and was pissed he wasn't home. "The pizza looks good. You want to have a slice before you leave?"

"Yeah, I can do that," he said, putting one of the potion-sprinkled pieces on his plate.

"Cool. I'll ask the waiter to bring boxes; you can take half with you," I said.

He looked up, alarmed. "No, um ... that's okay. Thanks, I um ..."

"Oh," I said, realizing he had, in fact, not told Mandy he was meeting me, as I had predicted, and that he couldn't come home with half a mystery pizza.

We ate in silence for a few minutes.

"This is good pizza," he said.

"Yeah, I like this place," I said.

Awkward silence is even more awkward when you know you've spiked your ex's food with weird magical herbs.

He ate another slice before getting up to leave. I stood too. We hugged.

It was odd. He smelled a bit different and had put on some weight, but the hug felt like every hug we had shared for fifteen years. It felt comfortable, warm, solid. I had loved his hugs. Part of me wanted to bury my face in his neck and pretend the affair, the fights, and the divorce had never happened.

Instead I pulled away before he did. Trying not to cry, I gave him my cheeriest smile, saying, "Hey, it was great seeing you, dude. Let me know when you want to stop by and see the cats."

"Yeah, you too, Sika," he said.

I sat back down and didn't watch him leave.

The next day I woke to a text from him at 9:00 AM.

NEAL: WILL YOU BE HOME TONIGHT, SO I CAN SEE THE CATS?

ME: No. TOMORROW OKAY?

NEAL: YEAH. 7?

ME: SURE

The next morning I woke to a text from him at 8:00 AM.

NEAL: I'M REALLY EXCITED TO SEE YOU

ME: COOL

NEAL: I'M BRINGING YOU SOMETHING!

He texted me off and on throughout the day, asking how the packing was going, telling me about some drama in his department. It was the kind of texting we had done every day for years. I used to like it, but now it was annoying. I had too much to do, and I didn't want to talk to him.

A few minutes before seven, he knocked on the front door of

"our" house. I let him in, and he offered me a bakery box filled with six beautiful cupcakes. My favorite. He used to do sweet things like that the first few years we were together.

I sat down on the couch and took one bite out of three different cupcakes: strawberry, key lime, and salted caramel. He walked around and petted all of the cats except for Toby, who hissed and ran away.

Neal sat down close to me, picking up each of the cupcakes I'd bitten into and eating some. He was too close, but it was also nice. I had hoped someday we would be civil to each other and was glad to see that starting to happen.

We made small talk again. Easy, enjoyable small talk this time. He asked what cosplays I was going to do for my next nerd convention, saying he missed doing those with me. We talked about old times, the places we had visited and the people we knew when we first started dating. Silly things we had done together.

He asked after several of *my* friends that had once been *our* friends, and he asked about my niece and nephew. He'd been there about thirty minutes when his phone started making text alert sounds, but he didn't look at it. After the fifth or sixth one, he turned the sound off.

"Do you still have the wedding scrapbook you made?" he asked.

"Yeah, I do."

"Good, I was afraid you'd have thrown it away. You worked hard on that. Did you keep anything else?"

"No," I said, not wanting to elaborate.

After a long pause, he said, "I'm sorry. About everything, about lying to you and the way things ended. I was mean; I didn't need to be that mean."

I wanted to agree, because he was right. He didn't need to be that mean. He didn't need to leave me just before Christmas, or take possessions that belonged to both of us without asking. He didn't need to call me names or talk bad about me to people. He didn't need to tell me he'd never loved me, that he'd never been happy, and that he had wanted to leave me since before we even got married.

I'd wanted an apology from him for so long, and now that I had it, I weirdly felt worse. It was like I was right back there, with him laughing as I begged him to stay. I felt sick thinking about how my heart had broken over this weak-willed, mean, dishonest, and frankly, boring man.

I didn't want to be around him anymore. I didn't want to be friends. I wanted him to leave. I wanted to finish packing, get away from this part of town, and never see him again.

"I don't want to kick you out," I lied, "but it's late. I have an early day tomorrow—deadlines, you know? Thanks for the cupcakes. They're delicious. I'm sure you need to get home."

I walked to the door. He stood and followed me, looking forlorn.

Once he left, I put the remaining cupcakes in the fridge and poured a double shot of tequila. I'd been mostly clean for six months, only drinking socially with some friends. But I needed a drink.

I went back to the couch, curled up in a ball, and cried. These weren't tears of loss, self-hate, fear, or regret that I had experienced so many times in the last year. This was a cleansing cry of relief. I guess I'd needed to hear him apologize to realize that I didn't need to forgive him, because I didn't want him in my life after all.

I drank a little more and went to bed.

A few hours later, I woke to knocking at my door. Looking at my phone, I saw it was 2:00 AM. I went downstairs.

Neal was there, and he looked like he had been crying. He also had a red puffy spot on his cheek. When I opened the door, he came inside without being invited.

"What are you doing here?" I asked.

"That bitch kicked me out."

"I'm sorry—"

"Mandy drove by here last night, while we were talking. She

said she knew I was seeing you, that she had seen my phone yesterday. When I didn't reply to her texts, she drove over here. She saw my car. When I got home, she started throwing stuff at me." He gestured to his cheek. "She hit me in the face with a bowl."

"You didn't tell her you were coming over here last night?"

"No. It wasn't any of her business!" he yelled.

I wanted to argue because I had hated his sneaking around and keeping secrets from me, but then again a little, vicious part of me was happy he was doing it to her now. I was also afraid because I knew how he could get when he was angry.

"I'm sure it's all going to be okay. She just needs some time to calm down, right?" I said softly.

"I don't care if she does. I'm done with her."

"Okay, that's cool too," I said.

He started pacing back and forth in the living room, ranting, telling me all the things he hated about his girlfriend. It was super weird. I wanted nothing to do with any of it, but I let him vent for a little while.

Once he had calmed down, I said, "You should probably get a room someplace. You need sleep."

"Can I stay here?" he asked.

"I'm sorry, but I already packed up the spare room. And you know, it doesn't seem like a great idea ..."

"No, I guess not," he said, looking hurt and confused.

I opened the door for him, and before he left, he hugged me, hard. "Thanks for listening. I love you," he said, kissing me on the forehead.

I stood at the door and watched his car drive away.

Standing there, feeling anxious, sad, confused, angry, scared, and nauseated, I realized how good my life had been since he'd left last year. My stomach used to hurt all the time, but that had mostly gone away. I'd figured it was because I'd stopped drinking, but maybe it was Neal. This same jumble of emotions in my gut was how I felt every day when I was married.

A cold chill ran up my spine when I thought about the love potion. That couldn't be why he was doing this, could it?

The next day he texted and called nonstop. The first few texts were him saying thanks for being a friend. When he started saying how much he missed me and loved me, I turned off the alerts.

I had physical therapy at 2:00 PM, and I stopped at the grocery store afterward. When I got home, Neal's car was in my driveway, and he was sitting on the steps.

"Hey, what are you doing here?" I asked as I came up the stairs, my arms full of bags, trying to not drop a case of Coke.

"I was wrong. I never should have left you. You're my wife, the love of my life. I made a commitment to you, and I messed that up. I don't want to be with anyone else. I'm so sorry. I want to fix things, to be with you. I don't want you to move away, you can stay in the house as long as you want, like I promised before. Please don't leave," he said.

"Yeah, you did say I could stay here as long as I wanted, and that you would love me forever and always take care of me. Then you filed for a divorce, and a judge signed the agreement, and I'm legally required to vacate this house," I said.

"I know, I'm sorry, that was all stupid. I changed my mind."

"You can't just change your mind. I've already closed on my own house. I have movers coming in a few days," I said.

"That doesn't matter. All that matters is that we are together again. And that we love each other."

I tried to stay cool, but I was freaking out inside, and scared. Was it the love potion? A few days ago he had barely wanted to speak to me, and now he loved me?

"I know you're upset and worried, but you and Mandy will probably work things out. You guys are right for each other. And if not, once I leave, you can stay here," I said.

"I don't want Mandy!" he screamed, pulling at the hair near his temples.

"Okay, okay, that's fine. You don't have to be with her. It's cool," I said.

"I want you. I've apologized, dammit, what more do you want from me? Why do you always have to make everything so hard?" he screamed.

Some of my neighbors were standing out in the cul-de-sac, watching everything. One of them might have called the cops already.

"I'm sorry. I don't want to upset you. How about you go, and we can talk about this tomorrow. I have some stuff I need to deal with, okay? I would really like to talk to you about this tomorrow, please," I said.

And, just like that, he calmed down. It was the weirdest thing. The anger was gone, and he said "Okay, yeah. Sorry. I'll call you tomorrow."

"Great!" I said, keeping it light.

He tried to hug me, but I was holding the grocery bags, so that helped keep him away. He said "I love you" before getting into his car and driving away.

I went inside, dropped the groceries on the floor, and hurried to my grandparents' books.

It had to be the spell. But it wasn't possible. But it had to be the spell! There was no other explanation, was there? Neal had always been a little unstable. Maybe he had finally cracked, and it had nothing to do with me? Magic wasn't real. People don't eat enchanted pizza and fall in love, that isn't a thing!

I found the spell and read it again. There was nothing on the page about an antidote, or a time limit before it would wear off.

There was a warning at the bottom of the pages, though.

Warning: Cast with pure heart and intention. The subject must be your true love.

I'd seen the warning, but I hadn't taken it seriously. I hadn't really taken any of it seriously. Magic was bullshit. It wasn't supposed to work.

I didn't love Neal. I hadn't loved him since before he left me. I hadn't loved him since he broke our vows. I hadn't loved him since I caught him lying, putting my health at risk having unprotected sex with another woman. I hadn't loved him since the day I realized he didn't care about me the way I had cared about him.

When he left, I had begged him not to go because I was afraid to be alone, because I was terrified that I couldn't make it on my own. I was afraid of change. I was hurt because I had been rejected, because some piece of shit I thought was the man of my dreams had dumped me before I was ready to dump him.

Now he loved me? But not in the healthy way I pretended he had loved me before, or in the way I used to love him. No, he loved me in the obsessive, crying, begging way I had felt a year ago when he left.

I looked through all the books, trying to find anything that would fix this. I turned my ringer off so I wouldn't have to hear his endless calls and texts.

I fell asleep, exhausted, surrounded by books.

I woke up with a start when I heard a noise at the door, the handle rattling like someone trying to put a key in the lock. It went on for a little while and then stopped. A few minutes later, I heard leaves rustling. Someone was walking around to the back.

Had I locked the back door? I didn't know when I had last even opened the back door. I jumped up from the couch and ran to the kitchen, checking that the door was locked. I could see a shadow out there, moving around.

I knew it was Neal.

I was afraid. More afraid than I had ever been of him before.

"Go away," I yelled. "I'm calling the cops."

I dialed 911, telling the operator that someone had tried to get into my house and that they were walking around in my backyard. They said they were sending someone over. When I looked again, the shadowy form was walking away, behind my neighbor's house.

I told the cops everything, except that I thought it was my ex-husband. I didn't want to get Neal in trouble. This wasn't his fault. I mean, it was his fault he was an ass and that he hadn't loved me when I loved him, but it wasn't his fault that he was in love with me now.

The next day when he called, I picked up.

"You have got to stop calling me. I don't want to talk to you," I said.

"You are punishing me for what happened before. You can't punish me forever. That isn't fair."

"No, I really don't want to talk to you. Please, leave me alone," I said as firmly as I could.

"Don't be such a bitch!" he started, but I hung up.

I spent the rest of the day reading books. I even went back to the occult shop and told the "witches" there what was happening. They all looked at me like I was crazy. Maybe I was. I hadn't believed in magic, so what had been the harm in doing a stupid spell? Now I believed, and I was terrified that I wouldn't be able to undo it and these people were not taking me seriously.

It seemed like my pagan grandparents had written down everything in their books: spells, poems from all over the world, fortune cookie sayings, short stories, song lyrics. I wasn't sure which of it was real, which of it was fake, and which was just them being verbal pack rats.

I found a spell to protect one from evil, but Neal wasn't exactly evil, just a lying, selfish jackass. I found one to make your partner stay faithful, which would have been helpful a few years ago. I found spells to bless a house, to exorcise a ghost, to increase creativity, but nothing to make a person fall out of love.

I needed him to stop loving me.

I checked my phone around dinnertime to find that he hadn't texted in a few hours. Maybe the potion was wearing off?

Still, I made sure all the doors were locked before I went to bed that night.

I woke to find Neal standing at the foot of my bed. Just standing there, not saying anything, staring at me while I slept.

"Neal, you shouldn't be here. You have to leave," I said.

"No, I'm never leaving you again. We are going to be together forever," he said.

I reached to the nightstand and turned on the light. He looked bad. He had a black eye. His annoying Hawaiian shirt was torn and bloody. His arms were covered in scratches, and he looked like he hadn't slept for days. The creepiest part was the big smile on his face, just like he had in my favorite picture of him from our wedding. He was a mess, but he looked so happy.

"You are my love. I told you I'd be with you forever—until death do us part—and I'll never leave you. I promise."

A few months after Neal had left, my friend Jane had convinced me to buy a gun. She was worried about me, a woman living alone. I had taken two safety classes with her, bought the one she suggested, tucked it between my bed and the nightstand, and never touched it again. I hardly ever thought about it.

Until now.

As he walked around the bed toward me, I grabbed the gun, pointed, and started shooting. I squeezed the trigger until it was empty. I heard him cry out in pain.

I called the cops before going to check on him. The operator told me not to go near him. But I did anyway.

I didn't hate him. I had loved him more than anyone in the world, then I had feared him. Then I had been angry with him. At some point, I had stopped loving him, and I think I was working toward indifference before I cast that spell. But never hate.

I knelt down, my bare legs in the hot blood spreading out from him.

He looked up at me.

"Sika, why did you do that?" he asked, his eyes filled with pain and shock instead of madness. His hand reached toward me.

"I'm sorry, I had to. I didn't want to," I said, taking his hand.

"I love you. I just want us to be together. You're my wife. We are forever," he pleaded.

"I know. It's okay, shh, it's okay. I'm here. I'm not going to leave you. I'm right here," I said softly. There was so much blood.

"I'm cold," he said.

I pulled the duvet off my bed, the one we had bought in Germany on our honeymoon, and put it over him.

Love Potion on a Large #9

"Do you love me?" he asked, closing his eyes.
"Yes," I lied.

Kitty Sarkozy is a speculative fiction writer, actor, and robot girlfriend. She is an Associate Editor and narrator for Pseudopod, an award-winning weekly horror podcast in the Escape Artists network. Several large cats allow her to live with them in Marietta, GA, where she cultivates extensive gardens into a perfect, tranquil place to hide bodies. For a list of her publications, acting credits, or to engage her services on your next project go to kittysarkozy.com or follow her on Twitter @KittySarkozy.

The World's Greatest Chef
CJ Erick

I met my friend Jace Teller for brunch a week ago at La Maison Fantastique, our favorite little bistro in North Texas. Knowing my predilection for a good story, he is seldom without something he feels compelled to share, generally some uninspired anecdote of dubious authority or value.

On the Saturday in question, we have glad-handed through the usual introductory pleasantries and sit opposite each other at a table the size of a large handkerchief, me with a Bloody Mary with extra garlic salt and a bourbon chaser, and him with a double-peach Bellini with three maraschinos.

"CJ," he says, "I have a story for you."

This is his standard preamble, like his personal favorite Hungarian chess opening, 1.g3, hinting he "will fianchetto his king's bishop," whatever that is.

"I'm all ears," I say, thinking that I'm really all taste buds at that point, watching him stuff lox and crispy potato disks with chives past his puckered lips.

"This story is about the world's greatest chef," he says between bites.

"How nice," I say, which is Southern for "Who cares?" But I do care, actually, because old Teller's stories are like spinning a narrative prize wheel, sometimes satisfying with a dollop of mental umami and sometimes difficult to digest.

"This story is about the world's greatest chef," he repeats, ignoring my comment.

"And who would that be?" I ask.

"Not a who, but a what."

"Animal, vegetable, or mineral?" I ask, feeling the rumblings of mental indigestion coming on.

"Mineral, I suppose, at least indirectly. Silicon wafers. Our chef was a computer. An artificial intelligence."

The burn beneath my sternum expands. "AI, eh? I have no issues with artificial intelligence. There's a great need, since there doesn't seem to be enough natural intelligence to go around." I take a long pull from the alcoholic tomato beverage, knowing it isn't a reflux quencher. "Carry on, Teller," I say. "I'm ready."

"You remember an acquaintance of mine, Maureen Orasmus? Executive for blah blah corporation?"

I do remember her. A businesswoman, president of a bank and a title agency, as I recall, and on several boards of directors and the local library foundation. She brings to mind a single word: formidable.

I acknowledge my familiarity.

"Ms. Orasmus is not one for faint interest in things," Teller says, "and the culinary field is an area she considered worth her attention."

He then relates an article that appeared in the DFW *Daily News*, an article that would prove to change her life.

Ms. Orasmus, seeking perfection in all things, had grown dissatisfied, according to Teller, with the restaurants she felt she was supporting morally and financially. In fact, they, like so many other service providers she'd been required to hold accountable, had failed to deliver a level of competence and experience equal to the commitment she had made to them.

In short, she had been paying too much for bad cooking.

But that was about to end.

The news article was for a new restaurant in the Uptown area of Dallas, a simple advertisement without adornment, one that spoke to Ms. Orasmus's no-nonsense aesthetic. No frills. No gloss.

D'Elite Kitchen. For VIP customers only. The dining experience of your life: We will prepare your perfect food. Guaranteed.

Perfection? For that, she was willing to pay.

Ms. Orasmus called to make a reservation the same day, as soon as she was finished firing two incompetent managers, one of whom was her soon-to-be former son-in-law. When she was told reservations were already months out, as Teller related, she "advised them of her connections and committed to a level of compensation with which they would not be disappointed."

After the negotiations in which she earned a reservation, the proprietors requested her precise physical measurements, a DNA sample, and a throat swab. No survey of her likes and dislikes, no questions regarding her favorite dishes at her favorite restaurants. Nothing even remotely subjective. Personalized cuisine designed by science.

She told Teller that she had been skeptical. But she'd been mistaken.

"You can probably tell the rest of this story," says Teller. "Our Ms. Orasmus arrives exactly ten minutes prior to her appointed time. She is escorted to her personal dining enclosure, a small cubicle shrouded in printed paper walls and 'reeking of feng shui,' as she put it."

Teller describes the simple wooden chair with a cushion of perfect softness, a square wooden table of just the right color and dimensions and height, a small cup of sake at the perfect temperature, all provided without asking or seeking her request, all determined by her bodily dimensions, DNA, and gastric biome.

"Let me guess," I say. "Her meal is perfectly flavored and textured, a brilliant tasting menu of course after course, each one just the right amount, the flavors lingering just long enough until the next is brought, accompanied by the perfect wine or aperitif. And the meal ends with a perfect level of satisfaction."

Teller sits back in his chair. I am expecting him to be annoyed that I have accepted his invitation to finish the story and have guessed the outcome, that I have stolen his digestive thunder. But his look is of one who has lured his prey into a trap and is about to spring it.

"Ah, CJ, you would think that, wouldn't you?" He smiles ingratiatingly and sips his Bellini, reducing the level in the frosted glass by fractions of a millimeter. He is one to nurse the same beverage for an entire evening, whereas I am one to indulge in several. I envy him his discipline but also question the point of such self-restraint.

"The problem, my dear friend," he says, "with indulging in the pleasures of the flesh is that reaching the point of perfect satisfaction is a fantasy. Just as one feels they are satisfied, the need to reach that point again comes along immediately."

"So, you're saying Maureen Orasmus developed an eating disorder. She became a food addict."

"Addict? Hmm." He ponders a moment, looks at the Bellini with newfound suspicion. "Something more profound. A disorder which may not yet have a name, I'm afraid."

Per Teller's narrative, what befell Ms. Orasmus was not a recognized eating disorder. She didn't crave this new, perfect food in addition to her usual diet. She found instead that she could stomach nothing else.

Her previous dining routines—morning oatmeal, lean salads and soups at lunch, fish and whole grains at dinner, regular but regimented enjoyment of red wine for antioxidants—all these were now not just unattractive but repulsive. Wretched. Vomit-inducing.

One look at a high-end filet of Alaskan sockeye salmon was enough to send her running for the toilet. Fresh greens brought on a burning rash. A sip of sparkling water with a twist of lime left her drooling like a rabid raccoon.

She called the restaurant begging for another reservation, but the contract specified one experience only. A one-time, life-changing culinary experience.

She couldn't eat. She lost weight. She couldn't sleep. She grew wan and sickly. Her calls to the restaurant were blocked. The police were called when she drove there daily, forcing her way inside past the valets, falling to her knees, begging for another meal. The hosts suggested she seek help for her mental illness.

She hired muscle to break into the restaurant. The bruisers confronted the owner as he was leaving late one Saturday night. They demanded to see the head chef. The owner led them to the kitchen, where he showed them the special equipment that prepared the ultimate meals.

There was no chef. Only four spiderlike robots, each with four metal-rod arms, multi-digit fingers and rod-mounted knives, all on rolling stands. Wireless connection to an advanced AI cooking system. A world-class database server. The culinary algorithm to beat all algorithms, based on chemistry, physiology, and food science. The black art of taste, now condensed into a self-developing silicon-based intelligence.

The owner had never expected to achieve perfection. Just the nearest thing, something good enough, as it were, to charge two thousand dollars for the experience.

"But it was bound to happen to someone," says Teller. "Call them Lucky Customer Number One Million, when the AI brains and the ideal human specimen cross forks and knives; the perfect meal."

It had happened once. It might never happen again.

"Where is Ms. Orasmus now?" I ask.

"In a ... facility. From what she has told me, she can now tolerate whole spoonsful of potato, leek, and carrot consommé. They hope to add Japanese fish flakes in the coming days. With luck, her caregivers will be able to remove the feeding tube in a few months."

I find it hard to swallow, my throat suddenly tight. I am thinking of a reservation I recently made, one for which I was required to prepay two thousand dollars. I was enticed by an advertisement that came just that day in the morning paper. The perfect meal for VIP customers only.

Dine by the Artistry of AI

D'Elite Kitchen

"You look pale, CJ," says Teller. "Feeling all right?"

"I seem to have lost my appetite," I answer.

He studies my sudden change in expression, and then the gleam of understanding comes to him.

"You must go, my friend."

"How can I?" I respond.

"Imagine it—the wonder of the perfect meal. The Holy Grail for gourmands like us."

"But the consequences ..."

Teller smiles like the cat who is about to eat the perfect canary.

"See if you can make that reservation for two."

CJ Erick stumbled into Dallas in search of love, great sushi, and access to big box stores. Having found all three, he now inhabits the city with his wife, Cee, and their sweet black-and-tan super-hero hound, SaberGirl. Mostly retired from the reckless adventure of engineering, he now designs and builds space fantasy, gothic horror, cozy mysteries, and even a little romance, among other unbalanced visions from caffeine-deranged nightmares. CJ has published three novels and sold short stories in multiple genres.

A Recipe for Home
Alicia Cay

Y ou can't ever go home again. Victoria looked up at the crumbling Queen Anne-style house and sighed. Gabled trim rotted off the rafters, and brittle yellow paint peeled from the wood siding. It looked as bad as she felt.

Victoria's red, strappy Louboutin heels clicked along the cobblestone walkway. In stark contrast to the moldering mess beyond, the lawn was neatly mowed, shrubs perfectly shaped, and her mother's prize roses, their yellow and pink faces open to greet her, filled the air with pastel perfume. Seems Mom had hired some help after all.

Her mother hadn't fared well after Dad's death twelve years ago, but the house was in worse condition than Victoria had feared. Her brother, Robert, lived out of state, busy with his growing family and his architecture firm, and Victoria ... well, she'd been busy, too—chasing dreams far away from home.

Victoria took the steps onto the wraparound porch, watching for her mom through the frosted glass panels in the heavy oak front door. She raised a French-tipped fingernail to the doorbell, then stopped. Who rang the doorbell to their own house? Victoria rolled her eyes, fished the spare house key out from under the planter, and let herself in.

A Recipe for Home

Her eyes widened. Stepping through the door should have felt like being embraced by an old friend. Instead, a heap of mail lay on the dusty floor below the mail slot, and matted cobwebs drifted from the crystal chandelier hanging in the foyer—a gift from Dad to Mom for their fifteenth anniversary.

"Mom?" Victoria called, brushing wisps of falling cobweb from her curled red hair. She left her suitcase by the door and went into the family room.

The same beige sofa hunkered in front of the bare fireplace, with Grandma's patchwork quilt thrown over the back. Victoria sunk into it and buried her head in a pillow.

The life she'd built far away from here, in Covington, was gone. The lawyers had settled it all. She'd trusted a man with her heart, and worse, her family's recipes.

"Vee?" Her mother's voice carried into the room.

Victoria tried to muffle her crying in the sofa pillow.

"*Shh, shh*, now. It can't be all that bad."

"It is that bad," Victoria said. "It's all gone. I lost everything."

"Oh, honey." Her mother made a small *tsk* sound.

"It hurts, Mom."

"I know it does. Come on, sit up and wipe your face. Get some tea."

Tea was her mother's answer to everything. "Ugh," Victoria moaned. This kind of heartache could not be mended with a mug of Earl Grey.

She sat up and wiped her face on the sleeve of her floral Chanel blouse. Sunlight filtered into the living room through a large bay window, and the porch swing outside leaned more than swayed in the summer breeze.

Victoria listened for the teakettle to whistle, hoping Mom was making her some. The house had never been so quiet. The noisy sounds of her family, long gone. She closed her eyes, fingers picking absently at the threads on the worn corner of the sofa arm. She'd sat in this very spot talking on the phone with Brandy and Emma late into the night until Mom picked up the line and told them to say good night. Victoria missed that. The insouciance of youth. She and her best friends, her only friends, had talked endlessly about leaving Shermer Springs. They were going to move to the big city. All their dreams would come true in Covington.

"Yeah, right," Victoria muttered. She opened her eyes. A dust bunny skittered across the floor, catching on the corner of the bookcase. Dad's handwritten journals cluttered the top shelf, each book full of recipes he'd spent years coaxing out of his Grammy, her sisters, and any of his cousins willing to share their family's baking secrets. Her father had lovingly recorded every recipe, waiting for the day he could retire and open his own shop. Until then, he'd spent hours in their kitchen making Bee Sting cakes, eclairs, and Struffoli that Victoria used to steal, still warm, off the tray, licking honey from her fingers and giggling when Dad feigned outrage at the theft.

A fresh crop of tears sprouted from her eyes. She took a deep breath. The smell of warm, buttery croissants fresh from the oven seemed baked into the walls of this house.

Her hands balled into fists on her knees. *Dammit.* Eli might have taken the condo in Covington and the bakery they'd built together, but he couldn't touch her here. This house was hers. First thing tomorrow, she would start repairs. Make it warm and inviting again. The way a home was supposed to be.

Memories, like forgotten bullies, lay in wait behind every corner in Shermer Springs, ready to jump out when Victoria least expected and punch her in the ribs.

Victoria pulled Dad's red Chevy truck into the driveway, sweating through her white silk tank top and scowling. She'd maxed out her only credit card at the hardware store. Old Man Vernon, who'd been old since she was a little girl, had seen Victoria and her AmEx coming a mile off.

A Recipe for Home

She lowered the truck's tailgate, pulled out a stepladder, then dragged out a five-gallon bucket of pale green house paint. A manicured nail caught on the pail handle.

Dammit! Victoria sucked on the finger, fighting back tears that had nothing to do with a broken nail.

A white pickup, "Nature's Way Landscaping" stenciled in black on the side, pulled into the driveway behind her, and a middle-aged man got out.

"Hi," he said, his voice warm like melted molasses on a griddle cake. "Didn't expect to find you here."

Victoria pressed her arms down to hide the sweat stains and slid her hand in her jeans' pocket. "Well, I am. What can I do for you?"

He chuckled. "I guess being gone for—what has it been?" He scratched the bald patch on his head. "Twelve years?—can make a guy forgettable."

Victoria tossed a lock of cherry hair over her shoulder and half-smiled. There was a time she had known everyone in Shermer Springs. Not anymore, thank God.

"Nick." He held out his hand. "Johnson. We went to Glen-brook High together."

His nails were crusted with dirt, and Victoria groaned inwardly as she shook his hand. "Sure. We had Home Room together."

A blush spread on the man's cheeks like strawberry jam. "Math and science, actually." He smiled. "You might remember me better as the pizza delivery guy?"

"Oh my gosh—Pizza Nick!" A smile broke across Victoria's face.

Pizza Nick, their nickname for the boy with the pretty eyes. The kind of eyes that made Brandy and Emma giggle when he delivered their extra-cheese pizzas on sleepover Saturdays. And he'd always thrown in a free order of garlic knots, although Victoria never figured out how he knew they were her favorite.

She raised a hand to shield the sun and get a good look at him.

His eyes were the same, hazel and surrounded by enviable thick dark lashes, and his skin had cleared up. Shame about his hair, though. Too far gone for even Rogaine's help.

Back then, he'd been cute enough in his own lanky way, but Victoria hadn't allowed herself to want things like him, didn't even join in giggling with Brandy and Emma. She knew what kind of girl she was.

At school, the boys didn't look at her, and the popular girls didn't speak to her, so Victoria, her chubby face covered in red freckles and wrestling with a body wrapped in "baby" fat that'd taken her three years of Pilates to get rid of, had perfected the art of blending into the background. Just another part of the Shermer Springs scenery she'd worked so hard to leave behind.

"You're still here, huh?" The words sounded harsher than Victoria had intended them.

"Yeah," Nick said. "Left for a little while, college and all that. Got my degree in technical engineering."

"Really?" Victoria's eyebrows shot up. Why was he doing yard work, then? "There's good money in that, I hear."

"I guess." Nick shrugged. "Until you get laid off."

"Oh," Victoria's eyebrows settled. "Too bad."

Nick snorted. "Best thing that ever happened to me. I did the big city thing." He shook his head. "Got married, bought the white-picket-fence house complete with two-hour commute." He shrugged again. "Guess the ex decided she couldn't overlook the weight I'd put on or the hair I'd lost." He offered a small smile and smoothed down the remaining strands of his hair.

Victoria nodded. Eli had a list of similar criticisms. He'd actually put "stifling his creative vision" on the court papers! *Jerk.* She crossed her arms. "So, you had to come back, too, huh?"

"No," Nick said. "I wanted to come back after I finished school, but Amy insisted on living closer to the city. Anyway," he said with a chuckle, "it all worked out. Got my own business now." He jutted a thumb over his shoulder at the pickup. "I do landscaping and such." He pulled out his wallet and fished out a soggy business card.

"That's nice." Victoria took the offered card, holding it at bay with two fingers. "Working outside. Lots of fresh air and ... nature."

Nick grinned down at his hands. "It's sure good to see you back, Vee."

At the use of her childhood nickname, a pit formed in the hollow of her stomach. Victoria frowned. "What brings you out here, Nick?"

"Oh, um." The color on his cheeks deepened to crimson. "City Council hired me to take care of the yard for your mom, when, you know ... it started to get a little out of hand. Neighbors were complaining, or whatever." He lifted a shoulder.

That explained why Mom's roses looked so good. Victoria shot a look at the pile of tools in the back of the Chevy. "That's why I'm back. To fix up the place, do some repairs."

"That's cool," Nick said. "If you need any help, I do handyman stuff, too."

"Really?" Victoria flipped her hair across her shoulders. "Oh my gosh, that would be a lifesaver. I practically cleaned out the hardware store, but I have no idea how to use any of this stuff." She picked up a wrench, slinging it from hand to hand, and flashed a smile full of whitened teeth. "Any chance you do plumbing?"

Victoria stood on the long ladder, pressed against the house, her knees wobbling every time she looked down. She pushed the scraper across the siding the way Nick had shown her, careful not to gouge the wood. Gray paint slid off in long pulls of old latex, falling in her hair and onto her tennis shoes. She was on the last corner of the house. It'd taken her an entire week, even with

Nick's help, but all the peeling paint was nearly gone. Then she'd have to do the ladder dance all over again to put the new paint on.

Victoria blew out the breath she'd been holding and wiped her sweaty forehead with the sleeve of one of Dad's old shirts. The ladder swayed. She grabbed at the rails with both hands, dropping the scraper. "Dammit! Stupid house."

She made her way down the ladder. It was time for lunch anyway.

The scent of warmed chocolate and brown sugar wafted through the back screen door, another memory lying in wait, and hit Victoria like a blow to the chest. That smell was her childhood, her family, and her home wrapped together in one sweet scent. Dad's cookies.

In the kitchen, tea stains mottled the countertop. Her dishes were still in the sink; Mom hadn't touched them. She must have left early that morning to play Bridge with the girls, her mother's Tuesday routine for as long as Victoria could remember.

A slip of paper was hanging on the refrigerator. Victoria's eyes landed on it like flies on butter. Dad's chocolate-chip cookie recipe. Right where he'd left it. How had she missed that?

The night after Dad's funeral, Victoria had hauled his journals down to the print shop and made copies of everything. Those recipes and a suitcase of her best secondhand clothing were the only things she'd taken. Her father hadn't been brave enough to leave Shermer Springs, so she'd left for him, carrying his dream with her in every puff of sugar mixed into his batters and every bite of goodness licked off the spoon.

She'd worked in Covington for years without making much headway. Then Eli had arrived—no, sauntered—into her life, with his French countryside accent and chocolate-colored eyes, his kisses canned-peach sweet, his fingers long and skilled, and all those damned promises. She needed only to sign over legal permission to use the recipes, ownership really—he *was* an award-winning chef with a reputation after all—and her confectionery dreams would become a reality.

A Recipe for Home

Lying bastard.

Victoria grabbed the recipe card, worn and food-stained, and traced a finger over her father's handwriting. She hadn't taken this one with her to the city. This one still belonged to her.

A sudden urge, a need, to taste one of Dad's ooey-gooey cookies filled Victoria from the soles of her feet to the ends of her chipped fingernails. She banged open cabinet doors. There was flour, brown sugar, and cinnamon, but no chocolate chips and no cayenne pepper—her father's secret ingredient. A pinch of heat to bring out the sweet, he'd say with a wink.

Victoria slammed the cabinets closed—*BAM! BAM!*—each one a defiant shout against the quietness trapped inside this rambling old house with its baked-in, crusted-on memories.

She hated the silence. It let the loneliness in far too easily. Dad's recipe card fluttered from her fingers.

Shoulders slumped, Victoria shuffled into the dining room and plopped into a side chair. She ran her fingers over the table's mahogany finish. How many Thanksgiving turkeys and birthday cakes had her family shared around this table? She looked up at the family pictures on the walls and the wallpaper behind them. Time had curled it at the seams.

Victoria reached over and flicked a finger at the curled wallpaper. She squeezed her eyes shut against the heat pressing on them, the smell of baked brown sugar seeping in along the edges of her senses.

She stood, grabbed an edge of the wallpaper, and pulled. The aged glue yielded its hold; the paper tore off in a large strip. This damned house, falling apart. Just like everything else.

Victoria stripped another swath of paper from the wall, then slammed a fist onto the bare plaster.

She and Dad had spent an entire weekend putting up this wallpaper. Why hadn't anyone taken better care of it? Victoria tore the strip in her hands into pieces. With both hands, she grabbed more.

The family cat, Banana, had insisted on trying to eat the glue-paste, and after being chased off one too many times, he'd stomped through the tray in a huff. Victoria looked down. They were still there—kitty paw prints running through the dining room—smudged in dust and worn with time, but still there.

She grabbed more handfuls of the brittle wallpaper. "Dammit!" Tears blurred her vision. Her hands scuttled across the wall, fingernails digging for leverage. Paper pulling away beneath them. *Scrrrrip!* Another swath of pearl-shimmer wallpaper tumbled down.

Mom had saved for a year for this paper with its velvet-soft fleur-de-lis pattern.

Victoria screamed. A sound so feral it kicked and scratched at her throat on its way out. She tore and thrashed through the dining room like a blender—shredding and ripping until her fingers throbbed, until old wallpaper lay in curled mounds around her legs.

Breathing hard, her heart beating an ache beneath her skin, Victoria retreated into the foyer and crumpled. The silence of the house settled on her again, pressing her into the floor.

The ceiling here was high. It made her feel a long way down, as though she lay at the bottom of her own grave. One she'd dug for herself. She stared at the cobwebs on the chandelier above her, drifting from the crystals in wispy trails.

She didn't move for a long time.

Her hips ached. Victoria dragged herself from the floor and moved to the sofa, waiting for Mom to come home, to rescue her with a cup of tea.

There was still no sign of her mother when the sunlight beyond the bay window began to weaken. She must have lost track of time, caught up in playing and sharing gossip, about Victoria no doubt, with the other old ladies.

Victoria's stomach grumbled. She couldn't wait any longer.

She grabbed Dad's truck keys and headed out the front door. Nick's battered white pickup sat in the driveway.

He walked around the corner of the house, the ladder she hadn't put away in his hands. "There you are." His eyes moved over her. He stopped. "Long day?"

"Very."

"Cool." Nick paused. "Well, everything out here's put away. You hungry?"

"Starving."

"I'll wait if you want to get cleaned up. We can go somewhere, grab a bite."

Victoria looked down at herself, then up at Nick. "I am cleaned up."

Nick's eyebrows shot up. "Okay. How about we eat here? I can grab a cheese pizza, for old time's sake."

Something warm, like the melted mozzarella from Sal's Pizza Shack, filled Victoria's chest, and the corners of her mouth flipped up. She nodded. "And garlic knots?"

"I would never forget the garlic knots," Nick said, a small smile slipping across his lips.

He was in his truck and gone before Victoria thought to offer him some cash. She wasn't sure what his buying dinner meant, but ... She looked down at herself again. Maybe she could find a clean shirt at least.

Upstairs, Victoria opened her closet. Designer jeans and blouses hung in tidy rows. Thousands of dollars spent trying to fit into a life that never hung on her right. She'd only been back a week and already these clothes felt like they belonged to someone else.

Victoria reached onto the top shelf and grabbed a peach Glenbrook High T-shirt. It was old, familiar, and comfortable. Victoria smiled. Just like Nick. The guy with the pretty eyes who'd spent every afternoon this week helping and teaching her and not once losing his patience or pushing her out of the way to do it himself.

Victoria thought she heard the front door. She called down

the stairs. "Mom? Hey, I'm up here. Nick is bringing some pizza over if you're hungry."

She grabbed a mostly clean pair of jeans off the tower of laundry growing from her bedroom floor, ran a brush through her hair, and gargled some mouthwash. There was paint under her nails, and her freckles were on full display, not a speck of makeup to cover them, but it was the best she could do for now. Besides, Victoria smirked, Nick had seen her look worse than this after that little plumbing mishap in the spare bathroom. She went downstairs.

The mess in the dining room was untouched, and the teakettle on the stove was cold. No sign of Mom. Must have worn herself out gossiping and gone to bed early. Outside, a truck door slammed.

Victoria hurried out. She met Nick on the porch, a warm pizza box in his hands.

"We eating out here?" Nick asked.

Victoria thought of the dining room and grimaced. "Yeah, it's a bit of a mess inside."

"Aren't we all?" Nick chuckled, pulled up a chair, and gestured to the porch swing.

"Oh, Nick. You fixed it!" Victoria clapped her hands and took a seat, already swinging her legs.

Nick unpacked slices and knots onto paper plates, the smell of cheese and garlic making Victoria's mouth water.

From the corner of her eye, Victoria caught a flutter from the curtains in the bay window behind her. She grinned. Mom would be standing there, watching her on the porch with a boy, a knowing little smile on her face.

These were the things Victoria hadn't even known she'd missed: the smell of Earl Grey, cheese pizza from Sal's, and her mother's roses bowing their heads over the porch railing in the evening breeze while the stars wrestled the sun for control of the sky. How had she forgotten these things?

"I forgot how beautiful the summers are here," Victoria said.

Nick waggled his eyebrows at her. "'Ery 'eautful," he said, around a mouthful of cheese pizza.

"Oh, please." Victoria rolled her eyes and grinned.

Nick blushed. "Sorry, I couldn't help myself. It really is good to have you back, Vee."

It was Victoria's turn to blush.

"So, have you decided?" Nick asked.

"Decided what?"

"When you're going back to Covington?"

Victoria thought of the dining room and the mess she'd made. Mom would tan her hide if she saw what Victoria had done to her wallpaper. A giggle erupted in her at the thought, and she threw her head back, letting the laughter burst from her like shaken-up soda.

Nick stopped chewing and stared at her.

"Well." She wiped laughter-tears from her eyes. "There's still a lot of work to do."

"You don't *have* to go back to the city, you know? I know it's a big house to live in all alone, but you could turn it into one of those B&B places." Nick cleared his throat. "Although, with your mom gone, I can understand if it's too painful to keep."

The laughter caught in Victoria's throat, strangled by the sudden surge of grief that rose from her chest. She put her plate down.

"Shit, I'm sorry, Vee. I didn't mean to bring up her death. I only meant … Gosh, I'm so sorry."

She glanced at the bay window. The curtains didn't move. Her mom was gone. Had been all along. Victoria had just … needed her to be here for a little while longer. Victoria's eyes filled with hot tears, and when the weight of them was too much, they fell, streaming down her cheeks like raging rivers.

Nick moved to her side on the swing. Victoria bent her head onto his shoulder. He put an arm around her and let her cry.

Shortly after her life had been settled away in court, divorce final, dreams broken, Robert had called to give her the news. Mom had passed away in the night. Her Bridge friends found her the next morning. On a Tuesday.

Victoria wept, and when enough of her guilt and sorrow had been drained for her to breathe again, she wiped her face with the napkin Nick handed her. He brushed his thumbs along her cheeks —his skin rough, his touch soft. Victoria raised her face to his, and as the sun dipped from sight, she leaned in and kissed Nick Johnson.

Victoria had laughed today, for the first time in too long. Now, in Nick's kiss, his gentle touch, more things she'd believed were gone forever returned. She'd come a long way in the past week, but there were still things that needed fixing. The house needed new paint, the dining room was a disaster, and there were still those cobwebs on the chandelier to deal with.

Nick held her close, and she rested her head on his shoulder. She was a mess, the house was a mess, but it was hers. She was home.

Alicia Cay is a writer of speculative and mystery stories. Her short fiction has appeared in several anthologies including *Hold Your Fire* from WordFire Press and *The Wild Hunt* from Air and Nothingness Press. She suffers from wanderlust, collects quotes, and lives beneath the shadows of the Rocky Mountains with a corgi, a kitty, and a lot of fur.

Find her at aliciacay.com.

The Honey Pie

Terry Madden

The pot was boiling over. Dionysios grabbed the lid with his bare hand and dropped it, expecting pain but feeling none. Red potatoes roiled with bubbles that burst and steamed his face. The realization that he was dreaming tried to wake him.

Focus. Get what you came for.

He pulled up the sleeve of his chef's whites and plunged his hand into the boiling water to retrieve a steaming potato. When he blew on it, the potato became a cupcake with lavender icing. He hadn't tasted anything like that since long before the Rain, and after one bite, he knew he'd have to figure out how to make it. But it wasn't what he'd come for.

With the cupcake in hand, Dionysios strode from the kitchen, through the restaurant dining room where he tasted a guest's parfait, then opened a door into a meadow flecked with butterflies, bees, and flowers of every kind.

At the far end of the meadow, she appeared as if on silent cue, dragging her fingers through the high grass and calling, "Dionysios! Where's your sweater? You gonna freeze to dead!"

Yiayia's thin gray hair was braided and looped around her head like a halo. She wore a flowered dress under her apron and a cardigan with only the two top buttons fastened. Taking her arthritic hands in his, Dionysios saw they were covered in flour. She smelled like strudel.

"The apples—too soft." She made that singsong whistle through her dentures, and a plate of strudel materialized in her hand.

Apples. What Dio wouldn't give for an apple off Yiayia's tree. He could even smell the cinnamon as he took the plate from her. But *he* was in control of this dream. He didn't have time for his grandmother's strudel.

Feeling the scratch of the blanket on his neck, he shifted, the sound of his own snore rousing him.

No, don't wake up yet.

"Melopita, Yiayia. Tell me how to make it."

"For Evander, I make melopita." A sad shadow clouded her eyes. "For you, I make strudel." She patted his cheek.

"It's for an important guest. She wants melopita."

"Ah, lady friend?"

"Sure."

A notepad and pencil appeared in his hand as he said, "I need your recipe."

She sighed and gazed over the meadow, her eyes misty. "I never use *recipe*. But the flour—you sift her twice. And the honey, you know, must be thyme honey from Crete."

"But the quantities, Yiayia."

"Your Aunt Zephyra used ricotta. You know better, Dionysios. Mizithra is only way to go. That Greek market on 25th and Castro. They have."

The pencil became a chewed stub, and as he wrote the address, the notepad became a meat wrapper and the sound of his own snoring began to dissolve them both.

"No, no."

The sleep mask pinched his ear. He shifted and turned, became aware that he was in his bunk in the commune and wasn't the only one snoring. Early morning light splashed through the mesh safety windows and cast a checked pattern over the cinder-block wall.

"Twenty-fifth and Castro," Dio said to the wire springs of the bunk above him. There wasn't a chance in hell that shop was still there. That whole district was dark.

He sat up and rubbed the sleep out of his eyes. He was missing something. Yiayia put something else in her melopita. Orange oil? Or maybe it was Cointreau.

"Dio, get your hairy ass outta my bunk." Harv worked nights in the soy processing plant, earning a salary big enough to send home to a wife, supposedly. Yet he was hot bunking in this cheap place. He smelled like booze.

Dionysios straightened his stiff joints and crawled out, hitching up his boxers.

Harv tossed the sleep mask onto the concrete floor. "Hey, don't forget your girlie blinders."

"Careful with that."

"What does it do for ya anyway? Show porn while you sleep, or what?"

From the upper bunk, Flaherty snorted a laugh. Her red face dangled over the side, hair a mess of purple spikes. "He can control his dreams. So, yeah, porn."

"How does it work?" Harv asked, taking back the mask to inspect it. "Maybe I'll give it a go."

"It takes a while to learn," Dio said, reaching for it. "I don't have it down yet."

"Yeah? Maybe I can go back to before the Rain." Harv flopped on the bed and pulled the mask over his eyes. "I'll give 'em back tonight."

Not all the plants had died in the Rain. Just most. Twenty years ago, the solar system passed through a biotic interstellar cloud. That, mixed with rising temperatures, meant that most farming was done inside these days. And the plants were genetically engineered to death.

Dio and Flaherty took the stairs to what had once been an underground parking garage. Passing through two airlocks and a disinfecting mat, they entered the walk-in cooler where the morning produce was sold. But Dio was thinking about the Greek market on 25th and Castro. Adrastos, that was the name. They used to sell those little Ouzo candies, all individually wrapped in silver and blue Mylar.

"Asparagus." Flaherty pointed to the slim, yellow-green spears. "It must be spring." To the salesman she said, "I'll take two kilos."

"That'll be forty-six bits."

Flaherty swiped her card—really their boss's card.

"What kind of sauce?" Dio asked, picking up the slim shoot and bending it to test its freshness.

"I'm thinking Dijon sage." Flaherty sniffed at some parsley and put it back. "Sebastian's pushing the lamb tonight. It's Friday."

Dio swallowed pooling saliva. "Isn't lamb on the menu for the mayor's dinner?"

Flaherty gave him a squinty, sidelong glance. "Well, yeah. So what?"

"Nothing. Just curious."

Everybody knew the new mayor would be hiring cooks along with bodyguards and secretaries and such.

"What about you?" Flaherty asked. "What's your dessert?"

"The mayor ordered melopita. Can you believe it?"

"Melopita? Jeez, you got a head start on me, boy."

"Never made it," Dio said.

"But you're Greek."

"So's the mayor."

"Damn." Flaherty grinned. "I hear the mayor's commune has two kitchens, one for her family and one for the staff. I'll put in a good word for you." She winked.

"Yeah, sure you will."

Dio's hand moved toward a basket of plump, perfect strawberries. The taste of the parfait from his dream still lingered on his tongue. A little triple-bourbon vanilla and the barest hint of nutmeg, like a remembered tune. Why hadn't the mayor wanted strawberry parfait?

"Still no lemons?" Dio asked the vendor.

"Lemons? You crazy?" The farmer scowled. Trees took space and deep soil and pollinators. Most tree fruit was extinct or nearly so.

"Just one basket," Dio said, and swiped Sebastian's card. He'd boost the whipped cream layer with extra lecithin and slice the strawberries thin.

"Have you run across any superior synthetic honey?" he asked Flaherty on their way out of the market. As sous-chef, Flaherty had accumulated some real hard-to-gets. But melopita with artificial honey might be a sacrilege even Dio could not pull off.

Flaherty set her jaw and sighed. "And I should divulge sources to my competition why?"

"Because there are two kitchens in the mayor's commune."

A smile broke across her square face. "Pillsbury makes a high maltose, corn syrup-based honey that *almost* tastes like the real thing, but the esters are off, in my opinion. Try Food Underground."

"Diooooo." The guard hitched his automatic to his shoulder and gave Dio the ritual backslap of comrades. "Save me some cake, huh?"

Dio smiled and clapped the kid's shoulder in return. "Sure."

The way the kid scanned the street in a swift, methodical sweep, Dio knew this guy hadn't been on street duty for more than a week. The adrenaline was still pumping from the training vids they'd been using since Dio had worked security fifteen years ago. This kid wasn't even alive during the last food riot, and people rarely killed for a sack of soy flour these days.

If it weren't for Sebastian, Dio would still be carrying a gun.

The restaurant was on the fifth floor of a chic entrepreneurs' commune in a skyscraper that had once been in the financial district. Dio flipped on the lights, and blinding fluorescence glanced off the stainless steel kitchen. It would be quiet until midmorning, so he logged onto the web.

Sure enough, a guy on Food Underground was selling honey he had socked away pre-Rain. He wanted a thousand bitcoin per ounce, and of course, none of it was thyme honey, just orchard honey. But what good would real honey be if he didn't have mizithra? Food Underground even had raclette, but no mizithra. There was no way he was going to substitute with ricotta.

Once he'd finished the cake and prepared the strawberries, he set out to create a new version of melopita. After jimmying the lock on Sebastian's liquor cabinet, he finally found the Cointreau, the cap crusty with dried sugar. He opened it reverently and sniffed. Oranges. God, how he missed them.

When the melopita was done, he plated a slice and drizzled a thread of artificial honey over it.

"Flaherty, give it a taste."

"I don't know what you're after exactly," she said, wiping her hands on her jacket. The spikes of her hair were encased in a chef's toque, making the ring in her nose a distraction.

"I guess I don't either. My brother was the melopita connoisseur."

Flaherty took a forkful and held it up. "Nice texture. I can smell the Cointreau. Is that what you want?"

"Maybe I'll cut it back."

The fork went into her mouth where she rolled the bite around, staring at the floor with a look of deep concentration.

Just then, Sebastian strode into the kitchen, sniffing like a fat basset hound. "What in the name of God is that smell? I could swear it's Cointreau."

"Melopita, sir," Dio said. "With a splash of Cointreau. I'm working the kinks out of the recipe for next—"

"The mayor's palate is as sensitive as a garbage collector's. Do you know how much that Cointreau cost? You won't be pouring it into a dessert for a client with no taste buds."

With that, Sebastian took the fork from Flaherty and scooped a bite of the melopita. He chewed and frowned. His eyes, glistening like a goldfish, rolled up to the fluorescent lights. He snuffed. One needed air flowing over the back of the tongue to taste properly.

"Serviceable," he decreed.

"Yes, sir."

"The mayor will love it."

Doubtful. In Dio's head, Yiayia said, "You call this melopita?"

But the young guard at the front door would like it. Dio left him a slice on his way home.

Dionysios opened the soy flour bin and peered in at rose petals. He could even smell them. Burying both hands, he scooped them up and let them fall, scattering them around the kitchen.

Don't get too excited or you'll wake up. Control this.

"What the hell?" Flaherty almost dropped her saucier.

"Smell." Dio held out the petals. "What does that remind you of? Huh?"

"My cousin's wedding. The flower girl threw them all over the people in the pews."

"See ya, Flaherty. I need to talk to Yiayia."

With that, he walked out of the kitchen, through the dining room and out the door, trailing a cloud of rose petals.

The front door of the restaurant opened into the living room of the tiny house where he'd grown up. He closed the door behind him. The TV blared a rerun of *All My Children*. Evander's painting of Mykonos hung over the sofa, and the dining table called to Dio from the small space it shared with Yiayia's pedal sewing machine. The table was covered with a green cloth, which in turn was covered with clear plastic, just like the sofa.

It was all so perfect, right down to the broken clock on the built-in china hutch and the sound of Petros, the neighbor, yelling at his dog.

"Yiayia!" Dio called. "Let's make some melopita, huh?"

His grandmother tottered from the kitchen, wiping her hands on her apron. She wore knitted leg warmers around her thick calves, claiming they helped her arthritis.

"Cook? You don't cook, Dionysios, you fish. Like man, you fish. Bring some fat bass, I make kakavia."

He kissed both her cheeks, smelling her face powder, then walked past her to the tiny kitchen and the ancient gas stove. Tins of various spices crowded the white enamel shelf above the burners. He lifted the lid of the pot and looked in. Kakavia. He laughed.

"I never liked fishing," he told her. "But you would never let me in the kitchen." He smiled at her, but she didn't return it.

"Like? Who likes? You like to eat, eh? You and Evander, you fish. I cook."

"Things have changed now, Yiayia. Evander is ... not fishing anymore."

"Change? Evander?" The look of confused horror on her face was exactly the look she'd worn the day the looters had come.

Dionysios wrestled to control the dream. He wasn't here to upset her.

He set to work, gathering everything he needed for melopita. Yiayia even had thyme honey, of course. And mizithra.

"Where is Evander?" she asked.

Dio couldn't let her remember.

"On the boat, Yiayia."

Her look said she didn't believe him.

"I'm going to cook," he said, "and you're going to correct me."

"Crazy boy."

He got out her hand mixer and began assembling the ingredients. The yellow tile of the counter had lost its grout, and a statue of St. Demetrios watched from the window sill.

"Two eggs, beat just a little, not too much air," he told Yiayia as he worked. "Sift two tablespoons of flour into it."

"Twice sift," she corrected.

"Ah, yes." He sifted the small quantity of flour into a bowl, then again into the beaten eggs.

Now for the test. He had indeed found a bottle of Cointreau hidden in her pantry, and he held it in such a way that Yiayia couldn't help but see his intent to pour a splash into the mix.

He eyed her as he poured.

"Cointreau is the secret. I knew it!"

With hands planted on her generous hips, she watched. A frown turned the corners of her mouth.

"No, no, no, Dionysios."

Her hand closed over his. He had forgotten the papery coolness of her touch, the worn wedding band, the way her fingers had been molded by working dough as much as the dough had been molded by her fingers.

"What is it, Yiayia? What makes your melopita so good?"

"Evander."

Dionysios focused. This was a dream. His dream. He could call Evander home. He looked at the front door, willing his brother to walk through it.

Someone did walk through it. The mayor-elect. She waved to the empty sofa as if an adoring crowd sat there, then took a chair at the table, her middle-aged hands clasped in expectation, her nails manicured and painted mauve.

"I'll have the melopita," she said.

"Right away," Dio said. "You must remember your own yiayia's melopita."

"Me?" Her finger buried in the lapel of her dove-gray suit, and her tattooed eyebrows jumped up. "Oh, no, my yiayia died before I was born. I did have the most exquisite melopita on Kythira once. I want to taste it again. Food of the gods. Make it for me, Dionysios."

He looked back to the now-empty kitchen. Where had Yiayia gone?

The mayor-elect was still talking when Dio set the mixing bowl aside and headed for the back door. From the landing of the rickety staircase, he saw Yiayia disappear behind the shed.

"No."

Clotheslines crisscrossed the brown sky that had begun spitting the Rain. A fig tree ruled the backyard and sheltered the herbs along the fence: rue, rosemary, chives, garlic. A grape vine Yiayia had brought from Mykonos trailed over the shed, the vine as fat as Dio's arm and the grapes but tiny green dewdrops. It withered before his eyes.

"Yiayia, come out."

The leaves had fallen from the lemon tree, leaving yellow globes the looters would soon strip away. He plucked one, the sharp smell of fresh citrus reminding him that he dreamed.

"Yiayia?" he called.

A shadow moved near the shed. A figure swung a baseball bat, over and over. The sound of a melon breaking on pavement. They had come.

Dionysios woke with a start. The fat lemon turned to a stone in his hand, and light peeked in from under the sleep mask.

He ripped it off and wiped tears away.

The honey arrived in a parcel that required a signature, and Dio knew this would be all he would ever get. When Sebastian found out he'd spent two thousand bitcoin on it, well, he might be looking for another job. But not before the mayor tasted it.

Flaherty looked over Dio's shoulder as he dug through the bubble wrap to find an unmarked jar the size of a nine-millimeter bullet casing. He held it up to the light, and the amber glow inside made his mouth water.

"I should have gotten two deciliters."

The mizithra had proven elusive in the daily listings of Food Underground. Who'd have thought goat cheese would be harder to find than honey?

After work, Dio hitched a ride with a produce vendor headed for the Bayview communes to the south. He rode between the vendor and his security man. The butt of the man's rifle swung past Dio's face as the guard scanned the vacant buildings that had once been a war zone.

Dio remembered the feel of the molded plastic rifle butt as it hammered his shoulder with every shot. The tide of the riot had swelled and broken here at 16th and Potrero.

Evander wasn't the only brother lying dead in the street that day.

Streamers of photosynthetic fabric snapped and fluttered in the breeze off the bay—the only things moving here anymore.

When the produce vendor stopped on the corner of Castro and 24th, Dio wasn't sure why he'd even come.

He kept a hand on the kitchen knife at his belt as he walked the block to Adrastos market. It was just where Yiayia had said it would be. The barred door had been pried off, hanging on by one hinge.

Dio slipped inside. Broken glass, coins, and Turkish cigarettes crunched under his boots. Everything edible had been looted long ago. Stairs at the back of the shop led up to what had once been the home of Adrastos Karakalos, by the look of the address on yellowing envelopes. Stairs beside the back door led down to a cellar.

Dio wiped the window clean on the back door and saw a flash of movement in an auto salvage yard across the alley. He opened the door and listened.

"*Fáte méchri mikrá angeloúdia mou.*" A woman's voice was followed by the sound of grain streaming into metal.

"Eat up, my little darlings," Dio translated in a whisper. He thought he'd forgotten his Greek.

The *baa* of goats, or maybe sheep, had him creeping across the alley to peer through a fence of corrugated sheet metal. A small herd of goats ate from a trough, their tails spinning in happy circles.

Clothed in filthy overalls, the woman who fed them stood with her hands on her hips, smiling down on them, dust circling her with a sudden breeze. Like Dio, she was in the evening of her youth, but radiant with a satisfaction that might come from caring for living things.

A braid of dark hair streaked with gray trailed out of a flowered kerchief. When she started toward the alley, Dio considered hiding. But from what? From whom? So he stood there and waited for her to lift the metal panel and slip out of her farmyard.

"Stay away, or I'll cut you." She said it with experienced malice, a knife held in front of her.

He held up his hands. "I mean no harm."

"Then get out." She started across the alley.

"My yiayia remembered a Greek market being here before the Rain. It was crazy of me to think it'd still be here." He started away, but turned back. "I'm sorry I frightened you."

She'd reached the steps of the shop. It was the tilt of her head, the suspicious smile that snared him.

"Dionysios?"

"Yes."

He stepped closer, remembering nothing about her but the leaf-green of her eyes. He did a reality check to make sure he wasn't dreaming. No, he couldn't fly.

He finally said, "I'm sorry. You are one of Adrastos's kids. But I don't remember your name."

"You've come for something."

"Mizithra. I thought maybe—"

"How much can you pay?"

After purchasing honey without permission, Sebastian had

banned Dio from using his credit and would garnish his pay until the price of the honey had been met. "Forty bits. Next month."

One eyebrow shot up. "Nice seeing you again, Dionysios." She turned and vanished through the back door of the market.

"Phedra!" Dio shouted the name while he was whipping cream, startling Flaherty into a string of curses.

"Her name was Phedra. *Is* Phedra."

"And she's got mizithra?"

"She has. And if you'd lend me some coin, I could make the most heavenly melopita you've ever tasted."

It had taken him two days to dig it from his memory. Phedra's father had owned the market, and the next day, while Dio rode between the produce vendor and his guard back to the Castro stop, he recalled Phedra as a child, or maybe he'd conjured her from all the girls he had known in school.

The elaborate barricade she had constructed to protect herself from looters wasn't difficult to traverse. But she opened the door to Dio. She had a little generator she used for nothing else but to run a refrigerator in which she stored her goats' milk and the cheese she ripened in the cool basement.

"It's a living," she said, her eyebrows speaking a language all their own. "Sometimes I make enough to buy greens. But you, Dio, you eat vegetables daily. Lucky dog. And this dinner for the mayor. If she likes your melopita, will she hire you?"

"I hope so." Sebastian was only keeping him on long enough to recoup the two thousand bitcoin he'd spent on the honey. "I just need the melopita to be right. That's all."

"Because of your yiayia? You think it will please her somehow, God rest her soul?"

"I'm trying to please the mayor, not my yiayia."

"Is that so? And Sebastian, he will pay for honey and mizithra to please this new mayor?"

"No."

Dio produced the asparagus he had taken from the restaurant. Phedra's smile was worth the risk of being caught.

"A down payment on the mizithra," he said.

She opened her fridge and produced a round of cheese the size of a baseball. She placed it in his hand, holding her palms over it for a second as if in blessing. She smiled, one eyebrow cocked. *"Kalí týchi."* Good luck.

He had started out the door when she said, "Hey, you had a brother. I remember him. Used to come by the shop all the time with fish."

"Evander."

"Yes, Evander. Did he make it through the Rain?" It was the way she asked, the hope sparking in her green eyes. She knew Evander. He remembered it all now. Evander and Phedra. They could not have been older than eighteen. That was why she reminded him of the past. She was part of Evander.

"No."

Dio made his way through the barricade and out into the twilight brown of evening, his boots crushing glass, the wind rattling through broken awnings. Dio liked to think Evander was at sea, pulling in yellowtail and skipjack, bonito and mackerel. And somewhere Yiayia would cook up a pot of kakavia for his supper.

"Get out of my bunk."

Dio peeled the sleep mask away to see Harv's big blue, bloodshot eyes inches away.

He checked the time. "Oh no, no."

Dio fell out of the bunk to find Flaherty already gone. He dressed and ran through a driving rain that smelled as yeasty as it had ever since the Rain.

He hated to rush something like this. Still soaked, he

constructed the six sub-perfect pies quickly, then spent the remainder of his time on the masterpiece. He whipped the synthetic lemon juice and Cointreau with the eggs and honey, then measured out the flour in the palm of his hand, sifted it twice, then folded in Phedra's mizithra, allowing himself a deep waft of the tangy goat cheese.

By the time the guests had finished the first course, the pies were ready. After the main course, Sebastian burst into the kitchen. "The mayor is overcome!" he announced with prayerful hands. "Dio, plate the melopita."

Dio decided that six pies would be enough for the mayor and her guests.

The seventh pie, he tucked in a pastry box and hid behind the lamb in the fridge.

The mayor raved about the melopita with the synthetic honey. Sebastian was right. No taste buds. He was glad he had not wasted the real thing on her. The chance of being selected as one of her personal chefs had lost its appeal. He wanted to cook for those who wanted to remember, those who could taste the past in his dishes.

The kitchen staff had all gone but for Flaherty and Dio. He removed the pastry box from the fridge and slid it open to reveal the golden top of the pie.

"Wait?" Flaherty said. "What's this? One you didn't serve?"

"*The* one. The real deal."

"You didn't serve it to the mayor?"

"Did she know the difference?"

He cut a very thin slice and plated it. "Taste."

Respectfully, Flaherty let her fork slide through the custard-like pie. She closed her eyes as she savored it, making noises that made Dio's mouth water.

"So?" he asked.

"Jesus, Dio. Is this for us?"

"No." He closed the lid on the pastry box and reverently placed the pie in a bag. The first produce vendor would be leaving for the south side. He had to catch them. Evander had wanted to marry Phedra. But her father had refused, saying she would not marry a fisherman. She would marry to improve her life.

Dio had concluded there was little in these times that could improve life. But he would try.

"It's for a friend," he told Flaherty.

By the time Dio made it to Adrastos's market, it was just past dawn. Phedra would be feeding her goats soon.

Terry's tenth-grade paper on the evolution of Frankenstein's monster from tragic construct to boogeyman set her on the path of writing about the weird and wonderful. As an award-winning fiction and screenwriter, Terry has worked with a variety of subjects from historical to far-future science fiction. She finds inspiration in the classroom where she teaches chemistry and astronomy. Her favorite question for her students is, "If technology could make you immortal, would you choose it?" Visit her at ThreeWellsoftheSea.com.

Space Without Breath

Jen Bair

The world is the size of a hummingbird but so much more vibrant and alive. The space constraints are not so bad, really. I prefer my confinement, existing in a dreamlike state, to the vastness of being everywhere. This is concrete. Not as concrete as living in my own body, but it's a close second.

I nudged my wife, pushing her thoughts aside to make room for my own. I wanted a chocolate cupcake. The kind from Sweet Tooth with tiny peanut butter cups sprinkled on top. The decadent kind that coated the tongue like sugary tar.

Lori has always been a healthy eater. I'm not sure she's ever enjoyed a cupcake like I do. Or did. Thinking back, I'm not sure I've ever seen her eat a cupcake. I wonder if the ability to enjoy certain foods is built into the tongue. Like maybe she can't taste the sugar. Or maybe her body doesn't absorb it. She's always been thin.

Well, not now, when she's six months pregnant, but before that. Right now, she looks like she swallowed a giant helium balloon and might float off if a strong breeze happens by.

I nudged her again, pushing my foodie desire against the pudding of her psyche, and I was hit by a wave of irritation. I've learned a lot about Lori since taking up residence in her head.

When I was alive, she had always seemed so calm. It had amused her to see me get riled up over little things, like when one of the shift workers at the restaurant I managed called in sick and then posted about their beach day on social media. Idiots.

It turns out Lori has the same emotional range as me, but she's got some kind of inborn Jedi power where stuff like that just rolls off her.

Not really off her. More like *around* her. She's a mental rock in a river of raging hormones.

I used to try to wrestle with my emotions to keep them in check. She doesn't bother. She ignores them. I'm not even sure she knows they're there.

"I'm trying to nap, Ron," she mutters. "I'm tired."

It was amazing how quickly she had grown used to my antics, her alarm becoming curiosity, then wonder. My constant presence had become a source of comfort. Except when I asked her to go on irrational errands for food that I couldn't actually eat.

She was stretched out in the recliner in our living room. It was the only seat in the house with good enough low-back support. I wasn't connected to the rest of her body very well. I couldn't control her or anything, but I could feel what she felt. Or at least I could feel it in a mental sense. She wasn't that tired. She was just meditating. It made me itchy.

My mind wasn't made to be sedentary. I was always the one going, doing, moving, pushing. I was the reason we ended up touring Europe the year before. She always said she was grateful for me. She said she loved experiencing the world through my eyes. Which is pretty funny now, considering our current circumstances.

"If I get you a cupcake, will you relax?" she asked.

I couldn't really reply. At least, not out loud. I could only give her my impressions. Emotions. I sent her my thanks and something like humility. I felt her smile, and warmth spread from her chest. Love. I reflected it back, and our feelings twined and merged like the blending of paint on canvas. I would have smiled, too, if I'd had a mouth.

She drove out to Sweet Tooth, and the heavenly sweet smell of baked sugar swept over me. I waited quietly as she had them wrap up the cupcake. She would eat it in the car, where we could be alone together.

"You know you're ruining my diet, right?" The pink cellophane crinkled as she opened it, and the smell of chocolate and peanut butter filled the small compartment of the car. I felt Lori's mouth water. "Are you even going to be able to taste this?" she wondered aloud.

Her craving hit just as hard as mine did, but again, it washed off her. Around her. Through her. It didn't affect her.

That first bite was heaven, the rich taste of chocolate melding with the warm, spongey cake dissolving on our tongue. It felt like home.

Though not my home. Not my home growing up, anyway. My home had always felt more like a prison. My parents argued a lot. They said they stayed together for my sake, but I would have been happier if they'd have gotten divorced. They'd have been happier, too.

No, the sweetness tasted like mine and Lori's home. It felt the way home was supposed to be. Where family members loved one another. Like birthday cake and smiles. Like late nights and old movies and sleeping in, tangled in the warmth of each other. The cupcake made me nostalgic.

I had only been cohabiting with Lori for two days, and this was the first time I'd asked her for food. I had been hit by a truck before I knew she was pregnant. Thank God she hadn't been there to see my brains all over the street or hear the screaming of the horrified driver. Things were a blur for a while after that. By the time I found my way back to her, I didn't know how much time had passed.

Five months. That's how long had passed. After wandering

aimlessly with no way of concentrating my thoughts, I crossed her path and felt a tug.

Actually, tug would be an understatement. It was a full-body haul down to the molecular level. Or, it would have been if I'd been made up of molecules. Whatever I was made up of now, it was pulled on. Hard.

I was sucked into a tiny space, and I was alive again. I could feel. I could think. I could breathe. And Lori was there.

I could feel her feeling me sitting in her head space. She thought she was losing her mind, but a memory surfaced. One I had forgotten. While we had been touring Europe, we had hit a bazaar. We spotted this olive-wood necklace. I don't care about jewelry, so I don't know why it caught my eye, but it caught Lori's attention at the same time. We touched it together. The German lady behind the table rambled something in her heavy accent about destiny and connection. She was teary-eyed by the time she was done. Some mystic mumbo jumbo designed to sell the piece. We bought it anyway.

The funny thing was, I could swear it was the necklace that pulled me into Lori. Like, I went *through* it to get to her. And now we were together again. Sharing a life. Sharing a cupcake. That necklace was the best money I'd ever spent.

In the car, Lori threw back her head and laughed. She felt my joy. Chocolate was joy. Life was joy. Life could also be irritating and inconvenient and hilarious and ironic and wearying, but all of that rolled off her. She was feeling joy through me. We were experiencing life together.

And we had company.

We felt the twinge from her belly. A kick.

The tiniest sliver of something. Curiosity. Wonder.

Lori's hand settled on her belly. Together, in the parking lot of Sweet Tooth, we felt our baby's first kick.

I radiated joy and felt hers rise to match mine. Then a white-hot blade of pain knifed through her.

We sat stunned for a moment. What had just happened? Had the baby kicked her kidneys or something?

But it didn't feel like a random stab of pain. Lori confirmed it wasn't a cramp. Something was wrong. Something was very, very wrong.

I felt the worry stronger than she did, and I wrestled with it. I didn't want to freak her out. She needed to stay calm.

She needed to get to the hospital.

She closed her eyes, trying to sense what was happening in her body. The pain had come and gone so fast that it left us breathless. The panic flowed past her. Around her. The pain was gone. Maybe it was nothing. Pinched nerve? Possibly. But everything was fine.

Everything was going to be fine.

She opened her eyes and cleaned the crumbs off her shirt where her belly made a convenient catch-all ledge. The trash went back in the pink Sweet Tooth bag. She started the car and put it in drive.

Another bolt of pain went through her belly. With her foot on the gas, the car lurched forward, nearly running over an old couple about to cross in front of her parking spot. Just like before, the pain was gone in an instant, and she slammed her foot down on the brake. She put the car in park and got out, checking on the old couple who looked at her with concern.

Something tugged low in her belly, and warmth flowed down her legs, pooling in her shoes. She was standing in a puddle of red.

"Something's wrong with my baby," she told them. "I need to get to the hospital."

They had her sit in the car with the engine off and stayed with her until the ambulance came. Dizzy, she tried to breathe through the pain, but I could feel the panic swirling around her.

This time it moved her. I did my best to send her soothing emotions, trying to keep my own panic from making hers worse.

The ambulance arrived, and the EMTs got her inside. Her

blood pressure was all over the place, and she was having bouts of nausea. The EMTs took turns telling her to stay calm and asking her questions. How far along are you? Have there been any complications before now? Who's your OB doctor? Should we call anyone?

The hospital was too bright. Frantic. Hospital staff hovered around her, wheeling her into a room where the curtain was pulled closed. More questions. They gave her a gown, but when she stood up to change into it, blood went everywhere.

"Oh, Ron," she breathed. My mind started to gibber, and I pushed back from her, trying not to let her feel my reaction. Was she going to die? Was the baby going to die?

Three nurses helped her into the gown and back in bed.

We couldn't think. We tried to focus on existing. On cradling the hope that our baby would be okay.

Words floated by outside of our comprehension.

Placenta. Baby's heartbeat. Wrong position. Too early.

A pinch in her hand told us an IV was in place. We waited in the swirling vortex of rushing bodies, beeping equipment, and muttered words. Lights flashed overhead as we were rushed into a spacious room where a sheet was draped over Lori's belly.

A man came in, a nurse on his heels. He had Lori turn on her side and fiddled with the back of her gown. He mentioned medication, and she felt a bone-deep jab in her spine, then her legs turned to jelly and the pain in her stomach faded.

We sank into each other, blocking out the world and clinging to each other and to that ethereal sense of wonder we felt from farther down the table, now narrowed to a thread. We hadn't even named him.

We'd played a game over the past couple days where I would give her impressions, and she would try to guess the name I was thinking of. I'd convinced Lori our baby was a boy, though I had no idea. Right now, his name didn't matter. He was part of me and Lori. A spirit child waiting to experience life. Every irritating, inconvenient, hilarious, ironic, wearying part of it. And joy. Because life was joy.

Space Without Breath

The sense of wonder flickered. Paused. Then spasmed.

The wonder turned to panic as our child struggled, clinging to life. I couldn't tell if Lori felt it, but I knew the second he started to die. The pulsing connection between us grew faint, like the receding tide. I feared it would never return.

I grabbed tighter to the tether that bound us, that vague sensation coming from down in her belly, focusing all my energy on it. The doctors were working. They were dissecting Lori in an attempt to save the baby. I prayed I wouldn't lose them both.

She had lost so much blood along the trail from Sweet Tooth to the ambulance to the hospital. Was that why the baby was dying? Blood loss?

Stay. I tried to will the thought at both him and Lori. *Stay.*

Knowing that death wasn't the end of all things didn't help. Without living bodies, we were existence without substance. Space without breath. We inhabited the emptiness between molecules, drifting from one place to another in an instant, without intent.

When Lori and I had visited Italy, we'd walked around Milan's city center and stumbled across the Duomo di Milano with its towering spires and open plaza full of pigeons and people. We didn't realize until after the tour that we had been only a mile from where Leonardo da Vinci had painted *The Last Supper* on the wall of a church.

I didn't want my child to wander aimlessly. I didn't want him to miss seeing *The Last Supper*. I wanted him to think and feel. I wanted him to live.

I had never been a God-fearing man in life, but in that moment I prayed to whatever force might hear me. Whatever might keep my child from fading, his spirit dissipating into the vast space between molecules.

It didn't help. The tether grew thin. The doctors quickened their motions, frantic to get the baby out so they could help him.

They were too slow.

I felt the tether snap.

I felt the moment of his death.

His soul drifted up from Lori's body. I could sense him flowing and expanding around me, like a slowly spreading cloud of dust. I knew it was too late. The doctors couldn't save him now.

My anguish washed over Lori, and I knew the moment she understood. The pain of it didn't go around her. It didn't wash over her. It didn't go around her. This time, she succumbed to the emotion, and it soaked into her. Drowning her. She screamed her anguish to the world, wanting to drown out this terrible reality.

That scream launched me out into the space between molecules.

Through all our years together, I had allowed my emotions to push me, to explore, to live life to its fullest. Lori drifted in the eddies of my life choices, content to come along for the ride. This time, it was her emotion that drove me, that forced *me* to action.

I lunged upward and outward, surrounding every last mote of my child's soul. My thoughts immediately became muddled with no neurons firing to focus them. I had a singular purpose.

Contain the soul.

That was easier said than done. The idea was simple enough to stay in my not-brain, but I had no muscles to move myself. Willpower alone could shift my perspective, but focusing that willpower was like trying to catch a cloud with a strainer. Anything I touched simply leaked through the spaces.

In the end, I'm not sure how I managed to accomplish my task. I like to think my child recognized me the way I recognized Lori. It clung to me, particle to particle. We drifted together at first, recuperating from our ordeal, but we weren't finished.

I needed Lori. Not in a cognitive way. More like an instinct. I could sense her through the necklace. It called me.

I floated closer, my precious cargo contained within the capsule of my soul. Lori was speaking, crying, praying.

"Oh, God, Ron. The baby. The baby. Bring him back, Ron. I can't lose him, too."

The baby. That's what I was holding. I was holding our baby.

Understanding came, sluggish and unwilling.

A doctor held a tiny bundle wrapped in a blanket. He moved to Lori. A precious doll face peeked out from within the folds, eyes closed, lips blue.

"I'm so sorry for your loss."

Lori cried harder, taking the bundle and cradling it to her bosom, her position awkward since she was laid out flat on the table. "He's here, Ron. Help him. Save him." She kept whispering to the room while the doctors and nurses went to work putting her body back together beneath the sheet, leaving her to her grief.

I drifted closer, trying to push the tiny baby back into the tiny body, but it wouldn't fit. His soul was scattered. The glue that held the particles together was missing. Every time I tried to push bits of him back into his body, they would spring away like magnets repelling one another.

Lori's head fell back against the table, exhausted from trying to look at the baby's face. She cradled the baby to her chin, one tiny ear coming to rest on the necklace sitting in the hollow of her throat.

It was like a doorway opened.

The tiny body, a shell of blood and bone and tissue, suddenly opened like a network of hollow spaces, waiting to be filled.

This time, when I pushed our baby back into his body, the particles stayed in place.

When the baby was half assembled, I knew something was wrong. Bits of him kept falling out like water dribbling from a straw. The container was open, but the glue was still missing. There was nothing holding him in place. Nothing holding him together.

My thoughts kept scattering like leaves in the breeze. I couldn't find a solution. I could barely comprehend the problem.

I heard Lori's keening, though I had no ears. I heard it as an emotion. The keening of her soul. The sound of a mother mourning her lost infant. Tears ran down the sides of her cheeks and into her hair, filling the hollows of her ears.

I had an overwhelming urge to hug her. To comfort her. To take her pain and bear it myself. The desire was basic and elemental and intense. Reflexively, my soul contracted.

And everything changed. My particles merged with my son's, becoming glue, blending us together. I felt some small measure of mental acuity return.

The sensation of my child taking over my soul particles was uncomfortable, and the realization of what had happened sank into my comprehension like water through cloth.

Greedy, my son clung to me with an alarming fierceness. What was unbearable to me was like breath to a drowning man for him. He was inhaling my soul. Drinking it.

He was taking me from Lori.

Lori, who was my joy in this world. Who I wanted to be with, to stay with, forever.

Even after death.

My child's need pulled at me. I could not choose to stay with Lori. Not at the cost of my child. *Our* child. I wouldn't bring her that kind of pain. Because that isn't love. Love isn't taking the easy path. My fractured thoughts were able to recognize that much.

I wanted to give my child a chance at life. At discovering his own joy.

Once I came to terms with the cost of the sacrifice, I threw myself into a desperate soul hug, feeling my identity dissipate as his grew more solid.

I could sense when I began to lose myself. My sense of consciousness.

Urgently, I herded him back into his tiny body, our conjoined particles finally staying firmly in place.

I no longer knew what I was doing, lost in the act of accomplishing my task, mindlessly unaware of the world. The last vestiges of my fading self registered a whoosh of breath.

Then a baby cried.

Space Without Breath

Jen Bair is an Air Force brat, Army veteran, and military wife. She loves traveling with her family to foreign places, real or imaginary, whenever she can. Her family is her life. Her writing is her passion. You can find her published works at JenBair.com, or write to her at author@JenBair.com. She'd love to hear from you.

Galaxy Edge Café
C. Michelle Jefferies

Lloyd Alexander stubbed out his cigarette on the brick of the alleyway behind the café and stared at the sky for a long moment. The icy air held a hint of snow. Such was life at the Edge—dark, isolated, and cold as hell. He blew on his hands before he stuffed them under his arms and headed for the café's front door. His shift started in fifteen minutes.

According to the galaxy-wide dictates, it was almost zero-hour startime, that moment when day turned to night even for those planets or colonies that never saw a visible change in light or dark. Here in this area of the Edge, it was always dark.

For Lloyd, it was the start of the busy hours as both starship crews—Spacers—and off-worlders frequented the café on their way somewhere else. The time where the local supernatural underworlders, or Unders as they preferred to be called, emerged. The time when most of the good guys were asleep.

Lloyd stepped from the alleyway but immediately shrunk back into the shadows as two men in black suits caught up with an unsuspecting man walking along the road. One of the suits pulled a black bag over the man's head while the other suit grabbed his hands and tied them together before shoving him into the back of a black shuttle, which disappeared into the depths of the city. Mafia.

The Edge was dark in more ways than one. That was a basic fact of life. To live here took a certain amount of guts.

Lloyd had built the café from the ground up—including the room at the back that held one bed, one desk, and one bookshelf. When the galaxy issued the new colonization rules, he'd claimed the land, salvaged what he could find, and made it a gathering place. He actually didn't need to work at all; he earned enough money from the café that he could hire a night shift cook and be done with it. But that would leave him with time to relive all of the stuff from his past he didn't want to think about.

So he clocked in every night at zero hour, hung his brown leather duster on the hook just inside the door, tied on an apron, and fed the Spacers, Unders, and off-worlders food like his grandma used to cook for him. Sometimes the only warm meal they would eat for weeks.

He paused inside the double doorway, opening the drawer in the handmade altar and selecting a handful of incense sticks. He stuck them in the nearby bowl of sand and lit them. He pulled a lone coin from his pocket and laid it in another bowl filled with rocks and water.

Most days, someone in need would fish the coin out of the water to pay for a meal, and he would put the coin back in at the beginning of his next shift for another person to use. Helping those who couldn't help themselves was one of the only ways he assuaged his conscience and expunged his past sins.

"Hey, Lloyd." One of the locals raised a hand as he stepped through the second door. "Still the best fried gerguns I've ever had."

"Glad to hear." He took a quick glance at the customers before heading to the kitchen.

Some off-worlders sat at the tables, and a pair of non-bipeds sat in a booth—if you could call what the non-bipeds were doing *sitting*. He'd have to mop the floor after they left. Slime was a hazard for everyone. A few pale-skinned Spacers in their traditional hoods and harnesses ate, as well as a smattering of locals, including two Unders. No one was waiting for food. That was good. It would give him a few minutes for some necessary prep.

He scrubbed at the Today's Special board with the attached fabric, tapped his chin for a moment, then wrote "Lloyd's Secret Surprise" in blue chalk on the black-painted wood.

"Morning," Ka'te said as she bustled by him into the serving area, carrying an empty plate and a pitcher of water in two of her four hands. "Ooo, Surprise night. I'm gonna have to save some for my lunch."

"We still have corn chips, right?" Lloyd added "Spiced Cherry Pie" to the board along with the prices.

"Pretty sure," she said before disappearing into the drink area.

Ruby had made the board for him the first year the café had opened. She'd moved on to better things since then, even going back to school with his encouragement. Getting a place for her and her kid in a safer area—and securing a better school for him later on—had been a priority for him.

"Lloyd Alexander—wasn't that an old fantasy author from Earth?" Ruby had asked as she sat in the chair for her interview.

"My mom liked to read," Lloyd answered.

She was small, even for a human. Thin boned, maybe five even on a good day. Pale like a Spacer, which made her chocolate eyes and warm brown hair stand out. She was definitely going to be a distraction if he wasn't careful.

One of the best things he'd done was hook up with her. A server with years of experience, she'd taken his plain little café and made it what it was now. She'd not only expanded the menu for the off-worlders and Unders, but she'd decorated too, adding a lil' Ruby touch to make the place more homey for those who found their way there through the dark and cold of the Edge. Lloyd hadn't thought that mixing rusty pieces of old spaceships, various other vintage items found on Ruby's adventures, and a little fabric and flowers would work, but it did.

He dropped two slices of bacon on the grill. He'd add the eggs and pancakes in a minute or two. He could eat his breakfast as he consulted the schedule and started on the special of the day. It wasn't a secret that Lloyd's grandmother had been from Earth and that her cooking had been award-worthy even though she had never entered any contests. People made the effort to stop by the café just to try the grits or the seafood, if the supplies were available.

While the bacon crisped, Lloyd pulled the bowl of white onions toward him and grabbed one, setting it on the cutting board. From the bag at his waist he unsheathed his tantō, a retirement gift from an old friend, and began to dice the onions into small pieces. Hiro would come unglued if he knew what Lloyd was using the blade for now.

He was finishing the last of the onions when he heard loud talking and laughter. He stood on his toes and leaned forward, but he couldn't see the side door from where he worked the grill. Most people came in and out of the front door where he could see them. His staff were the only ones who usually used the side door.

Ka'te approached the counter, her face flushed. She fanned at her pinked cheeks with one of her hands.

"What the hell?" Lloyd asked. "What's all the noise?"

"Oh, my gosh, I can't believe it. They're getting married."

"Who?"

"Marco and Amelia." Ka'te paused to grab four plates of pancakes. "He asked her tonight, and they're here to celebrate the good news."

"Here? You'd think they'd choose a better place than—"

"They met here. Don't you remember?" Ka'te turned and made her way into the dining area and placed the plates in front of some Spacers at a table.

Lloyd raised an eyebrow. No, he didn't remember a lot of what happened outside of the kitchen over the last ten years. Memories were something he tried not to entertain. The fast pace of short-order cooking kept his mind from wandering and thinking of things he shouldn't. Most of the time.

The light slanted through the tall buildings as the sun set. He stood in front of the hotel as the taxi descended from the traffic above and settled on the ground. Julia, his fiancée, stepped from the open door. She wore a long black dress and smiled when she saw him. They were celebrating his retirement from his job by going to the opera. Finally free from his past, they could focus on being a real family.

He heard the report of the rifle seconds too late. A bullet hit Julia's chest and knocked her to the ground. Another pierced his thigh. She was dead before her head hit the walkway, now splattered in blood.

No. Lloyd pressed a fist to his chest as the pain escaped the tightly controlled mental box where he'd locked it away.

He'd realized, as he slipped into the shadows that night, he'd never know why she smiled so widely. He'd never seen her smile like that before. Throughout the years, he'd wondered if it was the tuxedo he'd worn or the two dozen red roses he'd held. Maybe it was nothing.

He'd tied his bloodied jacket around his thigh and hobbled away from the scene into the dark backstreets of the city. To be caught alive and interrogated by his enemies would blow the entire Syndicate to pieces.

"Biscuits and gravy, a deluxe burger with cheese and bacon, and, oh, they want you to make the wedding cake."

"Wedding cake? It's like ... Do they know me at all? I'm not a baker."

"Your famous lemon bars would prove otherwise," Ka'te countered as she walked off.

"Still ... cake—especially wedding cake—is a completely different animal." Lloyd scrambled some eggs and flipped more pancakes. He placed his breakfast on a plate and, leaning against the counter, started eating while he watched the grill.

He plated both the burger and the biscuits and gravy, then added a small bottle of sparkling wine from his own personal stash.

"Up!" he shouted at Ka'te. He didn't want the wine to get warm.

"Black bob on the rail and a number three." Ka'te slapped the small paper onto the magnetic strip.

"Did you tell them the bob takes twenty minutes?" Lloyd asked.

"Repeat customer. He knows." One of her four hands pushed a pencil into her blue hair, the other two held plates.

Frances, his day cook, stepped next to him. "Why don't you do the bob, and I'll get the surprise started before I clock out." He grabbed the bowl of sliced onions and set it next to one of the stoves.

Lloyd opened one of the lower coolers. "Great, we don't have any bobs." He shut the cooler and grumbled a cuss word.

"What about Rufus?" Frances asked.

"He's supposed to be asleep," Lloyd answered, but opened the side door anyway.

Sitting on a nearby crate, holding the knife Lloyd had given him, sat a gangly teenage boy.

"Why aren't you at the school dorms?" Lloyd asked.

"You need me to fetch, and I need the money. A growing boy needs to eat."

"They're supposed to be feeding you." Lloyd groaned. "And you should be sleeping."

"Their food sucks."

"No, it doesn't."

"It's too healthy," Rufus answered. "What do you need?"

Lloyd fished some credits out of his pocket. "I need a few bobs."

"And some nermats," Frances added as he passed by the side door with a large container of ground meat.

"I can do that." Rufus jumped off the crate and held out his hand.

Lloyd placed the credits in the boy's hand. "Two minutes, or you're fired." Although they both knew he really didn't mean it. Rufus was a good kid in a bad situation. Lloyd intended to fix that.

"Two minutes. Got it." The boy bolted out of the alleyway toward the nearby dock.

Frances added the chopped onions into the pan with the meat. Lloyd knew he had ten minutes before starting the number three so the food would be delivered at the same time. He dropped his breakfast plate in the sink while the mechanical hands attached to the central unit picked it up, scrubbed it, and placed it in the sanitizer. Another hand hovered over the pan on the stove, hoping to be of use, although Lloyd and Frances did most of the cooking themselves. Man, his granny would have loved his automated kitchen assistant.

Frances finished patting the biscuit dough into three large baking pans, then hung his apron on the hook, shouted "Laters!" and left out the front door.

At the same time, Rufus opened the side door, placed a box of nermats on the kitchen counter, then opened the cooler and dropped two bob carcasses into it. "Seller pried them off the ship as I was running down to the dock." He looked over Lloyd's shoulder into the empty kitchen. "You need help today?"

"No. You need to go back to bed so you can go to school tomorrow."

"But—"

"We had an agreement." Lloyd shook his head. "You go to school because I am paying for it, and then, when you finish university, *if* you decide you want it bad enough, I will retire and you can take the night shift."

"You need the help now, though."

"And you need the education." Lloyd turned him in the direction of the door. "Now get out of here."

Rufus's shoulders sank, but he turned and headed the opposite direction, back to the school.

Lloyd turned to the kitchen and pulled out a bob. He pried open the bug's carapace to reveal the soft underbelly and numerous legs. Holding it open with one hand, he reached for the seasonings. Once he'd added enough spices to supposedly overcome the bug taste, he slathered on a bit—actually, *a lot*—of butter and let go. The carapace snapped back into the sectioned sphere it stayed in when the bug wasn't eating stardust off the local spaceships. Fifteen minutes in the oven, and it would be delicious. Supposedly.

Adding the Lloyd Secret Surprise seasoned meat mixture to the baking pans with the biscuit crust, he placed them in the oven and then started on the number three. French toast seemed so much more appetizing than roasted bob. Then again, not all of his customers were human.

"Are we still good on the Surprise?" Ka'te asked. "Table five needs two of them."

Lloyd settled two cheesy squares of Secret Surprise on plates, placed the corn chips on top, some steamed nermat on the side, then set them on the warming shelf.

"Number four and ten from the Black Menu." Ka'te slapped the paper onto the bar above the grill. The black menu listed all of the non-human food available to the customers—another of Ruby's ideas. "And don't forget you have the Tek'anha baby shower to cater tonight."

"I remember," Lloyd said as he eyed the counter with all of the supplies on it. "Boy or girl?"

"How about green and tentacled?" Ka'te answered. "And, yes, they want human food. The grandma is taking care of the food on the Vantuga side."

He looked at the clock; he had time.

Lemon bars first.

He knew the recipe by heart: one and a quarter cups flour, three-quarters cup powdered sugar, three-quarters cup softened butter, and a few teaspoons of water to make the dough workable.

The macaron cookies and eclairs for the shower had been in the fridge since yesterday. The charcuterie tray could be assembled while the bars baked or cooled.

Lloyd started on an order for a Monte Cristo and grilled pan fish.

Next, the lemon bar filling: four eggs into the blender, two-thirds cup lemon juice, a teaspoon of vanilla, one and a half cups of sugar, and a cube of melted butter.

Sandwich and fish on the warming counter, he poured the lemon filling into the pan and placed it in the oven. At 350 degrees, it would take about forty minutes.

The dining area cleared of lunch customers for a moment, he was halfway through placing a stack of sliced meats in a swirl across the wooden board when Ka'te stepped next to him, her face unreadable. Strange, she almost never came into the kitchen when she was on shift.

"They're back, and they won't leave." Her lips barely moved; two of her hands were shoved into her apron pockets, while the other two clasped each other hard enough her knuckles turned white.

"Let me guess. Pete?" He wiped off his tantō and pushed it into the bag at his waistband. The boy was stupid, thinking he could blackmail Lloyd into anything.

She nodded.

He rolled his shoulders and unbuttoned the cuffs of his shirt as he walked from the kitchen to the dining area. The wannabe gangster lounged in a booth, his feet stretched into the aisle, his leather jacket a little too big for the scrawny boy. His cohorts sat on the other side of the booth, grinning.

"Pete, Pete, what're you doing here?" Lloyd asked. "I have a 'No Soliciting' sign, or can't you read?"

The young man's poor excuse for a dagger dug into the table as he slowly twisted it in a circle, leaving a divot in the wood.

"Nice place you got here. Be a shame if it flooded or some of your employees got hurt." Pete smiled; his buddies laughed. "We can do something about that."

Lloyd nearly rolled his eyes. They had no idea how amateur they looked. "I told you last month, and the months before that, I don't need protection. I can handle it on my own."

"You don't understand. We own this area," Pete drawled. "If you want to keep doing business here, you need to start giving us our fair share."

With Ka'te safely hidden in the kitchen, he turned to Pete and swiped the knife from the table. He tossed it up, the blade lodging into the ceiling above them. Then he slammed the ornate tantō blade through the sleeve of Pete's jacket and into the table, pinning him where he sat. The other boys froze while Pete looked from the blade to Lloyd's face.

"No. I don't think *you* understand," Lloyd growled and pushed his sleeve up to reveal a tattoo on his forearm: a tiger stepping onto a lotus flower. "You mess with me, you mess with my tribe."

"Obiqua," one of the other boys whispered. *Syndicate.*

A rivulet of sweat actually slid down Pete's now-pale face.

Lloyd lifted his tantō from the table as if the blade had never been imbedded inches into the wood and turned back to the kitchen. "Get out of here, and don't come back."

The boys bolted out of the café, the bell on the door ringing wildly.

Lloyd pulled his sleeve down and entered the kitchen.

"They're gone?" Ka'te asked from where she was crouched on the floor.

"And if they're smart, they won't return." Lloyd opened the oven door to check on the lemon bars them resumed putting meat and cheese on the charcuterie tray.

With Ka'te standing at his side, Lloyd settled the wrapped charcuterie tray, macarons, eclairs, and lemon bars dusted in powdered sugar on the automated delivery platform. Everything looked perfect. He added a note of congratulations and swiped his credit device on the control panel scanner. It would deliver the food directly to the hotel about fifteen minutes before the baby shower was supposed to start.

He inwardly congratulated himself on a job well done and finishing on time, in spite of the hectic day and side complications. He would have personally delivered the food—Ka'te and his automated kitchen helper could manage the café for fifteen minutes—but he knew Pete, and he knew how stupid the kid was. Hopefully he had gotten the message and would leave the café alone.

He should call the local police and tell them to keep an extra eye on the place, but he didn't want the attention. Instead, he would pretend it hadn't happened, and be extra vigilant in secret.

Lloyd leaned against the counter as Ka'te walked away with the two plates with burgers and fries. It was early morning according to the galaxy clock, but for his patrons, it was the lull after the dinner rush. For Lloyd, it was time to prep for Frances's shift. He heard Ka'te open the little fridge near the drink dispenser and gather a handful of small cups of "fry sauce." It was an old Earth recipe his grandma had learned from two religious young men she'd found melting on the roadside in the Southern heat. Of course, he'd doctored it to his taste years ago. It was well-liked by his customers but was not as famous as his grandma's fried chicken.

He drained his water bottle and set it on the counter. He'd fill it later. Right now, he was enjcying the moment where no papers fluttered on the strip and the grill was empty.

The Secret Surprise had sold out, and the pans had been washed and stored for tomorrow. He had one bob in the cooler, and the supplies, delivered just before the dinner rush, were put away. The spiced cherry pie had sold out as well, and he had ordered a new round of desserts from his favorite bakery. They'd arrive tomorrow during the breakfast shift.

The sound of breaking dishes scarred the silence. Lloyd looked up, senses alert. Where was Ka'te? Was she okay?

"Hands where I can see them. Don't move," a voice said.

Lloyd pulled a handgun from under the counter, settled it in his waistband next to his tantō, and pulled his shirt over it. He'd try to talk to whoever it was first. Violence, the way he used to live his life, wasn't an option anymore.

Was this person trying to rob him? He had no cash in the café, and only a few paper credits in his pouch. Hardly anyone carried physical credits anymore. There were law enforcement eyes everywhere, and the penal system left much to be desired. Whoever it was, was desperate or insane. Maybe both. Perhaps Pete had decided to be brave and try another approach.

"You. In the kitchen. Come out here with your hands up."

He held his hands at shoulder level and stepped from the kitchen into the dining room.

Ka'te's body trembled as she crouched, arms over her head. His gut twisted to see her so scared.

The man was big. Not one of Pete's guys. Although Lloyd wouldn't put it past Pete to have ratted him out. This guy wore a dark suit and overcoat dotted with rain. Lloyd knew the look. Not just an average bad guy, but Syndicate.

He sighed heavily. His cover was blown, most likely by his own stupid, ego-driven interaction with Pete. Even if he survived this situation, the café was no longer a safe haven. They'd keep coming for him.

"You're making a big mistake. I don't have anything you want," Lloyd said as he stepped next to Ka'te.

"What I want isn't a thing. It's you."

"Me." He didn't question it. Revenge and payback were common in the underground. He had no idea who this man was, outside of being part of his past, but he assumed he had wronged him in some way. No one around him except this man knew his past. Not Ka'te, not Frances, not Rufus. Not even Ruby.

"Let her go." Lloyd nodded toward Ka'te.

"Not a chance." The man looked from Ka'te to Lloyd. "She's my leverage."

"You want me, not her. She just works here." He saw pain cross Ka'te's face at his words. Yes, they were coworkers, but the chemistry was there that could change that relationship to something more. But for her to live, this man needed to believe that there was nothing between them.

"You obviously value her life," the man said. "That gets me what I need."

Dammit. Lloyd wracked his brain, trying to place the man in his memory. Obviously, he couldn't just walk away from his past; too many people still wanted his blood. But this man was Syndicate, Lloyd should be safe within the network.

"I am immune. This"—he pulled out his tantō—"assures it." The small sword, his parting gift from his former boss, meant he could walk peacefully among his fellow associates. The blade glinted in the light of the café.

The man's face twitched, his pupils dilating momentarily. Good, the man knew what it meant. But then his face smoothed back into the calm emotionless expression before Lloyd had brandished the blade.

"Hiro is in no position to guarantee your safety. There's a bounty for your head. I intend to collect it." The man leveled his gun at Lloyd.

"Hiro's dead."

"Let's just say he's not in charge anymore."

At least Hiro is alive. Relief for his friend battled with the stark reality of his life now. He was no longer safe anywhere, not even within his own tribe. This changed things drastically. He had no option but to do something he hadn't done in years—put himself in the offensive position.

Lloyd caught Ka'te's eye and whispered, "The empty cupboard by the freezer—grab the white bag. Go."

The man moved toward Ka'te, and Lloyd barreled into him.

The gun, knocked off target, fired right next to his head, deafening him. The bullet lodged into the wooden ceiling as he and the man hit the floor at the same time.

A flash of pink that he hoped was Ka'te running toward the kitchen's side-door exit registered in his brain, but he dared not be distracted. Not with this opponent. If the man was trying to kill one of the Syndicate's best former assassins, he had to be at least the same level of skill.

The man struggled to point the gun at Lloyd, but a side swipe of Lloyd's elbow knocked the gun wide. The bullet headed in the general area of the kitchen. Bullet number three spiderwebbed a window.

Lloyd reached for his handgun as a fist connected with his cheek. He grunted, leaving his weapon holstered, and returned the hit.

He was going to play dirty? Fine, he could do that too.

He took a fist to the stomach, then slammed his knee into the man's sternum. Gasping for breath, the man attempted another hit, but Lloyd easily blocked it.

The man aimed his gun, and this time, Lloyd's swing was

seconds too late. The fourth bullet grazed his side, just under his ribs.

The assassin smiled at the blood blooming on Lloyd's white shirt.

Lloyd breathed in hard as pain raced across his chest. He detected a hint of gas wafting in the air. The second bullet must have hit the grill's gas line, just on the other side of the thin wall separating the dining area and the kitchen. The grill was off, but the pilot still burned.

He had a few minutes, maybe, before that leak took both their lives.

Lloyd scrambled to a crouch and rushed at his opponent, knocking him to the ground. The man's head slammed hard onto the ground with a dull pop. Seizing his advantage, Lloyd reached behind him and unsheathed his tantō, driving it into the assassin's chest and through his heart.

The man bucked once, then lay still as a puddle of blood formed beneath him.

Lloyd sheathed his knife and untied his apron, dropping it onto the body before he headed into the kitchen. He grabbed his leather duster off its hook, grimacing at the pain in his side as he threaded his arm into the sleeve. He could attend to the wound later. Once he was as far away as possible.

The door to the cupboard was open; the white bag was gone. Good. Ka'te had found it.

Inside that bag had been a stack of envelopes, each one containing a small severance and a note from him. The note for Rufus was longer than the others, and instead of money, it held details about an account Lloyd had set up in the boy's name that was his upon graduation. If he stayed in school.

Lloyd grabbed his bug-out bag from the underside of the counter and ducked out of the café and into the dark night of the Edge.

Behind him light and heat erupted as the café went up in

flames. He didn't pause or turn around. An assassin, finished with his job, never looked back.

The area cops would quickly sift through the debris, find a body and the remnants of an apron, and assume Lloyd Alexander had died in an accidental gas explosion that had destroyed the café he'd built from the ground up. Case closed.

For all intents and purposes, Lloyd Alexander *had* died tonight.

He pulled out his device and scrolled through a list of possible names and lives he could buy from the black market for a couple hundred credits.

This wasn't his first time, and probably not his last, either. He'd stick to the Edge, of course, but move somewhere several days' distance in the hyper.

Maybe this time he would open a bookstore.

C. Michelle Jefferies believes that the way to examine our souls is to explore the deep and dark as well as the shallow, to manipulate words in a way that makes a person think, and maybe even second guess. Her worlds include suspense, urban fantasy, and an occasional twist of steampunk. When she is not writing, she can be found on the yoga mat, hand-binding journals, dyeing cloth, and serving ginger tea. The author and creator divides her time between stories, projects, and her family of seven children. She lives in Wyoming.

Mission Impossible Burger
Mike Jack Stoumbos

T he subject's brain glows vibrant blue on my monitor. Gustatory and olfactory cortices so bright, I have to dim my screens and adjust contrast. I give a thumbs-up to Corey, my intern and this trial's proctor, seated in the sterile testing room opposite the glass.

Corey employs his soothingly smooth voice to tell the hard-wired subject, "I'm placing the plate in front of you now." He sets down an unnuanced plastic slab, supporting an equally lackluster ellipsoid lump. Its grayish-beige hue is anything but appetizing.

The subject, shielded by a headset and haptic feedback gloves, licks his lips. "Wow, that smells really good."

Corey shoots me a hopeful nod.

Sitting in the adjoining room, I'm more interested in the data on my screen. Several sensors relay hundreds of signals from the VR headset, each registering as little flares and mental fireworks. Joy, nostalgia, mouth-watering hunger—courtesy of two, tiny stimulator electrodes busy chatting with the subject's temples.

A scan of my own brain would show the same fireworks, but also the looming dread that plagues every scientist in their early tests. My anticipation and pulse continue to climb.

"You may touch the product," says Corey, much more evenly than I could manage. "And when you're ready ... take a bite."

The subject grabs supplement-283 on the first go, using more force than necessary, and testing the lump's structural integrity. It's common in VR; we're lucky the supplement's outer skin is so elastic.

The subject giggles, and I observe from his VR feed that his thumb went through the simulated contour. "Okay, got it." He opens his eager maw and chomps down, etching the grooves of his teeth through the lump as perfectly as if it were modeling clay.

"Mmm!"

First reaction. Good sign.

Indicator lights and measurements show exactly what I want to see—increased salivation and satisfaction.

"Oh, man."

Second reaction: louder, better. Followed by a second bite.

Never before have I so carefully watched the neck and jaw muscles working under a middle-aged male's layer of fat. Each swallow and subsequent bite moves me closer to the glass divide, inching toward the literal edge of my seat.

His digits grip the grayish-beige lump with practiced precision; his visual feedback indicates no disorientation. Like most subjects, this guy has checked "Very Familiar" with the Glove® Enterprises InterFace tech we're using.

But he still has not said the words. I know better than to suggest directly and scrub the validity—even though my monitors tease a 99.9 percent likelihood of total success. Nevertheless, I can't wait indefinitely while he chews.

I press the microphone button. "Can you tell me what you're tasting?" I ask, with my sharper, less elegant voice.

The subject laughs—actually laughs out loud—with food in his open mouth, a bit of supplement-283 stuck in his bottom teeth. "Oh, yeah! It's a hamburger. Absolutely perfect."

My fists shoot up, and I whoop. I've released the microphone, but I can see from the reactions of both Corey and the subject that the glass partition isn't soundproof.

At the moment, I don't care. I can be professional for the next nineteen trials. For now, I savor my moment, like the unctuous endangered beef that inspired the project. I have programmed an indisputable virtual-reality hamburger, and nothing will ever be the same.

"My absolute favorite was the vegan," says Corey, as he carefully removes the sensor pads from the inside of the headsets. "She kept lifting the visor to double-check she wasn't *really* eating a burger. I thought she was going to lose it!"

"I thought *you* were going to lose it," I interject from my console, remembering how frustrated Corey had been with that subject—a woman who looked about my age but in much better shape, with the kind of unnaturally magenta hair designed to mask any signs of gray. "You kept warning her that she'd disqualify herself from the experiment."

Corey shrugs. "I guess it's a reasonable reaction, especially for less-experienced VR users. It's good user data—right, T?"

Corey is nearly a decade younger than I am, and he's a student —working on my research venture for independent-study credit. Apart from his customer service manner and excellent fine motor skills, he brings little expertise or experience. Still, I have come to appreciate his "look on the bright side" optimism that hasn't been crushed by adult life.

Between our spurts of conversation, the only sounds in this veritable concrete bunker are the clicking of little mechanisms in the headsets, my muted typing on silicon keys, and the white noise of the HEPA filter.

Stooping over the prep desk, Corey carefully ejects and safely packages the stimulator electrodes, a proprietary element for my flavor endeavor. When he finishes extracting them from each headset, he walks to my side and places the clear plastic cases on top of my external hard drive.

"It all checks out?" he asks, pointing to my screens.

"Completely." I wear a ridiculous smile—equal parts smug and awestruck, as rare a combination as supplement-283 and my ingenious brain-hack. "Twenty trials, no anomalous readings. Everyone tasted a hamburger in VR." I run my finger down one line, where I've recorded the subjects' follow-up comments, which they'd made after, when not induced by the electrodes or virtual tech. "But, without assistance, they called it 'bland' or 'tasteless.'"

Corey says, "It *is* tasteless, T. It's just synthesized protein and fiber."

"This will revolutionize nutrition as we know it." I've said it before, but the claim has much more weight. Data like this is enough to seek funding. "People would kill for my recipe."

Having reminded myself of the importance of intellectual properties, I pull the traces of the experiment from the computer, which remains unnetworked during the trials. My trial data, as well as the formulas for the protein and brain stimulators, are secured on my personal hard drive.

While I work the tech, Corey resumes sanitizing the headsets. "You'll bank enough to retire on. Get yourself a place with real plants and animals even. Out of the sprawl."

I shake my head. Not that I don't enjoy the concrete-for-miles of the urban mega-sprawl, but I have much bigger plans. "This is only the beginning. Watch me tackle cheesecake, maybe foie gras."

The console wiped clean, I remove my hard drive and switch on the network in a single flourish. It's muscle memory, and I know better than most that nothing networked stays secret these days.

Corey reacts with surprise. "You're putting out the email blast now?"

"Strike while the iron's hot," I say, signing in. "Besides, it's not the formal grant request. Just chumming the waters to see who's hungry."

"You're including Glove, aren't you?"

"Naturally." After all, we're using Glove hardware, so it's a reasonable courtesy. Fortunately for us, and every other scientist, all discoveries, programs, and patents made using Glove tech belong to the original inventor—which is part of why every virtual user uses their tech.

I also add the fitness conglomerate, OmniGym, and the multilevel powerhouse, Nutritech, and the university, from whom I lease my lab space, among others. Fifteen recipients, each with generic *acquisitions@* and all in the *To* line, so they can see who else knows about the opportunity of the century. Corey doesn't comment on my list or the fact that I've left off Sustainable-Solutions, which I appreciate.

I keep the correspondence brief, brusque even, but within the norm for fast-flying, funding-seeking form letters. There's no need to exaggerate: the idea of a lo-cal, lab-grown, hypoallergenic, VR hamburger deemed "perfect" by all alpha testers sells itself.

My fingers move rapidly until they reach the product's name, which I've sort of spaced until now. "Supplement-283" doesn't exactly inspire excitement. As I scan the stark, concrete office for inspiration, my gaze settles on the nearest of our three Glove headsets. Each has the big, bold *InterFace* banner on the side, with the *I* and *F* in that bubbly, purple font used for kids' soda ads.

"You been in IF-World beta?" I ask.

"What? Like that sandbox program?"

So far, IF-World, or *InterFace*-World, is a free-explore game without objectives where users wander and chat with others' avatars in surprisingly immersive VR. Glove has already rewritten the rules on nightclubs, but they've barely scratched the surface of restaurants. They also haven't trademarked *IF* yet.

So I type:

Prototype Name: IF-Burger.

I hot-key my automatic signature, identifying myself as

Theresa Hunter, a research-scientist alumnus of a prestigious university, and add my contact info.

I hit *Send* before I can second guess myself.

"That's enough for today," I say, more to convince myself than Corey. In my excitement, I've worked later than planned, and it will be well after sunset on the surface.

The university provides great rental rates for alums, especially interrogation-room-style underground research labs. The single elevator with the sliding steel-cage door that jostles me four stories each way is a reasonable trade-off for a clean room without windows or outdoor allergens.

The second Corey and I step through the outer door and into open evening air, my eyes start itching from the June dander. Moss and mold are gleefully airborne these days, but it's a short walk to the light-rail, and I'm tougher than I look.

"Do you need me to come in tomorrow?" Corey's initiative is admirable, but I can tell he's hoping I'll decline.

"No, I know you have exams coming up. Besides, I might be out of the lab myself. Taking care of other logistics."

"Sure." Corey swipes his parking pass by the stalls. The one holding his bike unlocks and lights up green. He buckles his helmet. "Thought about next quarter?"

I know tuition has been tight for Corey, to the point that he's considering pausing his education to work twice-time for a few months.

"You know, Corey, if I get fully funded, I can turn your for-credit internship into a paying one, maybe even retroactively."

His expression of sheepish gratitude looks even more goofy on his long face when it's topped with a bike helmet, but it makes me smile.

We part with a quick, mumbled "Good night," reinforcing the theory that lab scientists are socially awkward. We are also inquisitive, which is why I look up at the streetlight when I see a flash in my peripheral vision. But I am also tired—I did alter all human experience as we know it today—so after a few seconds of veri-fying a normal streetlight, I continue home.

"Flood" is an insufficient term to describe the emails. "Flash flood" is closer. "Sudden Erratic Monsoon Waves" takes the cake.

I don't know whose data breached, or who forwarded what where, but I wake to buzzing notifications on my phone, and the stomach-clenching excitement that *everyone* knows about my prototype. Unlisted and blocked numbers have been calling for hours, and I'm glad my ringer was set to vibrate.

I push my hair out of my face and quickly thumb through inboxed subject lines, making mental note of the senders. The promise of a hot commodity, even unverified, has drawn far too many sharks too quickly to sort. I notice the message from Sustain-able-Solutions, begging to sit down with me and "start fresh"—which is a kind of vindication, but still elicits a groan.

Even as I scan, the sea of meeting requests continues to grow. I'm tempted to jump at the first one, but I'm waiting for a response for Glove or one of the other high rollers.

I see a breakfast invite from the safest, least binding opportu-nity: my alma mater. It's also the least lucrative, but I'd rather talk to someone than sit at home staring at the phone.

Without pausing for coffee or shower, I grab my bag with the experimental data and all of my anti-allergy measures. Despite my electronic deluge, the real-life forecast in the Seattle mega-sprawl is sunny and chock-full of spores and pollen. So, armed with my EpiPen, inhaler, and plenty of tissues, I start a brisk sunlit walk back to the light-rail and my rendezvous.

Each phone alert serves to spike my anxiety rather than excitement, so that by the time I arrive at the West Plaza Cafe, I'm feeling more burdened than advantaged by my valuable find. My lab is a moderate walk—or a short sprint—away, and I'd rather be there, cracking the next flavor code. But I know this part of the process—corporate sponsorship, official patents, playing the "game"—is essential for getting myself out of that makeshift research basement space and into a fully functional lab, which I would have been able to do ten years earlier if I'd been a little smarter about security.

This time, I am careful to leave nothing online; my cargo stays with me. The messenger bag's strap digs into my shoulder, and my elbow pins the blocky content to my ribs as I endure the short wait in line for necessary caffeine. There are too many people in sunglasses and headphones; a few wear face masks, either for personal health or echoing past trends. Hard to recognize or distinguish anyone like that, or to describe to a police officer in the aftermath of a bag-snatching.

My latte, like most beverages, comes out of an automated tube. And, like everything in our watered-down world, could use some flavor modification. I find myself wondering how to trigger the taste more than the money I could make. My brain is trying to work out the aroma and flavor patterns for coffee by the time I meet my university contact at a table.

Doctor Barker is balder and bigger than when I'd been his student, but he greets me warmly and gestures to a chair. "I understand congratulations are in order," he says in a scratchy voice.

"Thanks." I slide into the solar-heated seat, the metal legs screeching against the brick walkway. The outdoor cafe is bright enough for me to long for sunglasses. "It's a bit overwhelming."

Barker laughs. "That's what it's like being headhunted, T. Everyone wants what you're selling." He stirs his coffee with his spoon, his finger lifted daintily, contrasting both his appearance and the cheap, compostable cup. "So, you really made a burger work in VR?"

"Combination of augmented reality with immersive virtual assist, but yes." Though I'm not skilled or practiced in high-stakes negotiations, I try to segue smoothly into my aim. "And I am selling, by the way. Is the university making an offer?"

Barker laughs, shifts uncomfortably. "We're probably not able to match the corporate offers. But if the research is legitimate—"

"It's legitimate." I tap the bag still pinned to my side. "Twenty-twenty success, no discrepancies."

Barker literally scratches his pale, shining scalp. "We're all really curious: How did you manage it?"

It's tempting to tell him about the electrodes that hack into the mind to incept smell, taste, and nostalgia, but a glint on his shirt gives me pause. I squint at what might be a button microphone and realize the professor might be recording. Before I can object, nature intervenes. In the harsh daylight, surrounded by seasonal particulates, and spurred by a squint, I feel that undeniable nasal itch.

When I sneeze, I hear a rush of wind, and across the table, Barker reacts as if struck.

When I lift my head, I see a colored straw with a tuft, sticking point-first into his upper arm.

He wrenches the projectile free, but no blood spurts out. Hypodermic-tipped dart. "T, get down!"

I'm not slow, just stunned. Barker grabs my wrist and pulls me under the table, and I wonder if the dart had been meant for me. A *ping* off the table indicates a second miss.

"You gotta run!" says Barker, his eyes speaking volumes. He's worked out the situation. Closing and opening his hand, he remarks, "I'm fading." Sturdy frame or not, adrenaline or not, he's succumbing to the tranquilizer—which would have knocked my scrawny frame out in an instant.

I don't question hidden microphones or intended targets—that can come later. I lunge out from under the table but feel myself yanked back by the strap on my elbow. Someone's grabbed my bag. The shooter? Don't know, don't care.

Were I a secret agent, I would be able to extract myself

artfully using martial arts. But as I'm not, I utilize immediate resources and spray my hot latte onto my assailant.

Were he more professional, he might have held on. Instead, he yelps and loosens his grip on my bag.

I wrench free and take off, leaving Barker as collateral damage. It's okay, I tell myself. They aren't after him. It's hard to feel guilty about the prof turned corporate spy.

The outdoor cafe has erupted into chaos, and I'm one of many sprinting from the scene, hoping there were only two darts loaded.

I've hardly gone thirty feet when I trip over something. Not a graceful slide or tumble, but a full-on, ass-over-teakettle slam into the brick walkway. I probably would have broken a bone if my bag hadn't broken my fall—who knows what tech I've pulverized upon landing.

I finally see what tripped me: an outstretched leg, belonging to a wiry, magenta-haired woman with a stern jaw. The vegan who kept removing her headset had been a plant! Spying for who-knows-where.

She approaches, not to help me, but to roll me off my bag. "Give me that drive!"

I'm gasping from the sprint and spores—and now the sudden impact. Every good allergy-induced asthmatic has a quick-draw weapon at the ready, and we know how to wield it while panicking.

EpiPen out, cap off. Stab into the back of Miss Vegan's hand.

Warning, don't stick your finger or palm. Warning, don't hit bone.

I manage both.

Vegan jerks her hand back, which changes color to match her hair, but she has other limbs and a sneer of determination.

I start kicking, not caring where I connect, trying to scramble away before shooters, bag snatchers, or extra university goons arrive to help mug me.

She doesn't care about a few quick shots to her legs or torso either. But when she reaches for me again with her wounded hand, I go feral. The irony of sinking my teeth into a vegan will be funny later. Humor is not a current priority. But a burger, apparently, is.

A bite wound to a severely compromised hand doesn't stop her, hardly fazes her. Her heart must be racing from the epinephrine.

Crap! I juiced her.

Vegan looms over me, gritted teeth tacitly threatening to make me pay in more than patents. She's both athletic and willing to sacrifice a hand, and she probably has physical and financial backup en route.

I raise my arms in surrender and awkwardly try to shift off my bag to surrender it, too.

She seems to be debating whether to kill me, when a sickening *crack* interrupts, and her magenta hair fans. It's not a bullet or even a tranq, but a bike helmet. Holding the blunt weapon is Corey.

"You okay?" He extends a hand, very "Come with me if you want to live," and I accept.

Corey is also winded, but not enough to slow him down. Once he's picked a vector, I don't need to be told where we're going. "She's from OmniGym," he pants. "They wanted to grab the tech before you sold it somewhere else."

I glance back. Vegan is stirring but too dizzy to stand, possibly concussed.

Others are scratching their heads in confusion, not sure if they should be running. How many of them have called 911, and why aren't I one of them?

Neither Barker nor the bag-snatcher are visible through the chaos. When we turn a corner, down a concrete stairwell, we leave the whole scene behind.

I know the campus better than Corey does; it's home territory for me, especially the parking garages. This vast, underground array of pollution, which, ironically, does not interfere with my breathing, has remained my preferred headquarters.

Corey's long legs are leading toward my lab, and I follow. It's a safer, even more underground bunker to which only I have the key, and is the perfect refuge to regroup.

Of course, I hadn't imagined I'd need a hideout—or that the world could go suddenly bonkers over a VR-programmed flavor. Even Barker, an old prof, could have been luring me into a trap. Or, maybe, he was sincerely pitching the university when we got interrupted by a tranquilizer-dart-spraying lunatic, from—where? Nutritech? OmniGym?

No, the vegan was from OmniGym.

I peer ahead at Corey, hoping to be granted sudden X-ray vision into his mind. "Corey, how did you know where to find me?"

"Huh? Oh, I—yeah, sorry." He pauses at the exit door, just across the street from the lab entrance. "I tracked your phone."

Reasonable explanation. Corey could do it, but *would* he? Without calling first, on a day off? "I told you not to come in today."

He fumbles and babbles. "I figured—You know, I thought maybe you'd need help, then—Well, I found you at the cafe, with that woman attacking you."

"Right." Logical. Possible. Not realistic. "How'd you know she was from OmniGym?"

Corey doesn't try to lie. "She was attacking you, T!"

"How'd you know? Who told you?"

The slump of his shoulders provides the answer. I recoil. "No!" The word is a growl that escapes before I make a conscious sound. "You sold me out to Sustainable-Solutions? Are they planted at the lab, or are you robbing me yourself?"

"No, not that!" he protests, clearly offended by the accusation. "Just ..." He fishes into his baggy pocket and produces a phone:

shiny and new, but cheap. A burner. "They wanted me to arrange a call."

"Absolutely not!" I shove past him and stomp across the street without checking for followers. "I can't believe you! They stole my first patent—the last ten years from me—and you're colluding with them?"

"I know, but hear me out."

"No!" I'm in the foyer, planted between Corey and the elevator. "You don't get to follow me. You're officially fired."

"But T, they'll pay my tuition!"

I linger. Associated memory shout *reason* and *sympathy*, even if my ire wants to kick both to the curb.

"If you just take the call, they've promised me enough to get through next quarter." He desperately extends the phone toward me.

But I spy something else, behind Corey, across the street. Charging toward my trackable signal, one, then three, then maybe a dozen people—including a bruised and murderous vegan.

Catching my expression, Corey turns, then exclaims, "Go, T!" Good advice, and with it, a thrown burner phone.

I catch the device, sprint into the elevator, and pull the cage door shut. In those seconds, the horde has shoved Corey aside and would claw into the elevator were it not already moving. As I descend, I work out how to stop them from following me. There is, after all, only one elevator, and sometimes a crude solution is the best one.

Moments after I'm safely below, klaxons blare. Old sprinklers are working out their toxic, metallic standing water in the hallway where I've pulled the alarm. But no repeat elevator trip will follow me until the fire department has called the all-clear.

The door to my lab blocks out most of the sound, except for the vibrating burner phone in my hand. It pulses a call notification, waiting for me to pick up.

I accept. The screen populates a video-call interface for Elaine@SustainableSolutions.

"I didn't contact you on purpose." My fists clench, but I don't grit my teeth. That would be visible.

Elaine gives a pompous, pampered smile. "After we confirmed your results were legitimate, we couldn't let it go without putting in our own offer. How've you been, Theresa?"

We're not friends; I've never even met her before, but I know her company. "You stole my formula!"

"That was a long time ago. And I'd like to think Sustainable-Solutions refined your—what was it?—supplement-109?" She says it mockingly, disregarding that it was the first successful 3D-printed synthetic protein, and knowingly striking a nerve.

"Do you know what it's like to rebuild a career after you stole my patent?"

"You apparently recovered. Let's call it water under the bridge."

Her casualness boils my blood, but I seethe silently.

"I hear agents have taken shots at you."

"Was it you?"

"No, that's not our way. But we can provide some necessary protection. You start a contract with me, and we'll broadcast that you're safeguarded by our team. Our conglomerate is big enough that no one will go after you or your research. Some will try to reverse-engineer the design, but they'll know the original patent is ours. No one can fight our patents."

I am well aware. "Absolutely not."

She laughs. Not derisively—more like she's heard a joke at a cocktail party. "What is your pride worth to you? Your life? Because you're kidding yourself if you think you're not in danger."

"This is ridiculous!" I literally throw my hand up in frustration. The dam is broken; I spill my emotions like I would to a therapist or a girlfriend, not a bitter rival from a soulless corporation. "What kind of person would kill over a hamburger?"

As soon as I show my vulnerability, she shifts to biting cold. "Who wouldn't kill for it? You've made completely sustainable, virtual-reality endangered beef. Right now, nothing is more important. Everything is moving virtual, and anyone who wants a piece of the pie is taking it now. Isn't that why you switched your research focus?"

I start to confirm, but she cuts me off.

"Even Sustainable-Solutions is trying to ally with Glove for long-term virtual living. Why? Because people in VR leave a minimal carbon footprint. Really, Theresa, we're working on the same things but competing for limited space. This is your chance to join the revolution."

I'm not slow, just stubborn. "Not with you."

"They'll keep hunting you," she snaps. "They'll go after your research, try to get you out of the picture, reverse-engineer your design or steal it outright."

I scoff at the thief's hypocritical warnings.

"If these companies can have a controlling interest in something so valuable, they're going to fight dirty. I'm offering you a lifeline, Theresa, formally, before going to war. Who else has done that?"

I hang up. In many ways, she's right, and I don't have a plan to save me or my intellectual property. Every person involved in the testing might have been a mole, everyone could be trying to piece together my formula. And even if I do join someone's side now, who's to say they won't still try to get me out of the way, silence me, bury me—legally or literally. All over something new, exclusive, and valuable.

Then I see the solution. Like any good inventor, sitting alone in a concrete box, letting my thoughts ricochet off the walls, I've figured it out, and I'm not willing to wait.

My brain would appear bright red on an emotional scanner, an unhealthy mix of fear and frustration. But no panic, and some pride.

I know how to upload data. I understand security protocols. I've been part of the university system, academic forums, and online think tanks long enough to go wide.

In minutes, I have.

Mission Impossible Burger

The IF-Burger has been published, everywhere, online for free. The formula for the synthesizable supplement, the blueprints for my electrodes, the full program to trigger a real taste experience.

"There. Let's see them come after me now."

I decline all interviews, avoid all social media. I sequester myself in my lab, where not even an enterprising intern is allowed. Most people don't understand my desire to stay off-network for a while, and very few have my level of paranoia when it comes to security.

Less than twenty-four hours after the burger fiasco, I receive one more call. When my computer screen blinks to blue and a loading bar surfaces, I know someone's hijacked the system, which is hard to do when offline. It shows the strength of their hand immediately. I'm about to yank the plug—hackers can't hack a power outlet—when a familiar voice greets me. It's appeared in thousands of commercials, a few of which I've clicked.

"Hello! Is this T Hunter?" His enthusiasm is obnoxious and infectious, but he's self-assured enough to freeze me, even on audio only. "Glad I caught you. I am Colin Sarsparilla, Tertiary CEO of Glove Enterprises, and this is not a recording."

Part of me tries to draw back, while my head instinctively leans in. "What do you want? The burger is free—in other words, worthless."

But he laughs, the smug, self-satisfied laugh of a man who's not worried about losing a negotiation. "You mean it's *priceless*. But you, T, can name any price you want."

I'm not slow, just suspicious. "What?"

"Earth to T, I'm speaking on behalf of Glove with a literal blank check in my hand, and I'm offering you a research position."

My internal sensory overstimulates—frigid fingers, steaming forehead. My voice spikes at my ears when I bark back, "You wanna hire me? Why?"

A *tsk*ing sound responds through my speakers. "T," he says, with an ease that's too natural to be faked, "have you heard of long-term VR? IF-World? Perma-facing?"

A box populates on my screen. An invitation, not a mandate, to a video call, entitled "New Hire Meeting."

Colin Sarsparilla of Glove informs me frankly, "Where we're going, your burger is only the beginning."

I click "Accept."

Mike Jack Stoumbos is an emerging author disguised as a believably normal high school teacher, who lives with his wife and their singing parrot. He is a first-place winner of the 2021 Writers of the Future Contest and has been published in several anthologies, including *Hold Your Fire* and *Dragon Writers* from WordFire Press. He can be found online at MikeJackStoumbos.com and @MJStoumbos on Twitter, as well as in-person on many karaoke stages.

Roll the Dice

Mary Pletsch

Kelsi

This old truck flies down the open highway, my foot heavy on the gas; there are no streetlights here, only stars and my one working headlight to illuminate the road. If it wasn't for the glowing windows in the occasional farmhouse or barn, I'd almost believe I am completely alone in the world. I feel like if I drive just a little faster, my wheels might lift from the road and I'll soar into the sky, an airplane.

I'm startled to reality by a turn sign flaring golden out of the darkness beyond my windshield. Too late to slam on the brakes— I'd skid off the road for sure. I back off the gas and turn the wheel hard with both hands, hoping the truck doesn't roll.

Then I wonder if it matters.

Because I can't fly away, and I have nowhere to go even if I could. My stash beneath the seat is only an illusion of escape. I've stolen my step-uncle's truck, and part of me has known all along that tonight is going to end badly one way or another. What *if* it ends in a rollover and a rain of glass and blood?

It's an instant in which time stops. Hangs. Speed and motion and fear happen somewhere just outside of where I am.

Suspended in this moment that's more like a place, all I can do is wait to see how the dice fall.

Waiting irritates the hell out of me. That's how I know I want to live, at least for a little longer. There's a difference between making a choice and letting luck make it for you.

Forces shift me in my seat. Pressure builds in my temples. I blink. It's black for just an instant.

When I open my eyes, I'm back in the world, and time has resumed a linear flow. The truck rattles and slides onto the gravel shoulder, but I do make the turn. I guide the wheels onto asphalt just in time to enter the second curve: this time, a lot more carefully.

Everyone complains about this stupid S-curve in the middle of open farmland in the dark. Nothing ever gets done about it, though, because it's in the Rheinstadt village limits, and there's some stuff about the landowners and the municipal council, blah blah blah.

I glance in the rearview mirror and see a small light at the side of the road. A candle flickering at the base of a white wooden cross.

It's time I stopped flirting with Death. There's no guarantee that rolling the truck would have killed me. Or maybe I just don't want to die in the same place as Robert Halliday, with his stupid good looks and all-star smile captured in the portrait that hangs in my high school's trophy gallery, right behind the math trophy dedicated to his memory.

I never met Robert—I moved in with my aunt about a month after he died—but he was smart and popular and kind, and so people were still talking about him when I arrived. I've found that people who are only smart tend to get forgotten.

But luck went my way, and I'm not getting forgotten tonight. I've got all the freedom in the world, or at least the illusion of it, and I plan to enjoy it while I can.

My stomach rumbles loudly to suggest a destination.

Right. I haven't eaten all day.

There is exactly $1,367.40 in the glove compartment. I'm hesitant to spend any of it because I don't know when I'll get more, but I'm going to need to eat. I should learn a lesson about making wise decisions. Find a grocery store and load up on cheap food.

But I want a *break*. I want to forget everything and feel *happy* for a change. And, yes, I want to do something I know I shouldn't. So?

Freedom means I can eat chocolate cream pie for supper if I want to.

I turn left at the stop sign and head into town.

Autumn leaves collect around the base of a blue sign welcoming me to Rheinstadt, population 920. Behind the sign, the parking lot of Frankie's is half-full. It's unseasonably warm, and kids my age sit on picnic tables under halogen lights, snacking on fries and ice creams as the October sun sets behind the diner roof.

The last place I want to be is with the idiots I go to school with. Or idiots like them. I hope nobody recognizes my step-uncle's truck as I drive through town—a main drag lined with a bank, a convenience store, an antiques shop, and a gas station. I drive over a bridge, slowing down because there's fog rising off the river. The playground in the park on the other side is ghostly in the dimness. I can't see as far as the farm machinery dealership.

An illuminated sign leans out of the mist.

THE PAIR-A-DICE

RESTAURANT & DINING LOUNGE

I can almost taste the chocolate cream pie.

I signal, braking cautiously as I turn into a dense bank of fog. When it thins enough for me to see, the restaurant is still there, looming out of the mist. I ease into an empty parking space between a sea-green convertible and a pair of motorcycles.

I'm chasing my aunt's pills with my first swig of whiskey from the bottle under the seat when I start having second thoughts. I had *just* made a promise to myself about knocking off the stupid stuff and now I'm *here*. The right thing to do is to drive to the next town over and find out if *their* pie is any good. Before the pills kick in. Or maybe I should park on the side of the road and sleep them off first.

I weigh the taste of cocoa and whipped cream against the potential risk.

I roll the dice.

Meeghan

This is how to get to the Pair-A-Dice Restaurant & Dining Lounge: head down my driveway, turn right, and head up the block to Wellington, the main street. Once at Wellington, cross the road, turn left toward the river, and walk into the fog. If you reach the farm machinery dealership, you've gone too far. If that happens, you might as well turn around, backtrack to the convenience store, and get a snack there.

Twilight is falling as I turn onto the main drag. I can hear loud bass, laughter, and the occasional shout from up the street. Lots of kids from school hang out at Frankie's. If I walked there, I could probably find some people I know.

It's likely they'd ask me to go somewhere else with them, and I would have to say no.

Or maybe they wouldn't ask, and that would be worse.

It doesn't matter. Mom and Dad would throw a fit if they knew you walked across town to Frankie's. They don't even want you walking around the block.

I feel my heart hammering in my chest as I cross the bridge over the river. I don't want to think that Mom and Dad might have a point. My breath is coming faster, and I'm starting to feel dizzy.

But I can't stay home all the time. If I never go anywhere or do anything, I might as well be dead already. I've lost most of my friends. Nobody wants to hang around the sick kid who can't exert herself too much. No dancing. No sports. Always needing to sit and rest at the mall or the park.

Mom keeps telling me to be patient. Sooner or later, they'll find a match. I'll get surgery and a normal life.

If I can hang on that long. If I don't play it safe and die anyway.

If that's what ends up happening, how will I feel then?

I'll feel like I should have had the pie.

I pull open the front door of the Pair-A-Dice and step inside.

Most of the regulars are here tonight. Helen and Edith sharing a basket of fish fingers. Karl coming back from the bathroom. Little Carrie slurping ice cream, and Sparky tapping a cigarette into an ashtray. No sign of Sam and Fred, but I'd seen their bikes out front and I can hear the jukebox playing in the bar in back. No sign of Bobbie.

Winnie, the waitress, smiles when she sees me. "Have a seat wherever you like." We both know that will be the third booth against the far wall. It's got a great view of the door. When I was a kid, it also had a great view out the window to the main street, and I loved the way the stained glass insets glowed in the sun. I used to sit here pretending I was a princess and the glass was a rainbow of jewels.

These days there's nothing outside the Pair-A-Dice's windows but a heavy curtain of fog, and I'm seventeen and pretending is harder than it used to be. Still, it's easier in a place like this, where nothing's changed since I was a kid. The décor here is a rural style called "Things That Only Get Replaced When the Old Ones Break." The stools at the counter are from the sixties, the booths are from the seventies, and the neon signs have a definite eighties vibe.

"The usual?" Winnie asks on her way past.

I nod so I don't have to talk. I'm still catching my breath. My heart hammers madly, even though I'm sitting down.

Winnie walks behind the counter and murmurs to Mr. Allen, who's refilling the pennies in the cash register. The cook slides a burger platter through the window from the kitchen. I can already predict what happens next. Karl sits at the counter, where he always does. Winnie puts the burger platter in front of him, because that's what he always orders. Then Mr. Allen takes the chocolate cream pie from the display case under the register and cuts a slice, which, as always, is for me.

What are they going to think if someday I never come back?

The bell over the door jingles just as Winnie sets my pie in front of me. I turn my head and see something I could never have predicted.

I force myself to breathe slowly, rub my eyes, and look again. Nothing has changed, except that Kelsi Galinor has just said, "Hello," to Mr. Allen, and he is cutting a second slice of chocolate cream pie.

All of a sudden, nothing is familiar anymore.

I take the tip off my chocolate cream pie with the side of my fork and pop it in my mouth. It tastes incredible, even through a haze of Kelsi-bitterness.

I don't actually hate Kelsi. I just don't have any reason to like her. Kelsi clearly doesn't like *me*.

Then again, Kelsi doesn't like anyone. Doesn't talk to anyone, isn't on any teams, isn't in any clubs, doesn't go to games or dances. Doesn't bother doing any of the things that I wish so badly that I could do. It doesn't make sense that someone like that should be at the top of the class, but she is, bad attitude and all.

More importantly, Kelsi Galinor does not belong here.

Kelsi pays Mr. Allen for her pie, then picks up her plate and saunters toward the dining area without waiting for Winnie to seat her. I hope she'll walk right past me.

I'm not that lucky tonight.

She stops and stares at me. "Meeghan?"

I consider ignoring her. That's what she did in history class last year every time I tried to talk to her. This year, we're in calculus together, and I know better than to waste my time.

Kelsi will not be ignored. She sits down on the other side of my booth, turns her plate around until the tip is facing me, and starts eating her pie crust-first.

Roll the Dice

"Hey, are you feeling okay?" she asks.

I'm not, but it's none of her business. "How about *you*? I haven't seen you in here before."

"What, you come here a lot?"

She's made an assumption. I call her out. "I've been coming here since I was a little girl." She looks taken aback, but I don't stop until I ask her, "How did you even find this place?"

Then I realize what it must have taken to get her here.

Kelsi takes a deep breath, looks down at her pie—and then leans forward as she lifts her gaze to mine. "So, you know that everyone in this diner is dead, or close to it."

I lower my fork and lean forward myself until my nose is an inch from Kelsi's. "And I know the whole place burned to the ground when I was seven years old. I'll repeat myself: *what brought you here?*"

Kelsi sits back and flashes me a sudden wicked grin. "It's the pie."

Kelsi

It's the pie.

Which is a stupid thing to say, but I won't let Meeghan have the upper hand. If I sit in frozen silence, she wins. I've had enough of people winning at my expense.

There's motion in the corner of my eye. I turn my head.

The waitress is staring at us.

The man who cut my pie is staring at us.

The trucker at the counter. The ladies eating fish fingers at the table beside ours. The bikers loitering in the doorway that leads to the bar. The cook peeking out from the kitchen. The kid with an ice cream cone and the cigarette-smoking man in the gas station attendant's uniform; I thought he was the kid's dad, but they look nothing alike. It's been a long time since I've seen a uniform like that. The company rebranded years ago. And by the way, who smokes in a restaurant anymore?

They're all staring at us.

No.

At *me*.

They know Meeghan. She's a regular here. I'm the outsider.

I feel my gut twist into knots.

I'm worried about Meeghan *winning*? She's already won. I'm sitting in a diner on the brink of eternity, and I just found out this is *her* home territory.

Meeghan waves to the crowd. The ladies go back to their fish fingers, the trucker to his burger, the bikers to the bar, the attendant to his cigarette. The slim, pretty blonde who's challenging me for the top grade in calculus is also Queen of the Roadhouse of the Damned. Who would have thought?

I'd committed to doing something reckless the moment I hot-wired my step-uncle's truck. I did it again when I entered the Pair-A-Dice. I realize I am still hanging in moments out of time. It's too late for me to change the consequences. My dice are already rolling. All I can do now is wait to see how they land.

In the grand scheme of things it doesn't really matter if I live or die, but I'd rather do it on my own terms.

Meeghan looks at me like I'm a bug. "You'd throw away your life for pie?"

I shrug and take another bite. "It's good pie."

She rolls her eyes. "At least tell me what you died of."

She wants to look down on me? I can give her twice the attitude. "Dunno if I'm dead yet. Maybe I'll wake up on that park bench in the vacant lot tomorrow." I pluck the maraschino cherry off the top of my pie and pop it in my mouth. "Maybe I won't."

"I cannot believe you. How many times have you done this?"

"This is the third—as if you can talk. You're here with me, aren't you?"

Meeghan slams her hands down on the table. "I didn't *ask* for a heart condition," she snaps.

She really has a gift for making me feel like crap. First in school. Now here.

Roll the Dice

Meeghan

When you're little and your dad takes you for chocolate cream pie every Sunday after church, that's something you can count on in a world that feels big and random and scary. It's a promise that there's always something good to look forward to.

One night, you smell something funny, kind of like a campfire, but it's also sour and makes the back of your throat hurt. When you join your parents on the porch, you see all the neighbors standing on their driveways and decks, watching the lights on fire trucks and ambulances paint the town white and flashing red.

Your dad takes you to Frankie's from then on. It isn't the same. Frankie's chocolate cream pie has a graham cracker crust without any cocoa in it. The filling isn't very chocolatey, the whipped cream is watery, and there's no cherry on top. The waitress at Frankie's doesn't even bother to smile at you. But it's Frankie's or nothing. What you really want—you can't get it, ever again.

Except then you're a little older. Old enough to go around the block by yourself. You take a walk and all of a sudden, there's the Pair-A-Dice, with the little bits of stained glass in the edges of the windows and the sign with the two red dice. You go home and get your allowance, but when you go back, you can't find the Pair-A-Dice anymore.

You tell your dad, and he laughs. He takes you to the vacant lot where the Pair-A-Dice once stood and talks about the fire. You guess where the counter used to be. You pretend to walk up to it and order pie.

Later that week, you go back. This time there's change in your pocket and a restaurant on the vacant lot. Mr. Allen sells you a slice of chocolate cream pie with a cherry on top.

Mr. Allen has no hair and a nice laugh and likes to tell silly jokes. Your daddy said Mr. Allen died in the fire, but Mr. Allen is fine. You're fine.

The next day, you're in an ambulance.

I'm telling this story as a big old screw-you to Kelsi, who is watching me, open mouthed. I hope she feels really stupid for doing whatever she's done that brought her here.

You have everything I want, and you're wasting it.

Kelsi

"So how much longer do you have?"

Meeghan curls her lip. "That's tactful."

"If you've been coming here since the place burned down, then it's obvious you've been really sick for a long time. That's why you miss so much school." Which leads me to a conclusion I don't want to think about. "You'd probably be beating me in everything if you had better attendance."

"Ugh, why are you so obsessed with beating me?"

I slam my fist down on the table. "Because I need a scholarship to go to university. Because the big scholarships are based on grades."

Meeghan looks puzzled. "I didn't know your aunt and uncle had money trouble."

"They *don't*. I do."

Now Meeghan looks embarrassed, which is nice to see. I spell it out for her. "They never wanted someone else's kid." I want to pace, to bleed off the adrenaline that comes with anger, but I settle for spinning the pepper shaker in my hands. "You think I'm getting any help with school when they already told me I'm out the door the day I turn eighteen?"

Meeghan licks her lips. "And you were born in ..."

"April." I shrug, making myself look more casual than I feel. "It's not that bad. Summer's warm. I can pretend I'm camping." I'm actually trying to convince myself. Last year it snowed in April.

Meeghan looks horrified, and I hate her for it. She's never had to think about these sorts of things. Never given them a second thought.

Then I remember that Meeghan's dying. If I'm pissed at her

for having a nice family, she's probably pissed at me for being as healthy as I am.

I've always taken it for granted that I'll make it through whatever: days without sleep, my step-uncle's rages, eating week-old leftovers ... I can handle it. I don't think Meeghan could, and the idea terrifies me. Where would I be if I was that sick?

Probably already dead.

I feel like a jerk. I'm so cavalier, and Meeghan's so serious. But if I had to take my life seriously, I think I'd start screaming and never stop.

"That's why you want to die," Meeghan summarized.

"It's not about *wanting* to ..." I struggle for words. "I mean, I'm going to die sooner or later. Probably sooner. But I don't want to kill myself on *purpose*." I switch out the pepper shaker for the salt-shaker. "It would feel like something beat me—if I gave up and did it on purpose."

"So how'd you get here?"

I take a deep breath. "By accident."

I blink. The world flickers black.

By.

Accident.

The bell over the door jingles again. I open my eyes, and I see him come in the door.

He's wearing a different outfit from the one in his portrait, but I immediately recognize that all-star grin. Our aesthetic marks the difference between two smart kids: a boy who had a bright future ahead of him, and a girl with no future at all.

"Bobbie," Meeghan says with a wave.

I've never felt more like an outsider. Of course Meeghan had gone to school with Robert Halliday. *Bobbie.*

He walks over to our table. "Who's this?"

I stand up to say hi. "Kelsi Galinor."

Meeghan stands up too. "A friend from school who *shouldn't be here.*"

"Oh," Bobbie says. "Is *that* what's up with the ambulance and the fire trucks?"

"Fire trucks," I repeat blankly. I have done several stupid things tonight, but none of them involved fire.

"Yeah. Back at the S-curve. You know, where I dozed off at the wheel and—"

"Kelsi," Meeghan says, with a new urgency in her tone. "What did you do?"

I am once again suspended in that moment of hanging time— that precipice before the drop. My dice are rolling.

"I thought it was the pills."

Meeghan and Bobbie stare at me. I talk faster.

"That's how I got here the last two times. I steal my aunt's pills and my step-uncle's whiskey and I wake up in the vacant lot."

That's true, isn't it?

I remember it. It has to be true. I always park in the vacant lot before I open the whiskey and pop the pills. I never drink and drive. Never do drugs and drive. If my recklessness kills me, well, I have it coming, but I don't want to take some innocent person with me. Better to be forgotten than to be remembered for something like that.

I feel as though I am pleading my case before a judge and jury. "It's just supposed to be a one-night getaway." Is that so wrong? How can I justify myself? "One night when I don't have to think about how scared and angry and lonely I am. One night to rest up to face tomorrow."

My left leg is aching. My ribs are burning. My lips feel numb.

Bobbie Halliday shakes my shoulders. "Kelsi, you need to go. Get back to the curve. Now."

Have I ever seen the Pair-A-Dice through the fog *before* the pills and the booze? Have I ever seen *that*, before tonight?

Meeghan is staring at her pie. "At least you have a tomorrow. I'm running out."

I'm bolting for the exit when I stop in my tracks and look back over my shoulder at Meeghan and the half-finished slice of pie remaining on my plate. And I think about what's waiting for me on the other side of that door.

I know I'm supposed to make a run for it. For the truck, for the S-curve, for my life.

Except ...

When you don't choose, luck chooses for you.

The dice are still rolling. And I make a choice.

I turn around. Sit down. Take a bite of chocolate cream pie.

Smile at Meeghan.

Her phone rings.

Meeghan

I've been in a lot of hospitals in my life. X-rays as I grew, checkups and check-ins, and, of course, all those emergencies. I stare at the ceiling of my hospital room and remind myself that medical specialists will be watching me for the rest of my life.

It's just that the *rest of my life* is a lot longer than it used to be.

I run my fingers lightly over the bandages on my chest. It's going to leave a big scar. I don't care.

I think about starting applications to universities this winter. Part of me wants to get on with my new life as quickly as possible. Another part of me thinks it might be smart to spend another year in high school and boost my grades.

And, okay, yes, another part of me wants to spend another year in high school doing normal high school things. I want to go to dances. Join clubs. Hang around at the mall without having to sit all the time.

But I can still do those things this year. Three-quarters of a school year: could that be enough? If nothing else, I can give Kelsi Galinor a run for her money for the math trophy. Bobbie would get a good laugh if my name was on his trophy.

Tears sting my eyes. My throat closes.

Bobbie.

Until now, it's been almost as though he never died.

That's when the door swings open. Kelsi slips inside. She grins like she's not supposed to be here and she knows it and that's what's making it fun for her. She's carrying a white take-out box.

I wipe my eyes. "I didn't expect to see you here." Understatement of the century.

"I'm glad the surgery went well." Kelsi smiles and opens the box. "Will they let you have pie?"

I angle my hospital bed until I'm sitting up. "What kind?"

"What, there's other kinds?" Kelsi deposits the box on the fold-out table across my bed. It's a huge slice of chocolate cream pie with a cherry on top. Of course. For the first time since surgery, I'm truly hungry.

Kelsi hands me a plastic fork. She sits down in a chair next to me, holding a fork of her own.

"Where'd you get this?" I ask as I take the tip off the slice. "Frankie's?"

Kelsi helps herself to a forkful of crust and doesn't answer.

I lift my fork to my mouth and enjoy a very nice surprise. It's not gross at all. It's amazing.

I savor another bite. It's so good after awful hospital food. I feel guilty for enjoying it so much. It might well be the best chocolate cream pie I'd ever tasted, though I'd never tell Mr. Allen that.

It hits me, all of a sudden, that I'm never going to eat Pair-A-Dice chocolate cream pie again. Or, not for a very long time, and that's assuming I die inside the Rheinstadt village limits. I quickly set down my fork. My chest feels fine, but my eyes are burning.

"Meeghan?"

"This is stupid." I wipe my eyes furiously. "I'm not supposed to feel sad that I'm going to live."

"Luck doesn't think about how you feel. It just ... decides. Without even asking you." Kelsi skewers a chunk of crust. "That's why the best thing you can do is make a choice before luck makes one for you."

I take another bite of pie. As peace offerings go, it's a pretty good one. I don't know how to ask about her situation with her aunt and step-uncle, so I settle for, "How are you doing?"

"I'm still ticking." She says it lightly, but not sarcastically. "You?"

"I ..." I don't really know how to answer her. "I don't think I've had a chance to get my head around it. I've been on standby for *months*. These last few weeks I was feeling really bad, and I ... I guess I was starting to wonder whether I was even going to make it to graduation. Now, suddenly I've got years. *Decades*."

"But you're glad you're here?" Kelsi seems wary. "You wouldn't rather be with Rob—Bobbie—and the other regulars?"

I let out a rush of breath. "I'll miss them. I think I'll always miss them. But I know they want the best for me. They told me so."

Kelsi looks satisfied as she gets to her feet. "Then I should let you rest. We'll talk again."

She says it like it's a matter of course. But Kelsi and I aren't friends. Are we?

Is this how someone as tough as Kelsi Galinor says she wants to be my friend?

I smile as I set my fork in the take-out box and close the lid over the remaining chocolate cream pie.

The stamp on the lid depicts two dice.

The incision on my chest burns like fire.

My heart—my new heart—skips a beat.

And I remember the night I found out about the transplant, sitting in my booth in the Pair-A-Dice Restaurant & Dining Lounge.

Kelsi turning back to finish her pie. Bobbie growing increasingly frantic. My phone ringing. It's my dad.

They found you a donor. It's a match. We have to go to the hospital now. Where are you?

I snap my head up.

Kelsi reads the question—the accusation—in my eyes.

"Don't feel guilty. I didn't do it for you. My life. My business." She pauses, corrects herself. "My death. My business."

I'm speechless, not sure if she's given me a gift or hit me with a snub I'll never be able to match. And she's grinning, knowing damned well there's nothing I can do to change it now.

"Meeghan. Come on. You know we're going to be a great team."

Mary Pletsch attended Superstars Writing Seminars in 2010. In the years since, she has published short stories and novellas in a variety of genres including science fiction, fantasy, and horror. She grew up in rural Ontario, near a town very like Rheinstadt, and while she doesn't like pie, she'd roll those dice for fish 'n' chips with chocolate milk. She now lives with Dylan Blacquiere and their three cats.

Why I Will Eat Earth:
A Manifesto
M.R. Tevebaugh

I am about to eat the world the locals call Earth. Yes, I might be crazy. Most devourers won't even eat gas giants. And rightfully so. I pass nebulas for eons after consuming a gas giant, I won't lie.

But no devourer has ever eaten Earth. I mean, obviously, because it is still there. And why would they? There are so many delectable treats a devourer can consume. And most of them larger than Earth.

I used to love the sweet tang of a good moon, and I was a sucker for the crunch of a planetary ring. What kind of devourer would I be without the occasional sprinkle of asteroids and a comet for dessert? But then something happened to me that altered my yearnings forever.

I tasted water.

Before you ask, no, I am not concerned with the sentient beings inhabiting Earth. Some devourers are picky like that, but not me. I believe endings are the reason for my existence. Endings are what I do. Who I am. Whatever made me, whether chance or divine being or something else, endings are my purpose. I make way for the new. Perhaps the humans of Earth are taking up space from which the next great civilization will arise. I don't know. But every ending is a gift. An opportunity.

So, no, eating a sentient race is not what is protecting the Earth from me.

It's the water.

Not only is Earth almost completely covered in water, but the creatures on its surface are primarily made up of it. I mean, they drink the stuff!

If you've never eaten water, it starts off gloriously spicy, like the aftertaste of a moon. It burns magnificently on the way down, similar to a comet. And then it eats its way out of you as gnawing teeth. It is an utterly unique experience, and nearly inexplicable in its exquisite blending of agony and ecstasy.

The first water I ate was little more than a tidbit. I didn't realize a comet had ice beneath its surface, and I had already swallowed it before I realized what I had done. My entire awareness was agony until the water had passed. I couldn't devour again for five eons. It shredded me from the inside out. And I'm not talking gas-giant-flatulence here, I mean noxious stuff. True dark matter.

Yet a deep satisfaction lingered, leaving me with an insatiable hunger that no other food has since quenched. It was that hunger that drew my attention to Earth, a meal I thought I could never eat.

Instead of eating Earth, I spiced up my meals in other ways. I braised asteroids over a solar flare, but they tasted of ash. Toying with my food was an utter disappointment. Any time spent watching sentient beings scurry around just allowed the worlds they inhabited to grow stale before I ate them.

After fifty eons of miserable failure, I tried eating small moons with ice caps. Again, the agony was more than I could stomach. A fleeting aftertaste would sate me for a time, but the hunger for water inevitably returned, seeming more ferocious than ever. In the end, no matter how much water I ate, my thoughts always drifted back to Earth.

For a time, I grew so frustrated that I stopped devouring altogether. It was as if I forgot who I was. The hunger I experienced was a clawing at the depths of my being, a dark rumbling that threatened the fabric of the universe.

I grew furious, spitting insults at Earth and raging against the water that was both the source of my desire and that which prevented me from sating it. I watched the humans intently, finding a sick pleasure in imagining their panic if I devoured their planet.

Once, I nearly destroyed it. A small flick of an asteroid would have ended my torment. Perhaps if Earth no longer existed, I reasoned, I might again find joy in the taste of a simple comet. But in my gut, I knew I would never be rid of Earth, even if it was gone.

Ironically, it was watching the humans that led to my epiphany and the reason I will eat Earth.

I noticed humans consume plants and animals to repair their bodies. They refill themselves with water constantly, and they swallow their own atmosphere many times per solar cycle. They become masters at these activities in order to survive.

As survival is a foreign concept for us devourers, I will explain. Survival is the need to prevent an ending of one's existence.

Humans call their own ends "death." Though it is an experience common to all of them, they spend their lives scurrying around trying to avoid it, hence their constant consumption of air, water, and food. But the need runs deeper than that for them. In some cases, they visit death on other humans to escape their own.

I began to wonder if I had this need to survive. To avoid ending. Perhaps the desire to *not end* was the exact reason I couldn't eat Earth. Maybe Earth was coated in water for the very purpose of not being eaten.

But something else I learned from the humans is that if you believe you can't do something, you are right. The belief that I can't eat water is exactly the kind of thinking that keeps devourers stuck on a perpetually drab diet.

One eon, as I was watching the humans, I was idly flicking asteroids at a local gas giant called Jupiter when it hit me. Humans ate to survive. But they also survived to eat. They ate things they knew would bring them death.

How could any food be worth dying for? The answer came in the form of a more basic question. Could *anything* be worth dying for? That is when I realized some experiences must transcend survival. Eating Earth would end me. This, I knew. But the experience itself would outlast me.

The humans have a word that describes this—"legacy." I shall aspire to relate to you its meaning, for its nuance is strange, yet powerful.

Legacy is what remains after the end. The idea that outlasts. Legacy is that which endures, the part that transcends our very self.

I have found an experience worth ending for. Worth dying for. And the experience will endure beyond me. Eating Earth will be my legacy.

I won't lie, I am afraid of ending. I find myself wondering how much eating Earth will hurt. Undoubtedly it will hurt beyond imagining. But that question is trivial, the answer weak.

Who will I inspire? That's a better question, but I found one better still.

Is there a limit to what can be devoured? That is the question that drives me. That is the reason I will eat Earth.

In doing so, I will show all devourers that they can do more than they ever thought possible. I will show them that endings aren't just something we effect. They are something we can experience. By watching the humans, I have come to realize that endings have the power to inspire. To galvanize. To exhort.

Though we didn't know it, we devourers ate to survive. No longer. Let us survive to eat. Let no food be too lofty a goal.

Pursue a reality where water is a spicy sauce on a bed of asteroids. Envision a universe where singularities are a succulent appetizer. Dare to dream about the zesty fire of a star. The only limit to what you can eat is in your mind.

If you suspect I am stalling at this point ... well, philosophy is my most proven path to procrastination. I'm sure if the humans knew their end was nigh, they would dive deep into their own philosophies. But I will not toy with them. They have given me much. In return, I will give them a swift death.

Earth hangs before me, just as it did in my fantasies. Dirty brown crust slathered in spicy blue, frosted with white clouds of deadly water. Delectable. Soon it will end, and I with it.

I find myself at peace, blessed to have found an experience that transcends survival. I leave the universe knowing my actions will outlast me. I feel truly grateful to be the first devourer to experience a legacy. I leave my fears behind and embrace only the joy of my last devouring. A meal which promises a savory ...

End.

M.R. Tevebaugh is a learner, writer, and electrical engineer, as well as a few other labels. It has been theorized by many scholars that his practice of drinking lemon juice straight from the bottle is the cause of his sour disposition in public. He also has an affinity for making up stories, biographies notwithstanding. However, the bit about lemon juice is entirely factual, and some might agree regarding the sour disposition. As of this writing, he lives in Bozeman, Montana, with his wife and two boys. You can find more of his work on his website at mrtevebaugh.com.

An Obsession of Peaches
Bonnie Elizabeth

The weight of the peaches suffocated Nora. She was buried under a mountain of them, lying on her back on the green and gold grass. Through a rather artistic angle of round against round, she could see a tiny patch of blue sky, perhaps her last look at anything blue before the pile of fruit slid around and pressed down on her eyes and then her nose.

Beneath her back, the grass felt cool and dry. Thank heavens for small favors. She could be sinking into mud, drowning in that as well as being suffocated by the weight of peaches. The round fruits tumbled upon her, each little fuzzball weighing only a few ounces, but with so many, it added up to pounds upon pounds of them, as if the world of peaches had decided she was a witch to be killed under their combined weight.

Most people liked the sweet smell of peaches. Not Nora. She had hated the smell of peaches before, and this particular incident was only going to make her hate it more. The sweet clogged her nose and her mouth felt cloying as if she'd eaten forty peach pies in a row—not that she ever ate peach pie.

A particularly large peach was trying to force its way into Nora's mouth. The yellow and pale-orange and the darker, almost reddish color of its coat ground against her closed lips, squeezing the delicate tissue of her lips between the peach and her teeth. Nora hoped that the pressure would grind down the peach, letting the orange flesh pop free from the slightly hairy outer skin that was now scratching the tip of her nose.

She worried about the juices that would run across her face, so sticky and tacky, filled with fruit sugars certain to draw flies and, even worse, *wasps*. She was not going to open her mouth even if it meant she'd suffocate under the weight of the damned peach that would not get off her mouth or her nose!

At least these peaches were round and somewhat underripe. A ripe peach would have molded itself to her face by now, squeezing its soft inner meat onto her face and oozing into any open orifice, which seemed to be the desire of all the peaches sitting upon her.

Nora knew peaches were fascinated by her. She'd eaten her first peach under a tree when she was no more than six. She recalled the sunny day, the fluffy white clouds drifting across the blue. She had imagined a large cloud cat watching her, which quickly turned into a sheep. A cloud dog had appeared, rounding up said cloud sheep.

Nora always had a fanciful imagination.

That first peach had come fresh from the orchard where her family had gone to pick peaches. Her grandma had planned to make pie, something Nora's mother loved. First, though, Uncle Mark had wanted to let Nora enjoy the raw fruit so she could taste how amazing the peaches were.

Uncle Mark, so tall and already balding even though he was barely thirty, picked the perfect one for her from a branch too high for her to reach. The dirt beneath her feet was hard and dry, though the areas around the trees were dark with moisture. At the time, she'd wondered why it had only rained beneath the trees.

The fuzzy peach tickled her fingers, and she'd breathed in the scent of it. So sweet and something else, perhaps just a hint of sour. She'd worried about taking a bite through the fuzz, worried it would hurt her tongue, but her uncle had persuaded her. Trusting him, Nora took a tentative bite.

Juice flowed into her mouth, the flavor erupting across her tongue. Sweet and ever-so-slightly sour, the unique flavor made her smile. A hint of juice dribbled along her lower lip.

Nora didn't even stop to look at the peach but took another bite, a bigger one, enjoying the way the flesh held almost a crunch, but not quite. It was soft but not too soft like a banana, which she hated. It hadn't been hard and unforgiving like apples, which she also wasn't a big fan of.

The peach was even softer than pears, which, up until that moment, had been her favorite fruit.

As she chewed that second, larger bite, the peaches on the ground began to roll toward Nora and Uncle Mark.

Uncle Mark looked puzzled, watching the little rolling orange-and-yellow-and-red fuzzballs. As they started moving faster, he pulled Nora behind him.

She watched, fascinated, the peach in her hand forgotten.

The peaches rolled closer. One fell from the branch next to her head, landing with a plop, the flesh exploding from the skin. It splattered her lower legs and shoes, hitting Uncle Mark's heavy work boots and his thick khaki-colored work pants.

Uncle Mark picked up Nora in his arms as he started to run from the small orchard.

Unexpectedly, the peaches turned on them, giving chase.

The faster Uncle Mark ran, carrying Nora in his arms, her face peering behind them, the faster the peaches rolled.

"What's happening?" Nora cried.

Uncle Mark didn't answer, his breathing coming in hard puffs. When they reached the edge of the orchard, Nora thought the peaches would stop, like bees that chased you out of their home. But no. The peaches continued to follow them across the trimmed yard.

An Obsession of Peaches

One yellow and pale-orange peach, slightly green around the top where a hint of stem grew, flew from the ground and hit Uncle Mark in the back.

He grunted, stumbling and nearly falling on top of Nora.

Nora began to scream and cry.

The peaches kept flying at them. Not all of them hit Uncle Mark, but enough did that when they were almost at the small brick-and-whitewood farmhouse, he put Nora down and told her to run inside as quick as she could. The wide back porch, covered like the one in front, beckoned her to safety.

She was seconds from the two stairs—wide and white and not very high, that led up to the porch where the screen door was closed, but the real door was open—when one of the peaches hit her on the back of the head. It hurt a bit. The peach flesh had opened and oozed down her hair in what already felt like a sticky mess.

Mom and Grandma came to the door, drawn by Nora's screams, and let her in. Uncle Mark was lying on the ground, still groaning. Grandma opened the screen door to let Nora in, then tried to step outside to help Uncle Mark, but the peaches began to pelt the house.

The three of them hurried back inside, watching the fruits continue to fling themselves around.

It took at least an hour before the peaches gave up and stopped flying around the yard.

Grandma tentatively went out the door, her sleeves rolled up beneath her old-fashioned cream muslin apron, unbleached and unadorned, looking around. Nora remembered how the fat on her grandma's upper arms, normally so comforting, had shaken a little as she went down the two stairs from the back porch to find Uncle Mark.

She helped him up, and together the two of them limped into the house.

Nora didn't remember much of what happened after that. She

did know that she had blamed the peaches. She'd refused to go to the grocery store after that.

When she'd first moved into her college dorm at eighteen, there was a grocery store three blocks from the campus, a small independent thing that carried all sorts of interesting treats for college students without much money but plenty of hunger, particularly on days they didn't like cafeteria food.

Nora and her roommate, Julia, had gone to the store to get some chips and sodas. Nora hadn't forgotten the peach incident, but she was hundreds of miles from her grandmother's small orchard. She wasn't even in the same state. Plus, it was September, and that wasn't a good month for peaches.

Never having shopped for groceries, Nora didn't realize that things were often available even when not in season locally.

The grocery was a small place, not one of those large superstores, so the produce aisle was only two four-foot rows with fruit and vegetables on either side, the items against the wall climbing higher and being misted periodically with water that usually hit as much of the floor as the produce.

The peaches were at the end of the row facing the wall, away from the door. Nora didn't see them until it was too late.

She and her friend had walked quickly by the apples, which looked okay, bananas that were good for nothing except banana bread, and a pile of undersized oranges before turning down the aisle that held cereals and teas.

But then a loud sound echoed behind them. Nora didn't notice until Julia looked around.

Three of the two dozen peaches in the boxes behind the oranges had rolled off onto the floor. A fourth rolled out with a splat.

Julia frowned. "That's odd." She took a step toward the fallen fruit.

Nora reached out to grab her friend's arm as the peaches began rolling toward them.

Nora felt like she was in a horror movie, moving in slow

motion, unable to see quickly enough. By the time she had turned, six peaches were rolling toward her with shadows behind them suggesting more were coming.

"I have to go," Nora told Julia.

Nora practically ran out of the store, Julia following closely.

"What's wrong?" Julia had asked, but when Nora tried to explain about the peaches, all that got her was a new roommate.

Over the last two decades, Nora had found ways to avoid going to the store. Most grocery stores would deliver, and sometimes Nora relied on friends to "pick up just a couple of things." With the advent of online grocery shopping and curbside pickup, most of her problems had been solved.

Certainly, there was that time when the woman in the pickup lane next to her had gotten a bunch of peaches, and they'd all hopped out of her bag to go to Nora, but that was an anomaly. Fortunately, Nora's purchase was finished so she was able to drive off without incident.

She normally avoided farmers markets, but it was only late June. Peaches shouldn't have been available in her area for several more weeks.

Nora kept up on details like that.

That Saturday, Brad, her partner, wanted to pick up some fresh, grass-fed beef. Nora went with him. She'd gone earlier in the spring, and nothing had happened then.

The farmers market was a big place that was set up year-round, though in the winter there were fewer stands. Nora and Brad drove their hybrid SUV into the gravel drive that led to the two large parking spots under some shade trees.

It was a warm day for June, as the entire spring had been in northern Tennessee. Nora liked the area because it wasn't associated with peaches, but she could still enjoy the warm weather.

They walked by the first tent, filled with cut flowers in white buckets. A few vendors displayed bouquets in vases, but the vases themselves were extra. The smell wafting from the tent was pleasant, the occasional lily threatening to overpower the other flowers.

The bright sun warmed Nora's back, the light breeze a perfect foil. She pushed back her brown hair from her face as she hurried behind Brad.

Animal products, the grass-fed beef, the pastured chickens, and the pastured eggs—duck and chicken—were in the third tent down.

The tent in the middle held the fruits and vegetables. The ground beneath Nora's feet was covered in gravel, making her step carefully. Plenty of other people hurried along, but a few were walking as slowly and carefully as she was.

A mom drew close, her toddler daughter eating some popcorn from one of the vendors selling premade food at the far end. The mother walked so close that Nora's arm brushed hers.

Laughter echoed from across the field that doubled as the parking lot, the murmur of conversation, and plenty of birdsong.

Nora didn't notice the peaches at first.

"Hey, Mom! Look at that!" A young boy's voice. Nora heard him behind her but didn't pay any attention.

After all, peaches weren't in season, and what else was there for her to fear at a farmers market?

Then people started to make odd comments.

Finally, Brad glanced back. He stopped so quickly that Nora, who was following slightly behind him, nearly bumped into him.

"Look at that," Brad said, pointing.

Nora turned.

Her stomach sank as she saw the line of peaches.

Tiny rolling balls of yellow and orange, sometimes flashing a slice of red or pale green. There were donut peaches too, trying to roll like a wheel, but like a child unaccustomed to riding a bike, they kept falling over. As they flipped themselves up again and again, Nora had to admire their persistence.

"I need to go," Nora said as the peaches got closer.

She glanced at the parking area to her left. Brad had parked toward the entrance as the lot was getting full. They hadn't come early enough to get a good spot, and Brad had no patience for driving up and down the aisles searching for parking.

"Just let me get the beef," Brad said, frowning. He sounded annoyed.

"I really need to go," Nora said. How could she say that the peaches were after her? Who else had such a problem with fruit?

Early in their relationship, she had told Brad she didn't eat peaches and asked him not to even buy them, so when he'd had come home one day with three peaches for himself, she'd tossed them off the balcony of their condo, listening to the satisfying splat.

Brad had laughed then, but now, a decade later, Nora wondered if he'd laugh again or suggest she go to counseling. For all that she wondered, at least he never brought another peach into the house. He had brought home a piece of peach pie once, which he ate immediately.

Apparently, cooked peaches didn't attack her, or else Brad had eaten the pie so fast, the slices hadn't had time to remove themselves from the crust and attack her with their soft and spicy little edges.

Getting no help from Brad, Nora began to run.

The peaches were coming at an angle to cut her off from the parking area and the street beyond.

Instead, Nora ran toward the field beyond the market. Now and then, some farmers brought a few sheep or cows or even a llama that they put in a pen for the children to look at. Fortunately for Nora, there were no animals there now. The field was pristine, with green and gold grasses that came up halfway to her knee.

The edge between the gravel and the grasses was worn down to low grass and some thick, green clovers.

"What the hell?" a man said as Nora ran past.

She glanced back to see the peaches following her, rolling faster and faster.

They were faster than she remembered as a child.

She made it three more steps before the first one flew off the ground and thudded against her back.

She felt as if she'd been shot, the pain spreading across her back, echoing into her chest.

Nora's breath shortened, the air knocked from her lungs.

She panted, slowing.

This was it.

She was going to die in the field outside the farmers market, crushed by peaches.

Another peach hit her back, a bit lower.

A third hit closer to the first, leaving a large wet spot against her back. She felt the warm fruit sliding down her shirt.

The smell was strong and sweet. For once, Nora wished for lilies instead.

Tears threatened at the corners of her eyes.

Her heart beat both quickly and shallowly, as if it couldn't quite do its job while her back was being pummeled by the peaches.

Halfway through the field, Nora dropped to her knees.

She tried to pick herself up again, but peaches rolled around, leaping on her legs.

Others hit her in the back.

Nora fell, rolling onto her back trying to push the little fuzzballs away.

There were too many of them. How many bushels did the damned peach farmer bring to the market?

Nora's body was quickly buried, the peaches rolling up her chest and onto her face. She managed to swat some away from her eyes and her nose, but more took their place.

The peaches were trying to get to her mouth, to slide down her throat, perhaps to choke her.

"What did I do?" Nora tried to scream, but her voice came out in a hoarse whisper. The pressing weight of the pounds of peaches on her chest made talking difficult.

There was no answer.

An Obsession of Peaches

"I can't breathe. I'm going to die," Nora whispered again.

The peaches paused, then sort of rolled back from her face. The narrow triangle of blue became full sky. A few peaches rolled off her chest and onto the ground next to her. More dropped to the grass, then rolled close to the top of her head.

What was happening?

Nora's breathing became easier.

She picked up one of the little balls. The thing was almost vibrating like a purring cat.

Nora frowned. The peaches were moving, but this time, they were moving going toward her hands, rubbing her palms and her fingers. She picked up one and then another. There was the same vibration.

She held each one, gave it a little pat, and then set it down carefully, although part of her wanted to throw them against a tree. She was afraid she'd make the peaches mad if she did that.

Brad and a half dozen others were walking across the field toward her.

Nora didn't say anything to them. She just picked up or caressed each peach, her hands feeling the soft fuzz of their skin, the tender flesh beneath her fingers.

"What's going on?" Brad asked.

"I haven't got a clue," Nora said. It was the truth. She was just going with what she had to do to save her life.

After ascertaining that she wasn't hurt, most people left.

"Why don't you go get the beef and then come back," Nora suggested to Brad.

He nodded and went away, glancing back now and then.

Only the farmer whose peaches had followed her stayed behind with her, scratching his head.

"I think, if you bring the baskets, they'll go back now," Nora said. She wasn't at all certain about that, but it seemed likely.

The farmer hurried off to gather his empty bushel baskets.

Alone with the peaches, Nora continued holding and touching them. They seemed okay after being acknowledged, most of them staying still by the tree, but a few kept coming back to Nora.

She recognized one with two reddish spots on the top that looked a bit like eyes. It kept coming back up to her, demanding to be touched. Its vibration seemed stronger than the others. It vibrated so hard that when she picked it up, it moved in her hand.

The fuzz on its skin sort of tickled.

Nora set it aside.

A squirrel came up to her, clearly hoping to make off with a treat, but Nora glared at it until it ran away. The peaches gathered closer, but they no longer seemed intent upon suffocating her.

When the farmer returned, Nora helped him put the peaches in the baskets he brought. Only the peach with the double red spots like eyes refused to go into the basket. Nora had to put that one on the top herself and carry that basket for the farmer.

He shook his head in disbelief the whole time.

Back at his stall, Nora set down the basket. A few peaches that hadn't fit came rolling up behind her. Nora picked them up and placed them in the baskets.

"Damnedest thing I ever did see," the farmer said quietly.

"Not me," the woman selling strawberries next to him said. "Kid brother had the same damned problem with raspberries. It's why I don't grow the things. Darned vines practically strangled him once."

"Really?" Nora asked the woman.

She was older, with wild hair and a pleasant-looking face. She was rounded, but her body looked hard with muscle. Her skin was tanned and lined from working in the sun. "Really." She gave the word a nod. "Seems like you figured out your little fruit problem though. Have to suggest it to Billy Bob, but I doubt he'd be brave enough to try."

"I nearly died out there," Nora said. "I think it took me telling them that to let them know."

"Have to suggest it. In case he ever finds himself in a berry patch." The woman cackled like a cartoon witch and then turned back to her strawberries.

Nora went to find Brad, who was finishing up his purchase.

They walked in silence to the car where he loaded up the packages of beef he'd purchased. It was enough for a good six months.

"You certainly stocked up," Nora said.

Brad put his hands on his hips. "I always thought your peach aversion was a little eccentricity. I had no idea they were trying to kill you. And then you just calmed them down!"

"It was very weird," Nora agreed.

"I don't want you to have to go through that again. I got us enough meat to get us through until fall when peaches are out of season. That way I won't feel like I have to do this all alone and you won't be in danger."

"But you'll check, right? Just to make sure the peaches aren't around?" Nora asked. She might know what she had to do for the next time, but she didn't want to spend half a day petting fuzzy fruit to keep them from killing her.

"I'll check," Brad said.

Nora gave him a kiss and pressed her hand against his.

She went around to get in the car and saw the double red-spotted peach rolling toward her. Nora picked it up, rubbed it, and started it rolling back toward the farmer. Then she got into the car. She watched as the peach stopped in the middle of the lane between cars, as if waiting for her to say goodbye.

She gave the peach a little wave as Brad drove from the lot.

Bonnie Elizabeth writes the popular Familiar Cafe paranormal cozy series set in Kentucky. In addition to mysteries, Bonnie writes in a variety of genres, including paranormal police procedural, fantasy, and science fiction.

Like her writing, Bonnie has held a wide variety of unrelated

Bonnie Elizabeth

jobs from veterinary receptionist to cemetery administrator to licensed acupuncturist. As a teenager, she once told the local librarian that so long as a job involved books or cats she'd be happy. Writing allows her to involve both of those.

Bonnie lives with her husband in Kentucky. The two of them are owned by three cats.

Murder in the Roux Morgue
Chris Mandeville

D aniel gazed lovingly at his new Henckels chef's knife, emphasis on *new*. For almost a year, he'd squeaked a little savings out of each meager paycheck until he'd had enough to buy it. There were easier ways to get the money, quicker ways, but he was committed to his new life, his new way of doing things. A brand-new knife was an important reminder of that, especially when every day at work he was surrounded by *old* in the ancient kitchen of the Roux Morgue restaurant.

He placed the edge of his knife against the honing steel, making sure it was at the perfect twenty-degree angle, and scraped down exactly ten times on each side of the gleaming blade.

Tradition plus precision equals perfection. He could hear Chef's voice harping in his head as clearly as if the old tyrant were standing there, looking over his shoulder.

Chef was right about one thing—Daniel must be precise when it came to his knife. But Chef needed to get off his high horse about tradition and the "old ways." Daniel knew in his heart, in his soul, that embracing the *new* was the only way this restaurant was ever going to be known outside of Sacramento.

If only he could get Chef to see it that way.

Case in point, the *mise en place* he was prepping for tonight's traditional cassoulet: carrots, onions, and parsley. Could it be any more boring? As he diced the carrots into precise one-centimeter cubes, he dreamed about substitutions that would make this old dish new and exciting: leeks instead of onion, tarragon instead of parsley. He wondered for the thousandth time how he could convince Chef to give a little twist to the traditional, to try something, *anything*, to liven up the mind- and palate-numbing "classic" cuisine.

Daniel heard Chef's waddle before he saw him approach the prep station, and he braced for the morning lecture. No matter how "prepared, polished, and precise" Daniel was, Chef always found something to criticize.

Just as Chef opened his mouth to bitch, the sound of the French national anthem blared from his pocket.

Chef threw a scathing glance at Daniel's knife work, then answered his cell. "*Allô?* Zis ees zee Roux Morgue. Chef Prideaux *ici.*"

Spare me, Daniel thought. Celebrated French chef Jacques Prideaux was actually plain old Jack Wilson from Pittsburgh. Daniel was one of a select few who knew Chef's closely guarded secret. It was this knowledge, not his hard-earned culinary skills, that had finally landed Daniel a job after two months of rejections from fine dining restaurants in San Francisco. He'd even stooped to job-hunting in the East Bay, to no avail. The food industry was well known for opening its arms to ex-cons, but apparently not for *him*.

Man, that pissed him off. He'd done all the right things. He'd earned a fresh start, *deserved* it. He shouldn't have to resort to his old ways in order to get it. But they gave him no choice. And if he was going to fall back on his old ways one last time, he figured he might as well make it worthwhile. So, in addition to a new job, he'd *encouraged* Chef to give him a new identity, too. After all, who better suited to that task than Jack Wilson?

So Danny-boy Franks, graduate of San Quentin's inmate culinary program, had become Daniel LeFleur, esteemed graduate of

Le Cordon Bleu in Paris, and second-in-command in a classic French kitchen, even if it was in Sacramento.

"*Mais non!*" Chef said into the phone. "Tonight ees not enough time to prepare zee deeshes. It must be tomorrow."

What's he up to? Daniel wondered. There was nothing on the menu that couldn't be ready by tonight. For some reason, Chef was maneuvering to have someone come in tomorrow, when the restaurant was normally closed. But who? And why?

"*Oui.* Tomorrow." Chef jabbed the phone screen with his pudgy finger, then shoved the cell back into his pocket. "Daniel!" he bellowed, even though Daniel was standing a foot away and looking right at him.

"Yes, Chef," Daniel said, making a show of putting down his knife and paying attention.

"This is it. It's finally happening," Chef said with zero French accent. "The owner is bringing in a prospective investor tomorrow, and if he's impressed enough to come on board, he'll fund moving the restaurant into a brand-new, state-of-the-art kitchen. In the City."

Daniel's heart flipped in his chest. All his hard work was finally going to pay off. He was going back to San Francisco where he belonged. And not only that—he'd be in a brand-new kitchen. He could hardly breathe.

"Tomorrow's tasting menu decides everything," Chef continued. "We'll work straight through the night if we have to. Everything must be perfect if Roux Morgue is going to be a destination."

Daniel cringed as the name of the restaurant rolled off Chef's tongue. "Chef, maybe now would be a good time to consider a new name ..."

"*Again* about the name."

"This is our chance—"

"Enough!" Chef's pink face flushed red. "It's *my* chance, *my* restaurant. And the name is not up for debate. Now shut up and let me think."

Daniel clamped his teeth together. It killed him that Chef had no instinct for the business. How he'd gotten this far with the name "Roux Morgue" was baffling. The restaurant would never be a breakout success with a name like that. Especially not in the City. The critics would destroy them before even tasting the food. Daniel's dream was crumbling before his eyes.

"Let's see," Chef said, pacing between the flat top and the prep station. "I need something flashy, something to showcase the roux, something truly special." Pace, pace, pace. "What about ... *poulet en cocotte bonne femme ...*"

Seriously? It *sounded* fancy, but there was nothing flashy about chicken and potatoes. Chef needed to think bigger, bolder, if they were going to have any chance at impressing the investor.

"Yes," Chef Prideaux continued to himself. "*Poulet en cocotte bonne femme* and ... *boeuf à la Parisienne.*"

Boeuf à la Parisienne? It's beef fucking *stroganoff.*

Daniel had to do something, or the investor dinner was doomed.

For a couple of weeks, he'd been playing with a concept that *leaned into* the name Roux Morgue instead of running from it. It wasn't perfect yet, but if he didn't propose it now, he might never get the chance.

"Chef, I've been working on this idea for a theme dinner ..." Daniel started tentatively.

"I said *shut up*. How am I supposed to be creative when—"

"No, *you* need to shut up," Daniel said.

Chef gasped, eyes wide.

"Just hear me out," Daniel said quickly. "Give me five minutes, and if you hate the idea, I'll drop it. For good."

Chef narrowed his eyes.

"Please," Daniel added. "This opportunity is too important. Please, just listen."

Chef narrowed his eyes even further. "I'll give you *two* minutes, but that's it." He looked at his watch for emphasis.

Chef was finally willing to listen, so Daniel had to make sure Chef actually *heard* him this time. His entire future depended on it. He drew a breath to quell his jitters, and began. "Since you're sure you want to keep the name Roux Morgue, I've come up with a theme dinner that takes it even further, called ... wait for it ... Murder in the Roux Morgue! But in our case *murder* is a murder of *crows*."

Chef cocked his head, like he didn't quite understand, so Daniel pressed forward.

"For the starter we do *corneilles tartine* with San Francisco sourdough. Then for the soup, *potage crème de cresson*, subbing out the chicken stock. For the main, *corneille épicée aux épinards*. And cap it off with a traditional blackbird pie updated with black-berries, or juniper berries if you think blackberries are too on-the-nose."

Chef opened his mouth to reply, but no sound came out.

Daniel couldn't help the wide grin that spread across his face. He'd done it. He'd finally gotten Chef to listen, and his brilliant idea had rendered Chef speechless.

Daniel pulled his notebook from his breast pocket. "I have the details right here." He paged through, looking for his prep notes.

"You've got to be shitting me," Chef said finally.

Daniel looked up, confused by his tone. "Wh ... what?"

"I thought you were pulling my leg. But you're serious. You're actually serious. You want me to serve the investor *crow*. Actual crow."

"It's legit, I swear—like squab or pheasant," Daniel insisted.

"You wasted my time for this, this, this *new-age bullshit?*"

"It's not new!" Daniel had prepared for Chef's objection and knew exactly how to spin it. "Crow is totally old school. Historic. And it's classic French. The Frenchest. Who else would dare? Plus—you're going to love this—I designed each course with a different kind of roux. Like the *tartine* uses an olive oil roux, and the blackbird pie a duck fat—"

"*Stop*. Just stop it, Daniel. Murder in the Roux Morgue? A murder of crows, serving actual crow? That's already off the deep end. But now, now you want me to serve a roux that's *not made with butter?* This is a Classic. French. Restaurant. If I'd known you were going to pitch this *nouveau* sacrilege I wouldn't have given you even *two* minutes." He waddled away from the prep station muttering to himself and shaking his head.

"But, Chef," Daniel called after him. "It's *mostly* classic. You've got to take a risk if you want to make it big. Come on—open your mind."

Chef stopped at the door to the walk-in fridge and turned around. "When you have your own restaurant, you can throw ridiculous theme dinners serving crow, and you can use whatever bogus kind of roux you choose. But in the Roux Morgue, roux is made with butter. Only. End of story."

"But the investors—"

"Precisely. The investors appreciate the classics, and the classics are what they will get. So you will go old school or get out." Chef *humphed*, opened the walk-in, and disappeared inside.

Daniel turned back to the prep station and stared down at his new knife gleaming like a sharp silver promise alongside the uninspired ingredients of the classic cassoulet. Maybe Chef had a point.

Daniel ushered the restaurant owner and a buttoned-up investor to a table by the window, where he'd already set the teaser course he'd created for this moment. Even though the three men were the only people in the place, Daniel had tried to create ambiance with classic piano on the sound system and candles lit at every table.

Daniel waited while the other men sat and placed the freshly pressed linen napkins on their laps. When they were settled, he poured the wine and began his carefully crafted speech.

"The *amuse-bouche* you see before you is Chilean sea bass and spinach bathed in a lemon béchamel made with a traditional butter roux, which I've paired with this crisp Alsatian Riesling." Daniel held out the bottle for them to see, then placed it on the table. "While you enjoy, please allow me to describe the progression I've prepared for you this evening. The soup will be *potage parmentier*, a classic potato and leek soup updated with a smoked duck fat roux."

"This fish is delicious," the investor said, wiping sauce from his plate with his finger and licking it off.

Daniel gave a reserved nod, not letting the relief he felt show on his face. Thank God he'd decided to steer away from the "murder of crows" theme. He clasped his hands formally behind his back and continued with the description of the menu.

"The soup course is followed by *escalopes de veau à l'estragon* —tarragon veal cutlets with a pork belly brown roux. Then *côte de porc charcutière* with an avant-garde olive oil and tomato roux. And finally, the *pièce de résistance*, a duck *tourtière* featuring a blood roux. Each course is paired with a wine selected to bring out the nuances of each type of roux."

"Oh, roux, like in the name," the investor said. "You know, I'm not sure how I feel about the name 'Roux Morgue.' So morbid."

"I agree completely," Daniel said, thrilled to have an ally, though he knew he needed to be careful how far he pushed it. "I'd like to suggest you consider the name 'Le Moulin Roux.' It hits the roux theme, but is more lighthearted, more widely appealing." He'd love to ditch "roux" altogether, but the investor had gravitated to Roux Morgue for a reason, so Daniel had resolved to be less aggressive about change. For now. "I think an upbeat new name would highlight the fresh start you're planning for the restaurant."

"So it appears Chef Prideaux let you in on what's at stake here," the owner said, eyes squinty as he appraised Daniel.

"Of course. Now if you'll excuse me, I'll see to your soup." Daniel bowed and turned for the kitchen.

"Send out Prideaux when he has a moment," the owner called.

Daniel turned back with a sad expression he hoped wasn't over the top. "I'm sorry—I thought Chef Prideaux told you."

"Told me *what?*" the owner said in a suspicious tone.

Daniel shook his head apologetically. "I'm afraid Chef was called to France on a family emergency."

The investor turned to the owner with a grim look. "Then we'll have to reschedule."

"No, please," Daniel said quickly. "Chef knew the importance of this tasting and insisted I continue in his place."

"You?" the owner said. "Aren't you just a prep cook?"

"I'm the sous-chef," Daniel said, pulling back his shoulders. "I've been working closely with Chef Prideaux for years. I'm more than—"

"Jacques Prideaux is the reason I'm here," the investor interrupted. "I'm not prepared to go forward without him."

"You're right," the owner said. "Sorry to have wasted your time." He shot Daniel a dirty look and tossed his napkin on the table.

"Wait!" Daniel said, lurching forward. "You're already here, and the food is prepared. You said the sea bass was delicious—*I* made that. Please, just stay and eat. What have you got to lose?" Daniel caught the whiff of desperation in his voice and wished he could take it back.

The owner looked away, silent. Why wasn't he trying to convince the investor to stay?

A sick feeling blossomed in the pit of Daniel's stomach.

Had Chef Prideaux told the owner about his past? Had everything he'd done been for nothing? Defeat pressed down on his shoulders. Maybe he'd never had a chance at all.

No. He'd come too far to give up. He had to go all in.

"Look, I'll level with you," Daniel said, shedding the pretense of formality. "The truth is, you don't need Chef Prideaux. He's old school. A has-been. His ideas have no life in them."

"But you can't argue with classic," the investor said.

"There will always be a place for classic," Daniel agreed. "But that place is not at the top. The classics alone are too tired to make a splash in today's market. *But* ... if you take the old guard and cook it up with deft new techniques and unexpected new flavors? That's money. And that's what *I* can deliver."

The owner and the investor looked at each other.

Daniel pressed on before he lost them. "I'll prove it to you. Each dish I prepared for your tasting tonight is classic, but with a twist. Perfect for today's market. Perfect for a fresh start."

The owner shrugged, still looking at the investor. "The kid could be onto something."

"I'm not sold," the investor said. "I like it in theory, but I'd be afraid of losing the essence of what brought the restaurant to this level, what brought *me* to the table. And that something was Chef Prideaux." He turned to Daniel, his expression grave. "So, tell me. Do these new dishes still have that Jacques Prideaux *je ne sais quoi?*"

"I assure you," Daniel said. "You'll taste Jacques Prideaux in every bite."

Chris Mandeville writes science fiction/fantasy novels and short stories, as well as nonfiction for writers. Her fiction includes the time travel trilogy, In Real Time (*Quake*, *Shake*, and *Break*), *Seeds: A Post-apocalyptic Adventure*, and the short story "Bookend" in *Undercurrents: An Anthology of What Lies Beneath*. Chris can write anywhere, but her usual spot is a comfy chair at home in the Rocky Mountains where the only sound is the wind in the trees, her coffee cup is in reach, and her service dog, Oski, is snoozing by her feet. When she isn't writing, she loves to cook, travel, and teach writing workshops. She and Oski can often be found at events for writers and readers. To learn where you might spot them next, and to join Chris's Reader's Group, visit:

chrismandeville.com.

Somewhere Far

Ken Hoover

Because my grandparents live in the next vale over, I'm not surprised that they're the first to arrive for the family reunion. Grandma is in a pastel brocaded gown, and Grandpa is wrapped in his old green cloak. He fought in the First Great War against the bone witches and lich lords while wearing that cloak and is never without it.

When I shake his soft hand, mottled with freckles and blue-blooded veins, I feel the absence of two fingers. He likes to tell people they were bitten off by a ghoul during the war. I know some of the stories—long nights in unbearable cold, the dead rising from the mud, shadows howling in the mist—but he really lost the fingers from frostbite.

I'm several heads taller than my grandmother, so I fold in half to allow her to plant a soft kiss on my cheek.

"You're such a big boy, Runey," she says.

She hands me a pie dish covered with a linen towel and shuffles into the great hall to sit in her favorite rocking chair. It's the only chair low enough to let her feet touch the floor, and she'll probably stay there until dinner.

On my way to the kitchen, I peel back the towel and inhale the tart smell of cloudberry cream pie. It's my favorite, and I nearly drool at the thought of the sweetness touching my tongue. I break off a flake of buttery crust and pop it into my mouth.

I'm caught by my father, who glares at me from the entry, jabbing a dagger-like finger in my direction. "Get those fingers out of the food, boy!"

I bow my head and cover the dish. "Sir."

My father was a mage captain in the last Great War, a thick-bodied man who treats me like a soldier. Even now, despite being taller and wider than he is, I feel like a child. He wants me to be a mage, but I'm not interested. I'm sixteen, and I'm meant to do more in this life. I just don't know what yet.

He'll bring it up today—he always does in family gatherings—or maybe my Uncle Osburn will encourage me to become a soldier or a knight.

Thankfully, I'm not the only one they pick on. Uncle Farr never married, so he's always gossiped about, whether he's here or not. He's a cartographer, always off exploring exotic parts the world, so he rarely visits, even on holidays. This year, he's coming, and he's bringing a surprise. He's the only person I really look forward to seeing. I love hearing about his adventures, and I wonder what he'll bring this time.

As more relatives trickle in, I obediently take their pots, bowls, dishes, and pans into the kitchen. There are main dishes, side dishes, and desserts. I answer their ritualistic and repetitive questions: Is this your last year of schooling? Has a girl caught your eye yet? How about a boy? My, you've grown! How tall are you now?

When Aunt Leta and Uncle Osburn arrive, they're late. My aunt is dressed in a nice tunic and hose, and my uncle is dressed in his knight's robes of dark velvet. The symbol of his order is sewn over his heart in silver thread. They speak of their two-day carriage ride from the Wildwood—the roads were clear, and the weather here is just perfect. Mallon, their four-year-old son, runs through the tower like a bird that's flown in by accident and can't find its way out. I help my other cousin, Doryne, take food into the kitchen. She's a year older than I am and carries a confidence I can only dream of.

"This smells good," I tell her. It's the only thing I can think of to say.

"Greengage jam and crispbread," she says, clearly bored with me.

After we place the food on the butcher's block table, we go our separate ways. In the great hall, my grandmother is still rocking back and forth. Others are seated on benches around the hearth, which I had to scrub free of soot this morning. There is no place for me to sit, so I stand with my back to the stone arch, like a sentry.

Uncle Osburn is telling a crude joke in his loud commander's voice. I've missed the beginning of the joke, but it's about a farmer and a ghoul. When it's over, everyone laughs except me. My grandfather laughs so hard he begins coughing. Although I didn't hear the full joke, I doubt I would've found it funny. I never do.

Then, one by one, everyone stops laughing.

They're all staring at me, and I panic, wondering what I've done or said without realizing it. The air is sweltering. Despite this, my fingers nervously button up the collar of my green tunic.

I realize, moments late, that my grandfather isn't staring at me, but behind me. So is everyone else.

When I turn, I see Uncle Farr in the hallway, unshaven, wearing leather and fur. His thinning brown hair is pulled back into a ponytail. His arm is wrapped around a short, pale-skinned woman in a violet tunic over a black skirt that hugs wide hips and skims the floor. Black hair frames her oval face.

I've never seen a bone witch before, but the tattoos on her neck are unmistakable, creeping beneath her tunic collar like spiders. She is smiling warmly, though, and cradling a small sack in one black-sleeved arm.

Standing behind them is a slender girl. She looks to be my age, or maybe Doryne's. Straight, black hair hangs to her waist, lost in the striations of her velvet tunic and skirt. In contrast to her clothes, her skin glows white.

Uncle Farr smiles proudly. "Greetings, all. This is my wife, Alvina, and her daughter, Kyra."

They are met with slack-jawed silence.

Finally, my mother moves. "Let me take that," she says, reaching for the sack in Alvina's pale hands.

"Chokecherry wine, from the mountains where we live," says Alvina.

And just like that, the hall comes back to life. People rise from their seats. Greetings are exchanged.

While I wait for my turn to say hello, I overhear Grandfather. "I can't believe *those* people are in this tower."

"Da, keep your voice down," says my father.

"You are not my commanding officer!"

There is a fierce rage in Grandfather's eyes that I've seen only once before. When I was younger, he woke from a night terror and threatened to kill me because he mistook me for a wraith.

"I don't like it any more than you, Da," says my father. "Just go somewhere else. Quench your steel."

Nervous, I look around to see if anyone has heard this commotion, but the attention is thankfully on the newest guests.

Grandfather limps away, grumbling and slamming his cane onto the stone floor.

It's my turn to say hello, and I smile at my uncle. He laughs and gives me a bear hug, but he can't lift me off the ground. Not anymore.

"Rune, lad!" he says. "Have you met your Aunt Alvina and your cousin Kyra?"

"No, sir."

"This is my favorite nephew, Rune."

Hearing this brings me great joy, but I'm focused on shaking my new aunt's hand. Her hand is cold and bony, and I'm afraid I might break her hand if I squeeze.

"Nice to meet you," I say with a smile.

I awkwardly shake Kyra's hand next. Her grip is strong, and I try not to stare, fearful she'll look at me.

What she does instead surprises me. She reaches out and unbuttons the top two buttons of my tunic collar. "Better," she says, patting my chest with one hand.

Blood rushes to my face, but I manage a smile before she turns around. I can still feel her fingers at my buttons, a ghost tingling.

As Uncle Farr and his wife and Kyra mingle with his other relatives, I think they stand out like bright flowers in a boneyard.

We gather around the long table, which is just several shorter tables I pushed together this morning. We hold hands and close our eyes, while my father thanks the gods for bringing us all together. He prays for peace and our continued safety.

I stand between my mother and my grandfather. His eyes are closed, but his forehead is creased with angry wrinkles. He refuses to eat meat because it reminds him of the dead, and I worry that his anger will get the best of him. I worry for the newcomers standing across from me. The four of us are the only ones with our eyes open. Uncle Farr is pretending not to look around the circle while Alvina and Kyra stare at the food spread on the table before them. How strange it must be to see our foods. I wonder what theirs is like. I sneak a glance at Kyra, whose face is smooth and pale, except for lips the color of blood. A patch of sun falls across her hand, making her skin seem white as bone.

The food is spread before us on a long table that stretches beneath the span of the ancient oak tree. Earlier, I was instructed to sit with my younger cousins at one end of the table in the sun. I'm a giant among dwarves.

I listen to the jokes and tales coming from the other table as I eat smoked elk with gravy and caramelized potatoes. Between the giggles of the kids around me, I listen intently for anything concerning the newcomers. I hear fragments of conversation. Uncle Farr is living in the mountains where he met Alvina.

"You should see the snow," Uncle Farr tells someone. "Magnificent."

I try to imagine the mountains, but I've only seen the vales around us. Here, it never snows.

———

The Standridge maze is a family tradition. I help plot the proper path, which my father magically changes every year. As we walk, he shapes the hedges into high walls and impossible topiaries, while I hide silver coins for the kids to find. Uncle Farr hacks at stray branches with a machete to smooth the hedgerows.

"I'm surprised at you, Farr," says my father.

"What do you mean, brother?"

"The Valley of Mists. The unspeakable horrors Da battled there."

"That was ages ago! There has been peace for more than a decade!"

For a thin man, he has a loud voice, and I wish he'd lower it. I don't want anyone to feel uncomfortable, including me. The hedgerows are only six feet high. Surely the other adults can hear us.

"It matters not to Da," says my father.

"If anyone has a problem with it, they can talk to me. Even Da. Even you." With a crack, he severs a branch that is jutting low. He tosses the limb to the top of the hedgerow with a frustrated growl.

"You don't need to do that. I can smooth the walls," says my father.

"Not everything can be fixed with magic, brother."

I stop at the topiary lion my father has just created. I place a coin inside its red-leafed mouth. I like to make the coins easy to find, but some should be a challenge. The kids should have to work a little.

"Don't space the coins too closely together," says my father.

"Sir." My answer is automatic. He's never happy with my work.

Uncle Farr winks at me mischievously. "Are you still letting your da treat you like a baby?"

I shrug my shoulders. I don't like being called out, and I'm also afraid to answer in front of my father.

"You know, there are tribes in the southern jungles where a boy must make his father stop calling him by his child-name. It's the only way for the boy to prove he's a man."

"How?" I ask.

With a grand stroke, he slices through the hedgerow. Leaves twinkle to the grass at his feet. "Ha! They hit each other on the head with clubs. They're very proud of the scars. Maybe your da needs a good clubbing. Did you ever think of that, Rune?"

"No, sir." I imagine myself with long, jagged scars on my head, a club in one hand. But no matter how hard I try, I can't imagine hitting anyone on the head.

My father says nothing, eyes on the path ahead, but his scowl concerns me. Silence usually portends anger.

If we were in a tribe, my father would be deadly with a club. He fought in the wars. I've seen him hunt in the forest. I've seen him chop wood. He's tried to teach me how to hunt, how to fight, and how to use magic against an enemy, but I don't want to hurt living things. My father says I don't have the stomach for killing, but I know I don't have the heart for it. Lives should be saved, not taken.

I walk with my uncle, while my father storms ahead of us, changing the maze walls.

"Is your schooling just about over, Rune?"

"Two more years."

"Do you have a girlfriend yet?"

"No, sir."

"Why in all the Hells not?"

"They don't seem interested in me."

"Oh, sure they are, lad. You just don't know it. Wait until you go to University." He winks at me. "Prettier girls."

I grin sheepishly.

"Of course, your father wouldn't know anything about that, since he trained to be a mage. He doesn't know what he missed."

"A life of ease," shouts my father from around the corner.

"At University, they teach you about the world and its cultures," says Uncle Farr, too loudly. "If you ask me, that's better than murdering people in their own lands."

We reach the maze's center where a large stone fountain in the shape of a sea dragon gurgles and bubbles. Water streams up the dragon's spiraling torso and into its mouth, flowing in reverse.

My father slides a decorative short sword into the dragon's mouth and storms away. The hedgerows part for him, creating a tunnel through the entire maze, a shortcut. In his wake, the sconces alight in angry flashes.

We hurry after him. The walls begin closing behind us like curtains, forcing us to walk faster and faster until we're running.

A few moments later, we exit the maze and enter the court-yard, laughing even though we're out of breath. The maze closes with a shuddering crash.

Everyone is waiting for us. There is a quiet tension, and I know the adults heard the argument.

Uncle Farr spreads his arms wide with a theatrical flourish. "Who dares search the Standridge maze?"

The kids cheer and rush into the maze so quickly it looks like they're swallowed. A few adults straggle after them. I take the rear, ushering the younger kids in the right directions as needed. Ahead, I see Kyra and Doryne, smiling and laughing, and I wonder what girls talk about.

I notice my parents strolling down a path. My father is complaining about Uncle Farr.

A younger kid shows me a coin she's found, and I congratulate her. When I look back at my parents, my mother is walking alone.

Later, when the race is over, the kids count their coins. The true winner is Mallon, who reached the sword first. He holds it up triumphantly until Aunt Leta takes it away before he smacks someone in the face.

Desserts will soon be served, and I look forward to finally eating Grandma's cloudberry cream pie. The desserts are stored in the kitchen, and I can't wait to see the assortment—apple cakes, spiced cookies, semolina porridge with lingonberries, rice pudding, cardamom pastries, bilberry soup, smultrings, pyramid cake.

I want to sneak a piece of the pie before it's gone. I head to the kitchen, but a couple adults have beaten me there, so I freeze and listen. Aunt Leta and my mother are speaking in hushed voices.

"They're actually quite pleasant," says my mother. "Beautiful, really. Both of them."

"Is the girl even alive?" asks Aunt Leta.

Uncomfortable with eavesdropping, and not wanting to get caught, I head outside, disappointed.

Beneath the oak tree, my grandparents, my father, and Uncle Osburn are sitting with a few other relatives I don't know by name. They encircle a brazier for warmth, holding tankards and laughing in the red light. I sit beside my father, who is discussing local politics. Someone else speaks, and I seize the opportunity to ask my father for a sip of ale. He hands me the tankard, and I take a sip. It's putrid, and I can't help but make a face.

"Don't have the taste for it yet, eh there, Rune?" says Uncle Osburn.

"Apparently not," I say, sticking out my tongue in disgust. A few of the men laugh.

"Good," says my father grimly.

"When I was your age, I would not touch the foul stuff," says Uncle Osburn, holding up his tankard. "It was unknightly. But I am a knight no longer, and I am making up for lost time. So, Rune, are you ready to be a knight yet?"

Reluctantly, I shake my head. "No, sir." My voice sounds smaller than I intend.

"You are built for power, boy. Look at the size of you. You'll be legendary, like Sir Hugh the Ox or Sir Kapp the Giant. What is your weapon of choice?"

"I don't have one."

"Not even a sword?" Uncle Osburn looks to my father. "What are you teaching this boy?"

The men around us laugh, and my father shrugs as if to say, *I have done my best*, which causes more laughter.

Uncle Osburn continues. "He should at least like a sword. 'Tis only proper. Even Mallon fancies a good blade."

Uncle Osburn begins talking about legendary knights. He brings up Sir Hugh again. My grandfather bad-mouths Sir Hugh for being a savage brute, and a debate starts. Not caring about knights of old, I leave the circle.

I find Uncle Farr, Aunt Alvina, and Kyra sitting on a bench under the faint orange glow of a sconce. He's taken off his fur cloak and is dressed in a brown leather tunic. Alvina's clothing looks as though it's made from shadows. They're smoking pipes. Wisps of purple smoke swirl around us, and I breathe in the sweet smell. While hearth smoke bothers me, I've never smelled pipe smoke before, and I like it.

"Join us," says my uncle. "What's all the commotion over there?"

"Uncle Osburn wants me to be a knight."

"It never ends, does it?"

"No, sir."

Aunt Alvina smiles at me. "My, what a polite young man."

"Rune is a good lad. Unlike most his age. All these boys know how to do is what their fathers did, and their grandfathers before them, and nothing ever bloody changes." Uncle Farr says this to Alvina, then turns to me. "So, what does your future hold, lad?"

"I wish I knew."

"What are your interests? What do you like to study?"

I stare into the maze, where the orange lights illuminate some paths, but not others. How can I explain that I like to read, that I walk into the woods and imagine myself an explorer, just like him?

"I like to walk in the woods," I reply.

"Walking is good. It takes you places. Promise me you'll leave this bloody vale. Your father stayed, but he's never been happy here. And for the love of all the gods, do not become a mage or a knight. The last thing we need is another Standridge warrior."

There is a long stretch of silence, and I feel as though I should say something. "Are you enjoying your visit?" I ask anyone who will answer.

Kyra says nothing, and I assume she's miserable. I wonder what it's like to come to a strange place where no one knows you and you don't know anyone.

"I'm having a wonderful time, Rune," says Aunt Alvina. "I've never been to this part of the world before. It is very warm. So many trees."

"Where are you from?" I ask.

"The Zenbar Mountains. They are so beautiful that I ache to be away from them."

"What is it like there?" I ask her. Her description contradicts what I've heard from stories—mud, mist, and landscapes crawling with dead men.

"In the winter, the snow is so pure," she says. "When the world thaws, new life grows again. There are many wonders in my mountains. You shall have to visit one day."

"Yes. See it for yourself," adds my uncle. "Gorgeous country."

"I would like that."

With a rumpus, Mallon and several other younger cousins pour out of the maze, running as if they are pursuing the enemy. Over the noise, I hear Uncle Osburn's voice rise as he's finishing another tale. There is a lot of laughter from the group, and I can't help but feel like they're laughing at me.

"Why don't we mingle?" says Uncle Farr, pulling Aunt Alvina to her feet.

Kyra rolls her eyes.

I sit next to her at one end of the long table. The adults are speaking about the best way to grow corn in this climate. I listen, but I care little about growing anything.

"Da grows corn on rocks," says my father proudly.

"Only Da is stubborn enough," says Uncle Farr with a wide smile. The men laugh.

My grandfather's cornfield is a narrow strip on a hillside. The ground is a thin layer of soil with only rocks underneath, but the corn grows so tall I can hide in the rows. I like to believe I'm in a jungle or a dense forest.

The conversation quickly shifts to the local aristocrats before I realize it. The men argue about politics again.

"I didn't want to come, but they made me," says Kyra, leaning closer to me. Her voice is soft. "They thought it would be a valuable experience. My mother has always wanted to travel south."

"I wouldn't come if I didn't have to. And I live here," I tell her with a smile. I feel bad for her, as though somehow I'm to blame for her misery. She smiles, though, which makes me feel a little better. "Where would you want to travel?" I ask.

"Anywhere. I just want to get away from home."

"Where would you go?" I can't imagine living anywhere else because I never have.

"Somewhere far."

I can't imagine being anywhere else. Far, to me, is out of the vale. I wonder if I'm capable of moving away, if I possess such courage.

The voices at the other end of the table grow threatening. My father and Uncle Farr are arguing about the wars again.

"I did it to protect our land, our homes," says my father. "You should have, too."

"What about *their* land, *their* homes? Did you ever think of that?"

I look at Grandfather, who is perfectly still. His eyes are blank, but they suddenly grow animated, and he aims them at Aunt Alvina. Wrinkles spread across his forehead, like cracks in stone. In a flash of green, he rises from the bench. "Get my sword. We go to battle," he says. He points to his cane.

Aunt Alvina hurries away, one hand covering her mouth, eyes glistening, and Kyra runs after her.

I should do something, but I'm rooted in place.

"Don't threaten my wife, old man!" shouts Uncle Farr.

My father steps between the two men. "Peace, brother," he says, placing a calming hand on Uncle Farr's shoulder, who knocks it away angrily.

"Don't touch me."

My father presses close to Uncle Farr, smiling, his eyes wide with a crazy sort of challenge. The sconces flash. The hedge maze rustles.

"Whoa, whoa. We are brothers," says Uncle Osburn. He tries to intervene, but my father pushes him away.

My father bristles with power and rage, and there is no one to stop him.

Uncle Farr must see it too. He draws his machete from his belt sheath.

"To the death, then," says my father. The ground rumbles.

"To the death."

A rush of energy blooms in my chest, and without thinking, I rush forward. With both arms, I embrace my father in a bear hug from behind, lift him off the ground, and carry him toward the door, away from Uncle Farr. Uncle Osburn opens the door for me and follows us inside.

My father fights against my grip, writhing, twisting, cursing. He's incredibly strong, but I hold on. If nothing else, I'll hold him the rest of the night. I lock my hands together, and I close my eyes, seeing nothing but red, feeling nothing but my arms around my father.

"Ease up, lad," says Uncle Osburn.

Whether he means me or my father, I don't know. I open my eyes.

"Okay," says my father, his voice strained. He taps my forearm. "Peace."

"Not until I know this is over," I tell him.

"It's over."

"You're not going to hurt anyone?"

"No."

Uncle Osburn nods at me. "He's fine now, lad."

Hesitantly, I let go, and my father's feet touch the ground. I step back, fearfully, but when he faces me, the wildness is gone from his eyes.

He pats me on the shoulder. "You did good, son."

"Stay here a while," says Uncle Osburn to my father. "Weather the storm."

My father takes a big breath, paces. "Gods," he says, and takes another breath.

"Why don't you go outside, Rune? Make sure Grandpa is okay," says Uncle Osburn.

I obey, but everything outside is surprisingly calm. My grandmother is leading my grandfather toward the side gate.

"Goodbye, Runey," she says.

I kiss her on the cheek. Grandfather is staring down at the grass and cobbles, leaning on his cane. I close the gate behind them as they make their way around the tower.

Alvina is crying in one corner of the courtyard. Uncle Farr is holding her, and Kyra stands nearby, her arms folded. My mother is with them, apologizing.

"They didn't mean it," says my mother. "Their heads aren't right from the war, especially when drink is involved."

I walk past everyone and wander into the maze. The event is just now catching up to me. My knees quiver, my hands shake. Blood pulses in my ears.

It is dead quiet in the hedges. I see the glint of a silver coin resting on top of the hedge wall. The children missed one. To reach it, they would've needed to step up on a stone bench. When I pluck it from its hiding place, I hear weeping on the other side of the wall. I peer over the top and see my grandparents sitting on a stone bench by our front door. My grandfather is crying in her arms, while she rocks him back and forth.

I retreat into the maze. The dark paths are comforting. I find the fountain, which still gurgles, and I slump against the stone base. I focus on breathing, letting everything wash over me.

Soon, I hear someone approaching with soft steps. Kyra's silhouette enters the clearing. Half of her body is in shadow, half in light.

"Rune?" she says softly. I like the way she says my name.

I sit up straight. "Kyra. Um, hello."

She sits beside me, her legs tucked beneath her. In one hand, she's holding a pie dish. In the other, she's holding two forks, which glint in the sconce light.

"I brought cloudberry cream pie," she says. "There's one slice left. I've heard it's good, and we don't have anything like this where I come from."

"It's my favorite."

Together, we share the last of the pie. We talk about the food of other places, and I dream of going there.

Ken Hoover lives in New Mexico with his family. He is the wordslinger of *Midnight Agency*, a post-apocalyptic supernatural western series, and his short fiction has appeared in magazines and anthologies. He is a proud alumnus of NMSU and Superstars Writing Seminars. You can find him on Facebook, Twitter, and Instagram.

Royal Wedding

Kevin J. Anderson

Bells of rejoicing rang throughout the kingdom. Peasants and townspeople were called away from their tasks to line up and cheer the wedding procession of Prince Derek and Princess Lilac. The people wore their finest clothes and tossed flower petals along the path to the castle. Though they had no coins to spare, they spent time and money cleaning the streets, fixing their roofs, painting their homes, making everything beautiful for the royal couple. They cheered as best they could.

Up in the castle, Hedda had worked in the kitchens since midnight to bake wedding rolls, wedding cake, wedding puddings. The silverware had been polished until fingers bled. Hedda scowled even though she was supposed to be beaming with joy for what was sure to be the prosperity of the kingdom.

"Come now, all of you!" barked the head cook. "We have to prepare a feast for the eternal happiness of our prince and princess."

"How about our happiness?" Hedda muttered.

"That is not for us to worry about."

Jack, the scruffy young serving boy, came in with an armload of wood for the ovens. "This'll take care of the last breads and pies." He winced as he dumped the wood in the pile. His hands were red and inflamed, and Hedda hurried over to the sweet young man. They had grown up in the village, known each other since they were small children, though neither of them had many prospects.

"Let me see those hands," she said.

His fingers were blistered, every knuckle swollen. "It's the bee stings. Can't help it."

"You could help it if the royal couple didn't insist on honey-drenched bumblebees for an appetizer." On a whim, Princess Lilac had asked for the treat, which meant someone had to catch jars full of bumblebees, and bumblebees did not like to be caught. Jack had been stung repeatedly, but the appetizers were safe.

With each passing day, Hedda had grown to hate the prince and princess more and more.

"I made a salve for you. I know all the secret recipes." Hedda's mother had been an herb woman, a specialist in medicines and folk remedies, and she had taught her daughter every trick.

She gently rubbed the salve into his fingers. Hedda was sweet on Jack, and each night, the two would find a shadowy alcove in the castle and sit together with a meal scraped from the plates of the decadent nobles. Neither she nor Jack could ever scrounge the coins necessary to pay the marriage tax. The closest they would come to a fine wedding would be to hover in the banquet room and wait for the noble guests to demand more wine or another serving of broiled larks.

Hedda knew the other servants felt the same frustration. Everyone was instructed to keep up appearances no matter how much the prince and princess were despised. But she had had enough, and she saw her opportunity with the wedding banquet.

Nobles from across the kingdom would attend: counts, dukes, barons, and other titles that Hedda didn't entirely understand, except they all had to be addressed as "m'lord" and unquestionably obeyed. Hedda was an attractive girl, but too drab and scuffed to draw any nobleman's lusty attention; fortunately, Jack found her pretty. That was all she needed with the thing they had to do tonight.

She had planned for weeks, digging through forest mulch to find the right kind of mushrooms, the orange spiky ones her mother called Death's Daggers. One of the overworked cooks saw what she carried in her basket, and although the cook knew full well what the mushrooms would do, she turned a blind eye and whistled as she scrubbed a cauldron.

None of the other servants admitted they knew of the plan, but Hedda didn't need to give them any warning. Finally, when it came time for the meal, the breads, the soup, the roasted boar and venison, every course had a liberal dose of mushrooms, minced so small as to be unseen. When one serving girl tried to snatch a roll from a basket, the head cook had nearly screamed, swatting the girl's hand and scolding her never to taste the food of her betters.

Hedda, Jack, and the army of castle servants served the well-dressed and perfumed crowd. The handsome prince and blushing bride were too enamored with each other even to think to compliment the meal, which the guests ate with great gusto. Everyone stuffed themselves, but none of the servants tasted a bite, even though the food seemed luscious.

Princess Lilac was the first to groan and cry out in pain as she hunched over with stomach spasms. She spewed vomit into her plate. Her prince cried out for help, then he too doubled over. Very swiftly, all the nobles were retching, writhing on the floor, their skin erupting in boils, their throats constricted.

The servants waited patiently. The process was longer and noisier than Hedda had expected. Her mother had not given her all the details, but Death's Dagger was certainly effective.

Even before the victims all were dead, Hedda and Jack scurried about, pulling rings from fingers, snatching jeweled pendants, prying rubies and sapphires from goblets. Gold coins were piled up as wedding gifts, and Jack stuffed his pockets. Hedda filled a sack with necklaces and brooches, while the other servants scavenged their own riches. They would scatter after tonight.

This castle was dead, but now she and Jack could be free. They had all the money they could imagine, more than enough for the marriage tax, though she had no intention of paying it. They would be married in their own hearts and rich in their own souls.

In the dark of the night, they fled the castle and the dead bodies piled in the banquet hall. Hedda didn't think about the people she had just murdered. In her mind, they were a different sort of people anyway.

She and Jack ran off, and they lived happily ever after.

Kevin J. Anderson has published more than 170 books, 58 of which have been national or international bestsellers. He has written numerous novels in the Star Wars, X-Files, and Dune universes, as well as unique steampunk fantasy novels *Clockwork Angels* and *Clockwork Lives*, written with legendary rock drummer Neil Peart. His original works include the Saga of Seven Suns series, the Wake the Dragon and Terra Incognita fantasy trilogies, the Saga of Shadows trilogy, and his humorous horror series featuring Dan Shamble, Zombie PI. He has edited numerous anthologies, written comics and games, and the lyrics to two rock CDs. Anderson is the director of the graduate program on Publishing at Western Colorado University. Anderson and his wife, Rebecca Moesta, are the publishers of WordFire Press. His most recent novels are *Vengewar*, *Dune: The Duke of Caladan* (with Brian Herbert), *Stake*, *Kill Zone* (with Doug Beason), and *Spine of the Dragon*.

About the Editor

Lisa Mangum has worked in publishing since 1997. She has been the Managing Editor for Shadow Mountain since 2014 and has worked with several New York Times best-selling authors. While fiction is her first love, she also has experience working with nonfiction projects.

Lisa is also the author of four national best-selling YA novels (The Hourglass Door trilogy and *After Hello*), several short stories and novellas, and a nonfiction book about the craft of writing based on the TV show *Supernatural*. She has edited several anthologies for WordFire Press, including *One Horn to Rule Them All, Game of Horns, Dragon Writers, Undercurrents, X Marks the Spot,* and *Hold Your Fire.*

She currently lives in Taylorsville, Utah, with her husband, Tracy.

Additional Copyright

If You Liked ...

**If you liked *Eat, Drink, and Be Wary*,
you might also enjoy:**

Monsters, Movies & Mayhem

Edited by Kevin J Anderson

Unmasked: Tales of Risk and Revelation

Edited by Kevin J Anderson

Other WordFire Press Titles
Edited By Lisa Mangum

One Horn to Rule Them All

A Game of Horns

Dragon Writers

Undercurrents

X Marks the Spot

Hold Your Fire

Our list of other WordFire Press authors and titles is always growing. To find out more and to shop our selection of titles, visit us at:
wordfirepress.com

 facebook.com/WordfireIncWordfirePress

 twitter.com/WordFirePress

 instagram.com/WordFirePress

 bookbub.com/profile/4109784512